This book has to be dedicated to my mother, Gladys May Wills. When first married, she lived in a couple of gas-lit rooms in a shared house in Bedminster, but in the early thirties was allocated a council house in Newquay Road, Knowle West, Bristol. A proper house with indoor plumbing, electric lights and a gas stove. It was like moving into heaven. They could plug their radio into a power point; no more dragging a heavy accumulator (battery) up to the local garage to get it charged up. There was even a telephone box at the end of the street.

And they had gardens in which they could grow their own food. A number of people, including her, kept chickens and grew vegetables. Some neighbours kept goats, to which the council turned a blind eye. My mother-in-law who grew up in the Dings recalls a pig being brought through the house to be slaughtered out in the backyard. Growing and rearing your own food was not only a necessity but profitable. The neighbours were all willing to purchase the most nutritious meat they'd see all year.

They were tough times. My mother clothed her children from jumble sales, reusing adult garments and redesigning some old-fashioned items for herself – just like Thelma Dawkins

NEW NEIGHBOURS FOR CORONATION CLOSE

LIZZIE LANE

First published in Great Britain in 2023 by Boldwood Books Ltd.

Cover Design by Colin Thomas

Cover Photography: Colin Thomas

A CIP catalogue record for this book is available from the British Library.

Paperback ISBN 978-1-80483-400-8

Large Print ISBN 978-1-80483-396-4

Hardback ISBN 978-1-80483-395-7

Ebook ISBN 978-1-80483-393-3

Kindle ISBN 978-1-80483-394-0

Audio CD ISBN 978-1-80483-401-5

MP3 CD ISBN 978-1-80483-398-8

Digital audio download ISBN 978-1-80483-392-6

Boldwood Books Ltd
23 Bowerdean Street
London SW6 3TN
www.boldwoodbooks.com

INTRODUCTION

In 1936, Great Britain was an empire and the city of Bristol one of its bustling ports. Despite the harrowing ordeal of the Great War from 1914 to 1918 when three quarters of a million men had died, and despite hunger marches and poor housing, patriotism was a way of life.

King George V and his wife, Queen Mary, a former princess of the German province of Teck, presented themselves as a family and changed their name from Saxe-Coburg Gotha to Windsor.

The government was composed of a Tory elite led by Prime Minister Stanley Baldwin.

One occurrence shook the very foundation of empire and privilege.

King George V died on 20 January 1936. His eldest son was declared King Edward VIII and the coronation date set for 12 May 1937.

The new king was known as something of a playboy to those closest to him. They were also aware of his obsession with twice-married American socialite, Wallis Simpson.

Though international media printed the story, the British press were ordered to say nothing. The public were left ignorant.

Political unrest had followed the Great War. In Germany, a new regime was marching. In Britain, too, there were marches for change from both left and right of the political spectrum. An appetite for change was in the air.

An important sign of change for the working class was the building of council estates on the outskirts of the city. The houses had indoor sanitation, electricity and gardens front and rear. The first of these estates in Bristol was called Hillfields. There followed Knowle West and Southmead. All these suburban estates were a far cry from the gas-lit slums where water was pumped from ancient culverts or hauled from even more ancient wells.

Tenements hundreds of years old predominated in the centre of the city, their twisted floorboards creaking beneath the weight of too many people, rooms divided up to accommodate the poorest of the poor. The living space was often shared with rats, mice, cockroaches and fleas. As the old buildings were demolished, the occupants were moved out to houses with gardens and modern facilities. Their world seemed to be changing, but some things had not.

Set on one of those new estates was a quiet little cul-de-sac called Truro Close, which as a mark of respect for the new king, Edward the VIII, was renamed Coronation Close. The act of homage turned out to be a little premature. King Edward was never crowned but chose to abdicate so he could marry the woman he loved.

The name Coronation Close survived and a close-knit community evolved from the debris of the one that had existed in the city centre in an improved environment that inspired hope for the future.

1

THE PITHAY, BRISTOL JANUARY 1936

That morning of 20 January 1936 seemed very much like any other morning for Jenny Crawford who lived with her husband Roy and daughters Tilly and Gloria on the top floor of a ramshackle tenement in Blue Bowl Alley in a place called the Pithay.

She felt tired. She always felt tired and knew she looked it. Not that she took time to study herself in the handsome mirror that hung above the fireplace, the only thing of beauty and value her parents had left her. She knew without looking that her features still held the attractiveness inherited from her mother, the dark grey eyes, the glossy, dark hair and creamy complexion. Mary Webster's good looks had attracted a man of means, a tradesman who had called regularly on the elegant house in Clifton where she'd been employed as a lady's maid. Once married she'd moved into her husband's house in Montpelier. All had been well until the Great War from which he'd returned a broken man. Perhaps if things had been different Jenny wouldn't have married Roy Crawford who had also joined up and came to work for her father, Henry. Not that it did much good. Her father lost interest in the business just as Roy became interested in her. The war was to blame for him losing his mind and the business failing.

Falling in love and marrying Roy Crawford had been a form of escape. He'd promised her the world, but instead a life of genteel shabbiness had changed into outright poverty.

Montpelier where she'd lived with her parents was a palace compared to Blue Bowl Alley in the Pithay, the place where Roy had been born and sworn to end his days.

They inhabited a living room and two bedrooms on the top floor of the house. The main kitchen was on the ground floor, where a fearsome Victorian cooking range heated the water for baths and its oven provided the means to cook meals. A zinc bath intended for the use of all the residents occupied the smallest room on the ground floor, where moss grew between the flagstones and mice scuttled across the floor. The ground floor was taken up by a lean-to with a deep sink and a copper – a round, deep tub with a small fireplace beneath it. This was where everyone in the block was expected to do their laundry. Once washed it was hung out on one of the profusions of washing lines that criss-crossed the yard. Larger editions of the cats' cradles that her girls made from wool or string.

Rivers of condensation ran down the windows when the laundry was boiling away in the copper and hand washing done at the sink. In wet weather, the steam rose and condensed on the glass roof, adding to the humid atmosphere and leaving dirty puddles between the flagstones. It wasn't much better even when it wasn't raining. Black mould spattered the windows and green moss hung in ribbons from the cracked tiles of the sloping roof.

The other two rooms on the ground floor were in a bad way and barely useable and certainly not liveable. One was used as a coal cellar, the other was left to the fungus growing out of the walls. The living room of their flat was gas-lit and had a very small fireplace, the coal for which had to be manhandled from the coal hole out in the backyard and up six flights of stairs to the top floor.

The water pump was also out in the yard and buckets were needed to fill the flowery bowl in which they washed or to fill the kettle that sat permanently on the hob.

It seemed to Jenny that all she ever did was fill buckets and carry them up the stairs.

Before the children had arisen from their shared single bed in a room eight feet by four, she'd cracked the ice on the enamel bowl and washed her face. The water in the kettle, not yet even warm, she'd leave for her daughters.

In their absence, she patted on talcum powder to hide the bruise beneath her eye, the other reason she'd avoided looking in the mirror. Face powder would have been better, but she hadn't had enough money for such luxuries for a very long time. Talc would have to do.

Once the fire was going, she tore pieces of newspaper to stuff into the gaps in the window frames, the panes of which were patterned with frost.

She might have been privy to the momentous event that had happened if the wireless had been working. Roy had smashed it the night before, the toe of his boot ripping into the metal mesh protecting the fragile innards: the wires and glass tubes that lit up when it was turned on.

Around five o'clock the previous evening, she'd been humming along to the music, singing in places where she knew the words. According to Roy, the volume had been loud enough to 'wake the bloody dead'. He'd been on an early shift that morning and crashed into bed on his return from work.

Normally, he would have slept through until seven or so, then gone to the pub, then home and bed again. On this occasion, he'd volunteered for the night shift. A freighter was due in that night requiring a swift turnaround.

'Extra money,' he'd said to her. 'She's bringing in wood pulp for papermaking and suchlike. I weren't turning it down.'

'Of course not,' she'd said, though knew without asking that it wouldn't mean an increase in housekeeping.

He'd slumped into a chair and pointed at his boots.

She'd got down on her knees and began unlacing each one. Once she'd pulled them off, he'd staggered into the bedroom, pausing at the door, jerking his head towards the bed.

'Come on to bed.'

A tight knot had formed in her stomach, though she knew better than to let fear show on her face. Be amenable. Be submissive. That's what a wife was supposed to be. Even so, a small spark of reluctance caused her to shake her head. 'You've just come home from work. You're tired.'

His expression had darkened. 'I ain't that tired.'

'But the girls will be home soon.'

'Get in yer.' He jerked his head again, his expression leaving her in no doubt of the consequences of a refusal.

He'd jammed a chair against the bedroom door. 'That'll keep the kids out.'

The act of bodily intimacy was short-lived, the chair removed just before she'd heard the girls tramping up the stairs. She'd left him there snoring, glad he would sleep through until he was off for work again, glad he wouldn't be back until the morning. BBC music had taken her out of herself, away from this place, away from him. If only she'd kept the sound down.

He'd stumbled out of the bedroom, eyes red-rimmed and a surly grimace on his downturned lips.

Her apology was very necessary.

'Sorry. I didn't realise it was that loud. Anyway, I thought you were already waking up.'

'Well, you thought wrong!'

Knowing the girls were out playing, he'd raised his voice.

She attempted to laugh it off. 'No need to get like that Roy. It's only a bit of music. Soft music too. Should have helped you sleep.'

That was when he had lashed out at both her and the wireless. The wireless had come off worse, the music silenced.

Jenny had been heartbroken. The wireless had been her lifeline to the outside world. There was no electricity in the crumbling tenement, but with the aid of an old orange box fitted with pram wheels, she'd regularly dragged it up to the garage to have the accumulator – its inbuilt battery – charged up. That's how it was in a gas-lit property with an outside lavatory and no running water. Getting the wireless set repaired would have to wait until she had some money and that wouldn't be forthcoming until Roy got paid. If he got weighed on that is. That's how it was at the docks – if your face fitted...

Just as she was filling a bucket which she intended using for hand washing underwear, someone shouted at her from the tunnel that led from the alley and into the yard.

Lifting her head, she saw Isaac Jacobs coming through the opening, the sound of his footsteps echoing over the rough cobbles. As usual at this time on a weekday, a heavy sack weighed heavily on one shoulder. Isaac worked for a relative who ran a business in St Nicholas Fruit and Veg market. He started work early and was home by late morning. Leftover fruit and veg were shared out amongst those who worked there – a small bonus that helped supplement their low wages.

Isaac's bent legs, a consequence of childhood rickets resulting from malnutrition and lack of sunlight, gave him a swaying gait, like a ship caught in rough seas. Roy had said, unkindly, that a pig could run through Isaac's legs and not knock him over. Roy seldom said anything good about anyone these days, especially anyone foreign or different from himself. He'd taken on a morose disposition. She couldn't recall now when he'd first changed but concluded it had been gradual. Jobs hadn't come easy either. He'd had big plans way back when she'd first fallen in love with him. If she'd followed her mother's advice, she would not have married him. But the foolishness of youth and the hammering of her heart had overruled her advice and she now rued the day she'd married him. His dreams had come to nothing. Like many other working class men Roy laboured long hours for low wages. The strain of poverty had taken its toll on their marriage.

'Had a good day, Isaac,' Jenny asked, already wiping her hands on her apron, readying herself to receive a few bits and pieces from his sack. No matter what Roy said, Isaac was a generous man.

'It's not been a good day today, Jenny. Not good at all. The news took us all by surprise. Yes indeed!' He shook his head disconsolately as he placed the sack on the ground between his bowed legs.

Jenny feared he was going to say that he only had mouldy cabbages today – bits and pieces squashed beneath the wheels of a costermonger's barrow. He took a deep breath and stood with his fists clamped to his waist, his chest thrust forward like that of a pigeon. 'You could have knocked me down with a feather. I was shocked from my heels to my head, I was.'

He kept on shaking his head and muttering whilst dipping into the sack.

'Here,' he said. He passed her a swede, a turnip, two onions and a bunch of carrots. 'Those carrot tops should stew up well. Nice and green they are.' He went on making comment, shaking his head all the while. 'Shocked to me boots. I wasn't expecting it. Didn't even know he was ill.'

Jenny was too busy imagining the simmering stew she would

make to take in what he was saying. The mutton bones she had left from the Sunday roast would add a bit of flavour though little meat. It was a challenge to make a joint of meat last five days, but she did her utmost to stretch the housekeeping Roy gave her. Sometimes the cheap joint, mutton, brisket or breast of lamb only lasted three days. A shoulder of mutton went the furthest and having come from an old sheep needed a good stewing. Still, she thought, even though there was little flesh left on the bones, it should be tasty enough once the vegetables were added. She hoped that Roy would think so and shuddered at what he might say: '*A working man needs better than this.*' It was often on the tip of her tongue to say that the little housekeeping he gave her didn't run to much better.

'Mr Jacobs, I can't thank you enough. Let me give you something. You deserve payment.' She had about three shillings in coppers in her purse. Some needed to be kept back for the gas meter, but she could just about manage a few pennies. Four should do it. 'Here,' she said, the pennies in her hand.

He responded the way he usually did, flapping his hands in front of her. 'No, no, no. I do not take payment from friends and neighbours. Anyways, as I told you before, I get it free. It's what's left at the end of the day. And I am not out to make a profit as some believe of my people. It was free to me so is free to you.'

Isaac was more generous than a lot of others she knew. His heart was big. Giving her free produce had long been his habit, from the time he'd caught her sitting on the stairs tossing a penny from one hand to the other. On that particular day, she'd been working out whether to go and buy some scrag end for supper, begging the butcher if he had anything going cheap. Mid-morning was not a likely time for that. Selling off cheap happened at the end of the day. But there'd be hell to play if Roy came home at the end of the day and she was not there.

Isaac had worked a long day. St Nicholas Market began at about two in the morning and went on until nine or ten. Isaac was a wise old owl who stayed on to sweep up until mid-morning at least, knowing there would be leftovers. There was always some produce not likely to last another day and the leavings were shared amongst the men who worked there. All had families and made use of what they could glean to keep body and soul together. Some of whatever was in the sack went to him and Ruth, his wife. He also shared some with other neighbours in the same yard, and he always found something for her. To that end, he was her lifeline.

Wisps of grey hair floating on the morning chill, Isaac dug into the sack again and pulled out a small bunch of bananas. 'For your girls.'

She smiled at him. 'That's very kind of you.'

The corners of his eyes turned downwards, and their colour turned dark and still like glass.

Jenny saw the sadness and guessed bittersweet memories had come to mind of his own children – two daughters – who had died from diphtheria four years ago. They would have been the same age as her two daughters by now; Tilly was eleven and Gloria was nine. Consequently, he provided what he could to feed them as he would have done those he had lost.

'You were saying something just now, Mr Jacobs. I didn't catch what it was.'

'He's dead.' He screeched the word, raised his hands to shoulder level and waved them around.

'Dead?'

'I could not believe it. It is the end of an era. The end of an era.'

He was beside himself. For one worrying moment, it occurred to Jenny that he was referring to the death of the relative who owned the business. If so, he might have lost his job, but surely nobody described getting the sack as the end of an era.

'Oh, Mr Jacobs. What's happened to you?'

He looked astounded. 'Me? Nothing. Have you not heard the news?'

She frowned. 'No. I haven't got a newspaper and my wireless is being mended.' She could have said that the accumulator needed to go to Grundy's garage to be charged. But then Isaac would have offered to take it up for her. She didn't want anyone knowing about Roy's behaviour. Gossip spread like weeds in the Pithay. Fingers would be pointed. Her daughters would be the subject of pity. Pity could undermine confidence. Not that they were the only poverty-stricken family in the Pithay with a father too free with his fists and tight with his money. 'Such a nuisance.' Even to her own ears, the excuse sounded true. 'So, who's dead?'

'Well, this can tell you the news better than me.'

Isaac dived into his sack again and brought out the front page of the morning newspaper. He held it up. The headlines were bounded in a black border. 'Old Fred Crouch bought this. Heard the newspaper seller shouting it out. He can't read himself, so brought it in for us that can. We all read it. We were stunned to silence for a full minute or more.' Sweeping his cap from his bald pate amidst whisps of grey, he bowed his head and muttered, 'May his majesty rest in peace.'

Jenny's eyes skimmed swiftly over the front page of the *Bristol Mercury*.

THE KING IS DEAD

Even without the black border, the headline was sombre yet at the same time extremely striking.

She read through the article, noticing that, just for once, there were no advertisements for liver pills, corsets or shoe polish jostling for space on the front page, their omission a mark of respect for the old king.

She sighed and placing one hand over her heart expressed her wish that he rested in peace.

She asked him if she could keep it.

'Course you can, but only after you have read it to Ruth. She never did learn how to read and write and, much as I hate to admit it, she said that my voice is like the gurgling of an old drain.' He beamed. 'She likes the sound of your voice.'

'I'll come right away.'

'That's good.' He shook his head again, then shivered. 'It's freezing cold and the news makes it colder. Would you care to join us for a cup of tea in front of the fire?'

Accepting his invitation, Jenny followed him up the narrow staircase to the set of rooms he shared with his wife on the first floor. The narrow wooden treads creaked underfoot. Dust fell from worm infestations that had eaten the strength from the timbers and spiders scurried into dark corners.

As it swung open, the warped door to the first-floor room made a sound as though it was in pain. Jenny took shallow breaths. The room smelt musty, the furniture, all of which had been bought second-hand, had a worn smell, as though the cooking smells and debris of a century had permeated its thick, dark upholstery.

Ruth looked up as they came in, her moon-shaped face breaking into a smile when she saw who it was. 'Oh, Mrs Jenny! My very favourite neighbour. How are you today?' Then her face dropped. 'Have you heard the news? It was on the wireless.'

'I have told her, Ruth. I read it in the newspaper. This newspaper.' He flapped the newspaper above his head. 'The king we knew is dead. It is his son who will now be king.'

Jenny eyed the thick piece of velvet hanging from the mantelpiece. Pictures made from cloth hung on the walls. Most composed biblical subjects: Daniel in the lions' den, Samson wielding the jawbone of an ass, Moses found in the bullrushes. Ruth had explained to her that they'd once belonged to her mother.

The room wasn't as clean as it could be, but Ruth's health being bad, she did what she could; not that there was any way of totally obliterating the smell of five hundred years of decay. Every so often, a whiff of drains was also detectable. Even in her rooms at the top of the house, the obnoxious stench of decay often drifted up from the backyard and drains that were almost as old as the house.

'Mrs Jenny, please sit down,' said Ruth, gesturing at the nearest chair.

Jenny thanked her.

Ruth's lower body was wide enough to fill the chair she was sitting on. The sleeves of her dress were tight on her arms. Her clothes were clean though old-fashioned. Her black dress was complemented by a cottage loaf of black hair streaked with bands of white. It was rarely she moved from that chair, preferring instead to wait until Isaac came home to do what was necessary.

'Please make the tea, Isaac, while Jenny reads me the newspaper. I know I heard it on the wireless, but I'd like to hear it again. But get that cat off the chair first.' She flung her hand in the direction of a green velvet armchair with ornate legs and feet that resembled claws.

Jenny knew from other visits that the chair's stuffing was springing out from beneath the seat.

'That's it. And brush off those hairs. We don't want Mrs Jenny getting hairs on that nice skirt of hers, do we.'

Isaac flicked at the seat of the green velvet chair with both hands.

As she sat down, Jenny's attention was snatched by a cockroach climbing up the wall and she wasn't the only one watching it. Ears twitching, amber eyes bright with interest, the cat also sat watching the quick-moving creature's attempt to dive behind a loose piece of plaster.

Swallowing her revulsion, Jenny dragged her gaze away, cleared her throat and began to read the headlines, then the flowing words of a paper that represented the views of most people. A king had passed into history. The king would have a state funeral and in time the new king would be crowned.

Just as she finished, Isaac brought in tea the colour of mud. In direct contrast to the strength of the tea, the cups were of delicate porcelain and decorated with pink roses.

'Milk?'

Isaac held a tin of condensed milk above her cup.

She shook her head. 'I'll have it black.'

'Isaac. Let us have a drop of rum in our tea. Let's drink a toast to the king, both him who has passed and him who inherits the crown.'

A teaspoonful of rum was added to each cup.

A slight movement drew Jenny's attention back to the wall. The cockroach had fallen to the floor. The cat ate it.

Neither Isaac nor Ruth noticed.

With poised delicacy, Isaac raised his porcelain cup. 'God bless King George the Fifth. May he rest in peace.'

'And God bless the new king,' Ruth added, her little finger raised in a ladylike manner at odds with her thick, square hands.

'To King Edward the Eighth,' said Jenny.

Isaac finished the toast. 'To King Edward the Eighth. May God bless him with a long and peaceful reign.'

Their voices raised in unison.

'Amen.'

2

FEBRUARY 1936

Jenny looked up from stirring a saucepan of porridge over the fire when Tilly came running into the room screaming.

'Ma! Ma!.'

'Oh my God!'

Taking the saucepan from off the glowing coals so it wouldn't burn, Jenny Crawford threw up her hands in horror. Her eldest daughter, barely eleven years old, was covered in blisters gradually turning into crusted scabs. Tilly was covered in them.

She gathered her close, her head resting on that of her child. 'My poor little girl.'

Wrapped in her mother's fond embrace was not enough to ease the child's discomfort. Tilly continued to scratch her arms, torso, and legs. The bed bugs had had a feast and all because she'd only had enough money to buy a bed from Sam Fowler. A new bed had been out of the question. Nobody she knew could afford a new bed. Second-hand was all she could afford and now she was reaping the consequences.

Gloria stood defiantly in the doorway not scratching.

Jenny inspected her arm. 'You've been bitten too.' It was only to be expected as both daughters shared the same bed.

'But I ain't a cry baby.'

Jenny kissed her dear daughter on the top of her head. 'Eat your porridge and go outside with your sister and play.'

Tilly didn't need telling twice even foregoing her breakfast, preferring to get away from the infestation as quickly as possible.

With grim-faced determination, her husband Roy pounded the colony of bed bugs with a carpet beater. Not that it made much of a difference. The second-hand mattress continued to erupt with the nasty creatures, little black spots scurrying across the striped flocking, hiding beneath the fluffy fixings in indents.

Roy took a break from his fervent beating, a disgusted look on his face. He swiped at the slick of sweat trickling from his forehead into his eyebrows.

Jenny swallowed at the accusing look he gave her.

'You stupid cow. Didn't you check if it was crumby before you 'anded over the money?'

'It was cheap and didn't have any stains.'

What she really wanted to say was that she hadn't had enough money for anything better, but that would only have caused a row. The wireless had yet to be repaired – if it were possible. There was no knowing with his quick temper what he might break next.

'No stains, just a load of scurvy bugs,' he snarled, his top lip curling like a bulldog.

'I didn't know it had bugs.'

'I didn't know it had bugs.'

He was making fun of her, repeating what she'd said but in a wheedling voice she did not recognise as belonging to her.

Her marriage to Roy had never been a bed of roses, more thorns than flowers. Moments when things had gone well had been truncated too often by periods when things had gone wrong.

Mostly trivial things resultant from years of unrelenting poverty, but she'd taken the marriage vows. And that was what their relationship had become, a commitment to vows rather than to each other.

She attempted to put on a brave face, even a smile.

'Our girls needed a new bed. The old one had woodworm. You know it did. It fell to pieces.'

Roy had chopped up the old bed into kindling. It had burned well. Tilly and Gloria had slept on just the mattress for a while until the mice had burrowed into a hole and set up home. There'd been no choice but to buy a new one.

Roy had been in a good mood when she'd told him. He'd dipped into his pocket and given her a few extra shillings that week though it hadn't been enough for a decent bed from a reputable second-hand shop. She'd made up the shortfall by cutting down on meals – not that she had much scope for that. Ultimately, it meant Roy and the girls ate a cooked meal whilst she made do with bread and dripping.

Arms made brawny by physical labour, Roy made quick work of rolling up the mattress and tying it up with string. He patted the box of matches in his pocket and heaved the mattress onto one shoulder. 'A bloke works all day and then comes home to this,' he growled, surly in voice and manner. The bugs had made him bad-tempered.

She accompanied him out onto the bare boards of the landing. The boards were warped with age and creaked beneath every footstep. A mouse scuttled into a gap in the skirting. She was used to mice. Used to all the vermin that lived in these crumbling ruins.

'Keep yer eyes peeled,' he shouted over his shoulder.

'I am doing.'

She followed him from their top-floor rooms keeping her eyes on the mattress, ready with her heel to crush any bugs that might fall off before they could scuttle for safety.

Overhead, the bumpy ceiling, crazed with cracks and punctured with holes, hung low. There were times on the twisting stairs when it was necessary for Roy, almost six feet tall, to duck beneath lowering plaster. In some places, the sharp ends of dried-out laths hung dangerously from bare patches where the plaster was missing. Hitting them would result in more plaster falling or injury from the jagged ends.

At the bottom, he took a turn out of the lean-to that served as a laundry room. Boots clumped over the flagstone floor before the toe of one boot kicked open the back door. Other mean buildings of great age, almost identical to the one they lived in, loomed over a bare backyard where nothing grew except the gloom of a winter's day.

Only the very slimmest shaft of sunlight managed to break through the odd gap between the brooding buildings. All the tenements in the Pithay were divided into rooms on each floor, some into three and occupied by as many as six people. Three buildings and far too many households shared an outside water pump and three privies crammed against the end wall. The lack of sunlight lent the yard a perpetual air of damp and gloom. The feathery leaves of ferns poked through gaps in the mortar of the brick-built privies that leaned together, looking as though if one fell so would they all. The erosion of the buildings by wild plants and weeds was not confined to ground level.

Jenny lifted her face skywards to where a patch of blue slashed the narrow gap between crumbling parapets. The stalky branches of a buddleia waved from the rooftop next to a tall but twisted chimney. From this distance, she couldn't tell whether it was in bud but sorely wished it was. Oh, for a garden. She would really love a garden and often imagined what she would plant.

In the yard, Tilly and Gloria were attempting to build a doll's house from bits of broken stone and brick. On seeing their father, both girls sprang to their feet. Tilly, more wary, than her sister, eyed the rolled-up mattress carried on their father's shoulder, their mother marching behind. At the sight of the mattress, Tilly began scratching.

Gloria, hungry for her father's favour and most of the time his favourite, ran after him. 'Can I come, Dad? Are you gonna burn it? Are we going to 'ave a bonfire?'

Jaw firmly set; Roy acted as though he had neither seen nor heard her, but Gloria was not easily foiled. Before the gate could slam in his younger daughter's face, she slipped through. Slight, pretty and incredibly precocious, she did it easily.

'Get me supper on,' Roy demanded from the other side of the gate.

'It'll be on the table as soon as you get back,' Jenny shouted. So would some sandwiches to see him through the night shift. The night shift was always better paid than the day shift at the city docks and of late Roy had been lucky. He was on lates tonight where a ship had come in requiring a swift turnaround and the gaffer had favoured him. He'd been 'weighed on', as they said in common parlance. There had been a time when he hadn't been so lucky, but of late, with this new gaffer, he'd been favoured more regularly.

He'd been over the moon on the day it had first happened and he'd told her he was in with the man who mattered. Proud as a peacock, he'd boasted, 'We're of the same mind in a lot of things. He marked me out and didn't find me wanting.'

'Sounds as though you're his blue-eyed boy,' she had said chirpily, pleased he was in a good mood and hopeful he would stay that way.

Her comment had not been well received. He'd frowned and

rounded on her, anger darkening his eyes. 'What d'ya mean by that?'

It was as though she'd run headlong into a brick wall. She'd thrown him a nervous smile reserved especially for those moments when he'd taken something the wrong way. Flattery followed, the only sure way she knew to placate his anger.

'What I mean is if I was the gaffer, I'd give you the job every time. I've always loved your blue eyes.'

Flattery and flirtatiousness had always been her main defence against his quick temper and flying fists. Sometimes it worked. Sometimes it did not.

Lingering in the yard, apart from her husband and happy to be so, she rubbed the damp from her arms and tried to think back to a time when she hadn't walked on eggshells. Very early on, it seemed, but the exact moment when he'd ceased to be her Prince Charming was difficult to pin down.

In fairy tales, the prince marrying the princess was followed by the words happy ever after. *Only in fairy tales*, she thought as she made her way back into the house.

Before going back up, she shovelled some more coal into the brass scuttle she kept by the tiny fireplace that barely held enough of a fire bed to boil a kettle, let alone warm a room.

As she climbed the six flights of stairs to their rooms, she consoled herself with the fact that him getting work more regularly meant there'd be a bit of extra money. Hopefully he would hand some of it over. It would help, though it would still be shoulder of lamb for Sunday roast, not a rib of beef. Oh, for such a wonderful item.

The girls were getting bigger, growing out of their clothes. For their sake, she would ask him for a bit more. All she had to do was pluck up the courage. The girls' room was small so it was still a case of sharing a bed. What wouldn't she give for them to have a separate bed each, but circumstances wouldn't allow – not for now anyway.

Once the fire was made up with fresh coal, she ventured back downstairs again with the water bucket, where she found Tilly waiting for her.

Looking a bit lost without her sister to play with, Tilly offered to pump the handle.

'Thanks, sweetheart,' said Jenny. 'Give it a bit of time and we'll have a cup of tea.'

'And a biscuit?'

'That all depends on if the lid's been put down tight. If not, then we have some very fat mice scurrying in the skirting boards.'

'I put it back on tight,' said Tilly.

'Then we might have a biscuit with our tea.'

Still scratching her arms, legs and around her neck, Tilly followed her mother into the house as far as the laundry room. Jenny picked up a bucket and headed for the pump in the backyard. Tilly scratched all the way, her bottom lip quivering.

'I ain't sleeping in that bed again, Ma. I ain't.' Her bottom lip was thrust out further than her upper lip. She looked close to tears. Blood speckled her sleeve where she'd been scratching – and continued to scratch.

'You won't have to, sweetheart,' said Jenny, aggrieved by her daughter's suffering. All the hugs in the world wouldn't ease the intense itch. Jenny felt hapless and weighed down with guilt. She should have checked if the bed was infested, but her means were slender. She'd had shillings to pay for it, not pounds. The only reassuring point was that the cast-iron bedstead frame was useable – once she'd disinfected the joints, though it meant acquiring another mattress. She put on a happy face. 'I'm going to disinfect the frame and get you a new mattress. '

'Do I still have to share with Gloria?'

'I'm afraid so,' Jenny said sadly. 'But at least it'll be clean.'

Tilly looked slightly reassured. A bit more cajoling should help, though Jenny bit her lip at the thought of the guilt and the continuous struggle of keeping the rooms clean. She also baulked at the thought of paying a bit more, which meant asking Roy for more money.

'Now how about you stop scratching and pump the handle. I'm going to give that frame a good scrub.'

Tilly showed no reluctance to do as asked and Jenny hoped it would take her mind off her scabby arms and the nasty little brown bloodsuckers that might yet haunt her dreams.

It was heart-breaking to see the smears of blood on her arms and such a serious expression on such a pretty face. Her daughter's pale skin, pink cheeks and dark eyes never failed to remind her of the story of Snow White she'd read as a child. The resemblance to a princess from a fairy tale ended there. Tilly deserved to live in a castle, to feast on roast beef and wear silks and satins, not faded dresses and second-hand shoes.

* * *

Everything about my life is second-hand, Jenny thought to herself. Except Roy. Roy, the father of her children, had been her sweetheart from when she was sixteen. They'd grown to be adults together and she knew for sure that he'd never looked at another girl before they'd married. As for now, she wasn't sure. She dared not ask. His parents, her parents and everyone else who knew of their longstanding courtship had expected them to marry the moment he'd come back from the Great War. So had Jenny. But it hadn't happened. Not at first. He'd procrastinated, told her he needed time to readjust to civilian life.

Though there was never any evidence there might be someone

else he loved better, suspicion lingered like a dark shadow in the back of her mind. When she'd asked him outright, he'd assured her there was no one.

'You know it's only you for me. We'll get married eventually. Just give me time to get over the war. France was no picnic, you know.'

She thought about the coffee-coloured photographs sitting on the mantelpiece. One was of Roy in his uniform looking too serious for his years. Another was of them and their family. A third of him and his best mate back in the army. Roy had remained in contact with Simon Bruce Aylward after the war. Letters had gone back and forth for some years. Every single one was taken into the bedroom to be read, the door shut firmly behind him, the sound of the bolt being slid across. She'd once asked him if she could read one, it could help.

A fierce fire had ignited eyes that were usually brown. In a certain light, they looked blood red. 'No. They're private.'

About six years ago, they'd stopped abruptly. For days, weeks, he'd been taciturn until a postcard had arrived from Simon's mother to say that he'd passed away because of the mustard gas that had affected his eyes and his lungs.

'I'm so sorry,' Jenny had said. 'I know how it must feel.'

She'd been referring to the passing away of her parents.

The blazing eyes again. 'No you don't! You've no idea how it feels.'

She'd covered her ears and hunched her shoulders. 'No need to shout.'

'Every need! Every bloody need!'

The bedroom door had slammed. She'd dared place an ear against the door and heard something she had not expected to hear. Roy was crying and despite his bad temper it seemed something of the young man he'd been was still there and her heart went out to him.

Roy had been morose for some time after receiving the news. He'd barely spoken and sexual relations, even basic affection between them, had been non-existent. She might as well have slept alone.

As usual, she had carried on with household chores and the added chore of simply living.

Six months after receiving the sad news, spring had come and a blustery March wind had blown smoke back down the chimney and into the room. To reduce its effect, she'd left just enough embers in the fire to keep it going without making so much smoke.

Leaving the fire to its own devices, she'd gone out into the backyard to collect the nearly dried laundry hung out on one of the lines. Arms full, she had heaved herself up the winding staircase. Her hope was that she could air most of it in front of the fire without it ending up smelling of smoke.

At the living-room door, she had met with the sight of Roy's broad back blocking her view of the fire. Only one gas light was lit, its meagre flame dancing in the draught. A brighter light burned in front of him, flames and charred pieces of paper licking upwards into the chimney, the glow of the fire colouring his face.

'You've got it going?' she'd asked and began folding some of the laundry, spreading some of the other onto a wooden clothes horse that unfolded like the leaves of a book.

'You could say that.'

'That's good. This laundry could do with a bit of airing.'

He had made no response. In fact, he had hardly seemed to realise she was there.

Whilst folding a pillowcase, she had stepped to one side so she could see around him and into the fireplace. To one side of him was a small pile of letters. She recognised them as those sent from

Simon – the ones she'd never read. Not only had he never allowed her to read them, but the letters had also been secreted away in a locked tin box under the bed. Now here they were, out in the open. And there he was, feeding them into the fire one by one.

Feeling mystified and confused, she'd stayed silent, crept back out of the room and went downstairs. Better to breathe the foetid air out in the backyard than say anything that might hurt or incite him.

She'd looked up at the clouds billowing over the moon and made a wish. Please let things improve. Make our lives better.

Life had gone on. Simon was never mentioned again.

* * *

The change following the burning of the letters had come gradually. In times past, Roy had been reasonable enough and caring, though never truly passionate. At times, he had a faraway look in his eyes. She'd sometimes tackled him about it.

'Talk to me about it. Tell me about your mate and what you did together.'

The swift turning of his head and the fierceness in his eyes had frightened her. His words had been bitter.

'You can't know what it was like. Nobody can know what it was like.'

She'd tried to treat it lightly but with respect. 'I should imagine it was like Shakespeare said in Henry V – you were brothers in arms. Very close to each other amid all that horror.'

She couldn't read the look he'd given her. The shiver that had run down her spine made her knees shake. There was anger in his look, yet why should that be? It was such a well-known phrase – at least to Jenny, who had come from a house where books were prized possessions.

Over the years, his habits had also changed. In the past he'd not been one to make straight for a pub after work was ended and before going home. On one occasion, she had seen him in the public bar of The Hatchet, a pub approached down dark steps, close by. It had not been her intention to spy on him; she had gone there in search of a job – anything for a little extra money.

Before he'd spotted her and ordered her home, his laughter was the loudest, his voice carrying with an air of authority as he expressed his opinions on government, the working man and how foreigners were weakening the country and even the empire.

Tough men, not used to being scattered like pebbles on a beach, looked askance as he pushed his way through to her, his eyes blazing. 'Spying on me are you?'

She had shaken her head and just about managed to keep her voice steady. 'No. I've come for a job.'

He had looked her up and down, the pretty little knitted hat, the matching handbag, the collars of her white blouse taking the eye away from the faded neatness of her navy-blue jacket and skirt.

She had winced when he'd grabbed her elbow and guided her towards the pub door.

'Roy, you're hurting me.'

'No wife of mine is going to be a barmaid.'

'It's a cleaning job.'

Protesting did no good. He had bundled her through the double doors of the pub, slamming her against the brass handles and pushing her out into the street.

'You don't need a job!'

Outside in the amber evening, he had held her shoulders in a vice-like grip and turned her to face him. Her legs had shaken. She had smelt the beer on his breath, the sweat he'd worked up from a day unloading a ship with nothing except a metal hook and brute strength.

A vicious slap had sent her head to one side.

'I won't have you making a fool of me.'

'I—'

Another slap had sent her head in the other direction.

'I ain't 'aving nobody say that I can't put keep a roof over my family's head. Got that?'

It would have been wise to nod and say that she agreed, but she hadn't. All she did was hang her head forlornly, her cupped hands cool on her hot cheeks. Her friend Polly had suggested she got a job – a daytime job – not behind the bar. That's why she was here. She tried to make him understand.

'I need the money,' she'd admitted.

'Money? What the bloody 'ell do you need the money for? Don't I give you enough? And before you answer, I ain't got enough for luxuries, so don't you go wasting my 'ard-earned money.'

'I don't!' It was a sudden need to fight back that caused the shouted outburst and once she had started, she had to go on. 'I've barely got enough for food and the rent.'

'That's all you need.'

'No it isn't.' Tears had streamed down her face and into her mouth. There would be a price to pay for her outburst, but she couldn't stop. 'I've no money for clothes for the girls – not new clothes – second-hand clothes. I wouldn't buy new. And what about their underwear? Things for school?'

Drawing on inner strength swelling like a fountain within her, she had freed her arms and brought them down on his, thus breaking his hold.

'We live in a pigsty of a house, but that does not mean we have to live like pigs. I've still got some pride, Roy. I made a marriage vow and I'm sticking to those vows. I've made my bed and have no choice but to lie on it. But I want better for my girls, Roy. I want them well fed and well clothed. If I had my way, they'd be living somewhere better than Blue Bowl Alley.' She had taken a deep breath, surprised that he hadn't hit her yet. Now that, she'd thought, would be a first. The courage had kept coming. She held her head high, her chin defiantly thrust forward. 'Now if you want to hit me again, go ahead. I'm used to it.'

'Everything all right here?'

The accent was not local. There were three men, one of them standing slightly forward of the other two.

At first, they were dark figures against the illuminated lead paned windows of the pub. When the pub door had opened, a shaft of light fell on their faces, and on her own.

Roy was his usual surly and aggressive self. 'It's a private matter, chum. Shove off.'

The man who'd spoken had made no move.

'I'm fine. He's my husband.' She had licked her lip and tasted blood.

The man had hesitated. During the phase of light thrown on the group, his gaze had met hers. It might have been her imagination, but she had sensed a second of surprise. Most people on surmising that being the case wouldn't interfere.

The stranger's expression had made her think that them being husband and wife didn't cut much ice with him.

'As long as you're all right.'

She had heard the concern in his voice, though the stranger had kept his eyes trained on Roy, almost as if daring him to lash out at him or her. When nothing happened, all three had doffed their hats and walked off, the one who had spoken glancing back over his shoulder. It wasn't long after that meeting outside The Hatchet that Roy gave her two shillings extra in her housekeeping. There was a catch. She was to accept that a woman's place was in the home.

'You don't go out unless you must. Stick to the local shops. Don't mix with anyone.'

At first, she hadn't fully understood what he'd meant. Not mixing? At pubs like the Hatchet? Was that what he'd meant? 'This helps,' she'd said, referring to the extra money. 'I won't be going for a job.'

'I want you 'ome yer and my tea on the table. It ain't just about a job. No gallivantin' about with nosy neighbours. You got that? They're sluts, just sluts, the bloody lot of them.'

His comment was both unfounded and unfair. Without friends, she would be as trapped as a canary in a cage. He'd already laid down laws about not fraternising with the local women. Now he was restressing his wishes. Soon she'd have nobody to talk to at all – except for Isaac and his wife downstairs.

She disobeyed when she thought she could get away with it. Polly Gifford and Grace Shelley lived in one of the other tenements overlooking the yard. They chatted together when hanging out the washing. Last summer they'd taken their kids to Brandon Hill, chatting and knitting as the kids ran round and around Cabot Tower, the memorial commemorating John Cabot's discovery of North America, until they were dizzy. It was a trip she still looked back on fondly. Now all she dared do was meet up with them in the small park in front of St James's church.

The conversation seemed to carry on where they'd left off back on Brandon Hill in the summer before. Both of her friends still had something to say about men frequenting pubs.

'I told my Joe to take a bed down to the pub. He spends that much time there.'

Polly had a cheery disposition and a face covered in freckles. Her hair was so red, it looked as though it was on fire.

There was laughter and agreement. Grace added that she

wouldn't mind so much if her husband, Roger, could find his way home after drinking too much.

'The number of times that someone's 'ad to bring 'im home. Drank so much, the silly sod couldn't remember where he lived.'

'And straight from work. A pint to wet their whistle, and them still in their work clothes.'

Jenny frowned. 'Roy used to do that, but now he comes home and changes before going out.'

The others raised their eyebrows. A knowing look passed between them. Jenny knew what that look meant. She read pity in it, and she didn't want that. Her attitude turned defensive.

'It's not another woman,' she said, shaking her head vehemently. 'If that's what you're thinking. Roy isn't like that.'

Judging by their eyes lowering swiftly onto the knitting, it was exactly what they'd been thinking.

Polly chewed her bottom lip, her knitting needles thrusting determinedly in and out of the stitches. She was using a fine four-ply wool, but the way the needles were stabbing it might just as well have been string.

Grace had done the same but in an effort at recompense shouted to one of her youngsters who was halfway up a tree. 'Get down from there.'

A pair of dirty legs, socks in grey folds around the ankles, began descending before her son's torso and finally his grubby face appeared. It amused Jenny to see that once Grace's attention had returned to her knitting, he resumed climbing.

The clickety clacking of knitting needles vied with the cawing of crows and the rustling of leaves. From close by came the sound of barrels being unloaded from a brewery dray and the yawning mouth of a pub cellar. A liveried nursemaid walked by pushing a sparkling perambulator. She ignored Polly's cheerful 'good afternoon', her manner aloof as though the snaking of the path was more to her taste than three working-class mothers with noisy children and laps full of knitting.

The passing of the nursemaid was enough to charge their silence.

'Too good for the likes of us,' Grace said.

Jenny laughed. 'Did you see that collar? Starched so stiff it could have cut her throat.'

'I hope it does,' Polly added. 'She's the sort who only looks after somebody else's children. She'll never have any of her own.'

'Not a looker,' Grace remarked. 'Not like our Jenny here.'

'Thank you, dear friend,' Jenny said, her dark eyes flashing in mock humility. 'You've made my day.'

'It's true,' Grace said and Polly agreed with her.

'I've seen the way men look at you, not that you seem to notice. Head in the air and faraway, that's you Mrs Jenny Crawford.'

Jenny felt her face turning pink. 'I've no need to notice the attention of other men. I'm married to Roy. One man is more than enough in my life.'

Grace nudged her. 'Just because you're tied don't mean to say you can't loosen the knots a bit.'

'Grace! Really!'

Although she joined in with their laughter, Jenny felt an element of pain. What would her life have been like if she hadn't married Roy? She'd been barely sixteen when he'd returned from the war back in nineteen eighteen. They'd married two years later. What if his procrastination had lasted longer? The simple truth was that if it had, her affection might have melted with the years. She'd been too young and knew that now. The only saving grace about her marriage were their two daughters.

Polly's voice broke into her musings.

'I notice your Roy's grown a moustache. Must admit it suits him.'

'I thought so too,' Grace said. 'Reminds me of Clark Gable. Looks right 'andsome, 'e does.'

Jenny was used to women finding her husband handsome. The moustache had come about at around the same time as he'd begun dressing very smartly. These days the black moustache looked almost as though it had been drawn on with black paint. He'd also taken to slathering his hair with a copious amount of Brylcreem. He wore it slicked back and from a distance it looked like a glossy cap set on his head. It gave him a military look and to her was slightly frightening. His manner also had changed. Questioning his authority and his rules were not allowed. In the past, he'd been just about tolerable to live with, but of late he'd become more demanding. Rules had crept in. He expected his meals at a definite time, demanded if she'd been out that day, where to and what for.

'A woman's place is in the home and don't you forget it.'

'But I do have to go out and buy food...'

On that first occasion she'd questioned the new rule, his hand had left a red mark across her cheek. She had never talked back again if she could help it, but sometimes it was hard to avoid. She did what she had to do regardless.

The striking of the clock on the church tower startled her into packing up, shouting at the girls to help.

'Oh my goodness. I didn't know it was that late. Roy will be wanting his dinner.'

'It won't hurt 'im to wait,' stated Grace nonchalantly.

No. It's me that will be hurt.

'I must,' she responded, and once Tilly and Gloria were with her, both pleading to stay longer, she gathered them like sheep and headed home.

It was gone six o'clock by the time she got there. The girls peeled off to join their friends sailing a paper boat in the water running along the rainwater channel at the side of the lane.

The first thing Jenny did on entering was to pop into the kitchen. She'd made a mutton, onion and potato pie from the bone and bits left over from Sunday and topped it with pastry. To her chagrin, the range had gone out. Her hands flew to her face in dismay. Hadn't anyone thought to keep it lit?

Just as she thought that Isaac Jacobs came in.

She turned to him; her hands poised in a gesture of total helplessness.

'The fire's gone out.'

He stopped dead in the doorway. 'Is that so,' he said in his calm and slightly accented voice.

Jenny was frantic. 'The girls will have bread and cheese, but Roy will want a proper meal. I made a pie. I thought I'd be back in time to put it in the oven.'

'I was going to clear the clinker with this,' he said, raising his hand. The metal rod was about five feet long and flexible. The range needed such cleaning now and again. 'It wasn't burning so well.' His pink face glowed like Santa Clause on a Christmas card. 'But I thought to cook your pie off first. It's still in the oven.' He opened one of the solid iron doors of the range and pointed at the pie. 'That's a lovely golden crust you've got there, Mrs Crawford. It's a wonder I didn't gobble it all down myself.'

His grin was infectious. Smiling, Jenny shook her head as she took the pie out of the oven. Even though the fire was out, the oven compartments had remained warm. Her pie was perfect. Relieved beyond measure, she heaved a sigh of relief as she wrapped it in a clean tea towel.

She paused long enough to express her gratitude. 'I can't thank you enough. Must go now.'

Turning fast on her heel, she bounded for the stairs. Hopefully Roy had been late getting away from the docks.

Hope was cast aside as she opened the living-room door. Roy

was washing his face in the blue-rimmed enamel bowl specifically kept for the purpose.

'Where the hell have you been?' His voice was muffled by the face towel as he patted himself dry. The smell of Lifebuoy soap was strong. The towel he'd just used was thrown on top of the one he'd used to wash the rest of his body.

'Getting your dinner,' she exclaimed as brightly as she could.

His clean-shaven face shone as though beeswax had been applied.

She tensed at the displeasure in his eyes. A wrong thing said and displeasure would become anger.

He came behind her as she set a knife and fork to either side of a dinner plate. Salt and pepper pots were placed just so.

'Before that. Where were you? I wanted a bath. I wanted a hand with the water.'

It took two people to fetch water from the pump in the yard, heat it on the range and fill the bath, but she had an excuse.

'The water's stone cold. The range has gone out. It's being cleaned out even as we speak.'

Again, the bright voice. Hope intervened again. Hope that she would get through this without him losing his temper. Such a small word, hope, but so big in her life.

'So you've been down there all afternoon baking this pie – with no fire.'

His breath on her neck was warm; even so, she felt a feeling like icy water run down her spine.

'I wasn't there all afternoon. I took the girls out to Brandon Hill with Grace and Polly and their children.'

'Grace and Polly.' There was contempt in the way he mimicked her voice, his intention to make her feel small, inconsequential.

Just for once, she stood up to him. 'There's no need to be like that. They're my friends.'

'You don't need friends. You've got me. You've got your family.'

'But everyone needs friends!'

It was the wrong thing to say. He spun her round to face him. 'You don't. You've got a home to run and me and the girls to look after. That should be enough and will be enough. Have you got that?'

He'd made it obvious from the moment they'd moved in when the girls were young that he didn't hold with neighbours just 'popping' in.

This was one of those times when she felt as though she was drowning and had no recourse but to force her way to the surface.

'That's ridiculous.' She shook her head so hard that her hair escaped from the tight bun she'd bound it back in today. Like a mountain torrent, it fell from around her shoulders. 'They're my friends. I've known them since we moved here. It's small compensation for living in a place like this.'

The muscles of his face tensed. She guessed he was only just about holding his anger back. The truth about where they lived was unpalatable. They'd been thrown out of the rooms they'd first occupied in Montpelier, a neighbourhood just a few miles from the Pithay. She'd never got to the bottom of exactly why the landlady had thrown them out. The suspicion that the woman's daughter was involved weighed heavily on her mind. The landlady would not be drawn, standing tight-lipped when she'd asked. Her husband had made himself absent for comment.

'You deserve better,' the landlady had at last conceded. 'I'd get rid of him if I were you.'

But he's the father of my children, she'd wanted to shout and that was why she hadn't left him.

Strong fingers gripped her arms so tight; she knew she would have bruises. 'Be it ever so 'umble, this is our 'ome and this is where you live. With me. I puts the wage on the table, and you will do as I say. Now, to start with, I don't want that Grace Shelley and Polly Gifford in my 'ome. Got it?'

As he ate his evening meal, she rubbed at the sore spots on her arms. Of course, she got it, though whether she would obey his order was a different matter.

Jenny picked up the empty water bucket and headed for the door.

'Where the bloody 'ell do you think you're going?'

She stopped in her tracks and held up the bucket. 'Where does it look like?'

He looked surprised, not necessarily about the bucket, but the tone of her response. 'Well, get on with it. But don't be long! Hear me?'

Yes. She heard him.

The further down the twisting staircase she went and the further from him, the better she felt.

Something was going on that he wasn't telling her about. There was still the possibility that it might be a woman. Never would he admit to that, of course, but there was a definite gleam in his eye and a new vitality and aura of self-importance. As though he'd grown bigger and had finally made his mark in the world.

'You just wait,' he'd said to her the day before when he'd come in late after working the day shift, washed, changed and went out again.

Where did he go on those nights when it wasn't the pub, why did he sometimes return later from the day shift and earlier from a night shift, sometimes with raw knuckles and a cruel gleam in his eyes?

***

Jenny's mind continued to wander, and she rubbed at the small of her back as she watched Tilly pumping the handle. Her eyes roamed to the ramshackle tenements surrounding her like a high wall between her and the outside world. Like a prison! That's what her home would become if she wasn't allowed to go out or have friends. The very thought of it was unbearable and untenable. She had to go out. Seeing the world and friends outside this quarter was what made her life bearable. Absorbed in her thoughts, she didn't notice that the water level in the bucket was nearing the brim until it began splashing her feet.

'That's enough, Tilly, darling. You can stop pumping now.'

She poured the excess into the drain. Hopefully it might diminish the smell.

She heard the front door slam and guessed it was Roy. The timing was right. He was off out.

'Right,' she said, ruffling Tilly's hair. 'Let's give that bedstead another good scrub. Then I'm off to buy a new mattress.'

Her daughter trailing behind her, she made her way back into the house through the laundry room and up the stairs, pausing on each landing to regain her breath.

Top to toe was the regime for that single bed on account of the room being so small. The luxury of her girls having two separate beds was out of the question. Tilly slept at one end, Gloria at the other. Although Gloria had been bitten, she was neither scratching nor complaining so much, her way of claiming superiority over her sister. Gloria was cocky, a definite chip off the old block, an offshoot of her father. That's why they got on so well. Whilst they'd had no bed one girl would sleep on the sofa in the living room, the other on the two armchairs pushed together to give it some length.

Setting the bucket down on the floor, Jenny poured half a bottle of bleach into the water. Bleach and scrubbing brush were a routine part of her weekly chores, both kept on a shelf out on the landing.

The bleach stung her eyes and hit the back of her throat.

Tilly wrinkled her nose at the strong smell and began to cough.

'Darling, it's not good for you to breathe in this smell. It's bad enough for me. Why don't you go outside and play? It's cold, but you'll be fine if you wrap up well.'

Tilly shook her head. 'I want to be with you.'

The sound of footsteps heralded her younger daughter's arrival. The two siblings exchanged looks, Tilly wearing a pained expression and Gloria's face wreathed in smiles, the kind usually reserved for her father when she wished to get her own way.

Together but standing slightly apart, the sisters watched their mother.

'Are you crying, Ma?' Gloria asked her.

Jenny swiped at her misted eyes. 'No. It's just the bleach. It makes my eyes run.'

On this occasion she was telling the truth. The bleach was responsible. Life made her cry at times. So did Roy.

'At least that old nasty mattress is gone. Did you enjoy watching your father burn the mattress the other day?'

Gloria laughed. 'I heard them pop. Dad said there were a lot of people he'd like to burn.'

Jenny clenched her jaw. She wasn't so sure that he was joking.

As she regarded her hands, getting redder from the burning bleach, she thought about that brief slash of blue sky, the buddleia, and her wish for a garden. What wouldn't she do for a garden?

'Ouch. Don't do that,' said Tilly. 'She pinched me.'

'Behave yourself, Gloria.'

Jenny didn't look up but carried on scrubbing. She just couldn't stop herself, obsessed that the bugs would not come back. Until she bought a new bed she wouldn't stop scrubbing. Her eyes stung and her hands were sore. But she had to do this. She had to do what she could to give her girls a comfortable life. A clean house and bed mattered.

The two girls continued to bicker. There was a marked difference in character between the two of them, though they both had her glossy brown hair and wide blue eyes, the same build, the same taste for music inherited from their Welsh grandmother – or at least that was what Jenny chose to believe.

Tilly was sensitive to her father's moods and close to her mother. Gloria was cockier, and although only nine years old was of a manipulative nature, aware that she was pretty and using all the tools in the box to wind her father around her little finger.

Jenny glanced at the two of them. 'Why don't you both go out to play?'

Tilly wore a worried expression in her eyes that could be merry but mostly held a steady seriousness.

'Can I sleep on the settee tonight? Gloria slept on it last night. We should take turns.'

Gloria tilted her snub little nose with disdain. 'I don't mind sleeping on the settee, but only if it's by meself. I ain't sleeping with 'er!'

'Her,' proclaimed Jenny, who liked to have her girls speak well. She threw Gloria a warning expression. 'Her begins with an aitch.'

Gloria lifted her head that bit higher, expression ripe with disdain. 'I'm not sleeping with Tilly. She takes up all the room.'

'There's no bed or mattress. Until I get a new one, one of you will have to sleep on the settee, one of you in the two armchairs again.'

'No!' Gloria had a way of wailing that set her nerves on edge.

Jenny was exasperated, tired and the bruise beneath her eye ached. She could do without this. 'All right, all right! You can have the settee to yourself.'

Gloria's expression was one of triumph. 'Goody, goody.' She turned to Tilly. 'You've got the armchairs. I've got the settee!' She poked out her tongue. 'Nah, nah, nah, na nah!' With a final thumb on her nose and a wiggling of fingers she was gone, her feet thudding down the stairs accompanied by her mocking laughter.

Jenny sighed. The girls had been closer when they were younger but seemed to have grown apart these last few years.

Still on her knees, she straightened rubbed at the small of her back and eyed Tilly's crestfallen countenance.

'There's not much room in the armchair. I don't want to sleep there,' she said.

'You don't need to worry, my love. Your dad's on night shift. There's a ship in. Got a lot of unloading to do, so you can sleep with me. How will that be?' She flashed her daughter a warm smile.

Roy was on night shift later but was now out with his cronies, attending a meeting that might or might not have something to do with work. He'd not been forthcoming on the subject. All he'd told her was that he was well thought of by those that mattered. She was unsure as to who these people were and wouldn't chance prying too deeply.

Tilly stopped scratching and looked a little happier.

'Just for tonight,' Jenny added, scrubbing brush in hand. 'Tomorrow I'll get you a new bed, but for now, open that window. These fumes are choking me.'

Once one half of the small casement window was open, Jenny got up from her knees and pushed the bedframe as close as she could to the source of fresh air. Though not exactly odourless, the air was as fresh as it could be and preferable to the stinging smell of bleach. Then she was down on her knees again, soaking the joints of the bedstead with the obnoxious mix of water and bleach for a second time and scrubbing for all she was worth.

She needed another mattress, though wouldn't be going to Sam Fowler to buy it. He could keep his crummy stuff. Five bob had been cheap, though was certainly not the bargain she'd thought it to be. Gladys, at Hubert's Empire Store at the junction of Stokes Croft and City Road, had offered her one at ten shillings. She'd passed because she'd not been able to afford it. Now she had no choice but to go back. She needed a mattress as cheap as possible.

3

Gladys Hubert was smoking a clay pipe when Jenny pushed open the door of the second-hand furniture shop on the corner of City Road, the next day. Second-hand furniture at Hubert's was more expensive than Sam Fowler but of better quality. A handwritten notice in the front window proclaimed that all furniture for sale was guaranteed flea, cockroach and bug-free. Whether it enhanced trade was an unknown, pound notes and shillings in shorter supply than vermin in the sorry area known as the Pithay.

Hubert's second-hand shop and pawnbroker, grandly termed 'Empire' stores, was a lighthouse for those in need. Beds, tables, chairs, and sofas made up the bulk of the stock at the front of the shop. Behind that was the pawnbroking business where the most valuable items were kept behind an expanse of double layered galvanised wire.

Gladys sat within sight of the shop door and amongst the second-hand furniture, her bulky figure close to filling a two-seater sofa.

Jenny felt the force of one eye scrutinising her like a fly beneath a microscope. The other eye was screwed up against smoke winding up from a bowl of W. D. & H. O. Wills Navy Shag, a tobacco as black and pungent as tar and much favoured by seafarers.

Jenny perceived intelligence in eyes of liquid mud peering from between the folds of fleshy eyelids above a bulbous nose and flaccid cheeks.

'Well, if it ain't Jenny Crawford. You didn't come back for that bed the other day.'

'I had to think about it.'

'Course you did. I 'eard you bought one from Sam Fowler.'

Jenny felt her face warming. Gladys was one of those people who seemed to know everything that happened hereabouts.

'It was all I could afford.'

Gladys nodded sagely. 'So, what now?'

'A mattress,' Jenny said breathlessly, rushing to get the words out whilst she still had the courage. 'I need a single mattress.'

'Do you now.' It was a statement, not a question.

Jenny took a deep breath. 'The bedframe I bought is fine, but the mattress... it was... well...'

'Lousy,' Gladys exclaimed. 'That's Sam Fowler for you. Crummy bloke, crummy bed.'

Jenny looked down at her shoes. Gladys was indeed the font of all knowledge but being scrutinised by someone who knew so much was unsettling. Gladys Hubert had lived a long time, long enough to observe the best and worst of human nature. One look, often with only one eye, and she sized people up, knew what they wanted and what they were likely to get – from her anyway.

From somewhere, certainly not from her shoes, Jenny found the courage to continue. 'As I said, the bedstead is fine. I've given it a good scrub. I just need a mattress.' Raising her head, she looked Gladys direct in the eye. 'Do you have one?'

The scrutiny continued, almost as though Gladys was trying to recall who she was and what she knew about her. Finally, she said, 'You used to go to school with my Robin, didn't you?'

Jenny nodded. 'Yes.'

'You knows he was sweet on you, don't you?'

Jenny's face reddened. 'We were friends.'

'Childhood sweethearts?'

'I'm not so sure about that,' she said with a light laugh. 'He pulled my pigtails and made fun of the way I used to speak. My mother insisted.'

'Yer mother would. Wanted to be a nob, she did. But there you are, just because you work for the nobs in a big 'ouse, don't make you one.'

Jenny thought of her mother. She'd worked with Gladys in a posh house up in Clifton, an upmarket area of grand houses. The one they'd worked in overlooked the Clifton Suspension Bridge spanning the Avon Gorge, connecting Clifton with Leigh Woods on the other side. Her mother had been besotted with those people, their lifestyle, their houses and the way they spoke.

'He didn't bother you once he was grown,' Gladys continued.

'No.' Jenny found herself feeling embarrassed by the memory. 'He didn't.'

Robin had been the bad boy in the class, even a bit of a bully, but never to her – not once he'd got over the pigtail pulling, that is. Her mother had advised her to marry him, but by then she'd become besotted with Roy Crawford. Against her mother's wishes and despite his frequent moods, she'd been in love with him, was sure she could make him happy and nagged her mother until she'd relented.

It came as a shock when only two weeks following her wedding, her mother had died suddenly. Her heart had stopped, the doctor had said.

Once the funeral costs were paid, there wasn't much left.

For a time, things had gone well enough, Jenny and Roy clinging together, both orphans with no surviving family, but in 1926 the General Strike and the uncertain times had undermined their brittle happiness. Tilly had been born and Roy had almost to beg for work. That was when things had taken a downward turn.

Gladys tapped the stem of her pipe on the furniture arm. 'Always surprised me that you married Roy Crawford.' Her look seemed to turn inwards as though rummaging through her vast store of memories to find the reason she thought that.

'Well. That's life. I hear you've got two grandchildren.'

Gladys kept one eye closed, head cocked to one side. She nodded. 'Marry in haste, repent at leisure.' She chuckled to herself. 'Trouble with princes, and princesses for that matter, is they likely as not turn into frogs ...'

There was something in the way her voice trailed off that made Jenny think that Robin's marriage was far from being a bed of roses.

'I suppose so.'

'But there. Love is blind, ain't it, chick?'

Jenny shrugged. 'We were young. I was young.'

'And now you're married and the romance flew out of the window a long while ago.'

'Well, that's marriage for you,' she said, tossing her head as though she accepted her lot. She had done, but now? She wasn't so sure, though wouldn't admit to it. She shrugged. 'That's the way it is.'

One eye narrowed and incisive, the other squinting almost shut, Gladys nodded in that wise old woman way of hers. 'For better or for worse. Till death do you part. Only sometimes marriage can be a living death.'

Jenny resisted the urge to squirm. She didn't want to be asked anything more about her marriage. She decided to treat it lightly and said, in a jokey manner, 'I heard a rumour you were getting married again. Could that be true?'

Now it was Gladys who was under the spotlight.

She responded by throwing back her head and cackling as witches are supposed to do. Jenny wouldn't have been at all surprised that she might be the real thing. She looked the part. Three wiry hairs sprouted from the wart on her nose. In the process of throwing back her head, gaps between yellow teeth in pink gums were clearly visible.

The searching look descended again. 'Let me tell you this, me dear. I wouldn't marry another bloke if 'is rear was 'anging in diamonds or 'is mouth was full of gold teeth. Money made a bloody big 'ole in my old man's pocket. Georges' Brewery got the biggest share. I got the bloody work!'

Jenny smiled and rubbed her cold fingers together. She knew the history. It was common knowledge that Herbert Hubert had shaken off his earthly coil when staggering out in front of a brewery dray. The accident had occurred after a lengthy session at the Greyhound, an ancient coaching inn in the heart of the city. An ongoing joke had passed into local legend that Georges' Brewery much regretted the fact that one of their own drays had run over and killed one of their best customers.

With her son Robin's help, Gladys had carried on with the business and due to not having a husband spending all the profits was doing all right. If anyone wanted anything Gladys could get it – for a price of course.

Though the old girl had done very well for herself, you wouldn't think it looking at her. Thick black stockings lay in folds around her ankles covering up varicose veins which ran like threads of purple silk over her legs. Her belly wobbled. Her clothes were ancient. All the same, she was regarded as the heart of a community where money was scarce and women's purses were kept even lighter by feckless husbands or their own unpleasant habits – mostly cigarettes and gin.

'As I've already said, all I want is a mattress. A single. I've got the bedstead.'

Gladys regarded her thoughtfully and at length. The searching look and silence made Jenny ill at ease. 'You should 'ave married Robin.'

Jenny felt her face warming. 'Look, Gladys, have you got a mattress or what?'

Gladys carried on regardless. 'He would 'ave made sure you 'ad somewhere decent to live, not that filthy place in Blue Bowl Alley. Full of rats, mice and cockroaches. It's no place to bring up kids.'

'He's got a wife and children.'

'Hmm,' growled Gladys. 'Met 'er at the seaside. I'd throw 'er into the sea if I 'ad my way.'

Jenny headed for the shop door. 'It seems I'm wasting my time.'

'I've got a single mattress.' Her voice rang out.

Jenny stopped. Fingers touching the door handle, she braced herself to calm down. After all, she was here for her children's sake. She walked back to where Gladys was sitting.

'You do?'

Gladys waved one hand in a dismissive manner. 'Problem is I only got one and that's spoken for.'

'Oh.' Hope plummeted.

'Customer concerned needs a single bedstead. Mattress ain't no good without a set of springs to put it on.'

Jenny gritted her teeth. Gladys was playing with her, raising her hopes then crashing them. Her resolve stiffened. 'Do you have a mattress or don't you?'

Smoke no longer rose from the clay pipe, but it remained gripped between the shop owner's teeth – few as they were.

'Are your kids sharing a bed or 'ave they got one each?'

'The room's too small for them to have a bed each.'

Though it was hardly a rare occurrence, Jenny found it hard admitting that her daughters were sleeping top to tail.

What Gladys said next threw her off balance.

'How about a three-quarter bed? Would that suit?'

A vision of the box-like bedroom spun in Jenny's mind. A single bed measured three feet. A three-quarter bed measured four feet. It would just about fit in. The girls wouldn't need to sleep top to tail. There was just about enough room for them to lie next to each other.

'Yes,' said Jenny, hardly daring to get too enthusiastic in case she couldn't pay the price or the bed was rusty and far beyond its best. 'It's a very small box room but should just about take a three-quarter.'

'In that case, I've got something you might be interested in.' Gladys rocked in her chair as though about to get to her feet but didn't. It was just a gesture preceding a casual wave pointing her to the far end of the shop.

'It depends on the price,' Jenny blurted.

Her rocking ceased, Gladys eyed her quizzically with that one shrewd eye, the one not hidden in folds of loose skin that had once been an eyelid.

'I could do a part-exchange. I could do you a deal on your single bedframe – if it's in good nick, that is.' The scrutiny continued. Thought furrowed her broad brow. 'See that brass bed over thur?' She pointed a sausage-like finger to the glint of brass resting against a walnut wardrobe off to her left. 'Now that is a nice one and I can do you a fair price. As I said, it ain't a single. Funny size. Foreign, I think. Falls between being a single but not quite three-quarter. Came from a posh 'ouse out Keynsham way. Woman I bought it from said it was French.' She nodded in the general direction of the bed. 'Go over and take a look.'

Jenny threaded her way through a forest of gate-legged tables, hall stands and marble-topped washstands. Sight of the brass bedstead took her aback. The brass gleamed. A porcelain oval of pale pink roses and blue cornflowers inset into the brass headboard was matched by one in the footboard.

Mesmerised by the sight of it, she reached out and ran her fingers around the largest oval. The delicately painted flowers reminded her of her mother's garden. She'd always grown flowers, but then she'd had a garden – not much of one, but much more than the yard at Blue Bowl Lane where the sun never penetrated and most of the wetness came from the damp ground.

'Do you like it?'

Jenny ran her fingers over the shiny brass. It was beautiful and meant that her two girls could sleep alongside each other – for a while at least – until they'd grown too big to do so. By then, she hoped they'd be living in a house with bigger bedrooms, perhaps even one where they no longer shared a room, let alone a bed. A dream, but one she clung onto.

The bedstead was beautiful, like something from a fairy tale. If it was possible to love an inanimate object, this was it. The bed was the stuff of dreams, the brass bright and shiny, the mattress striped with ribbons of pink silk. She wanted it.

Money. All hopes of buying plummeted at the thought of what it might cost. How much would Gladys want for this?

Hidden behind a broad wardrobe, Jenny took her purse from her shopping bag and examined its contents. Eighteen shillings was the total of her housekeeping. There was also an extra two shillings she'd gained from sacks of worn-out woollens she'd taken to the Red Cow Yard on three consecutive Saturdays. The Red Cow rag-and-bone man had given her two shillings. It wasn't much, but every little bit helped. However, she couldn't afford to spend all that on a bed. She needed to buy food. Roy had passed on some of the extra he'd been earning but had told her to go carefully with it. There was no guarantee he would do it every week. She had to make up her mind about buying the bed quickly, do some shopping and get home. To avoid a row – and a cuff around the ear – she had to be back in Blue Bowl Alley whatever time he came home.

The acrid smell of Navy Shag drifted over to her. Gladys had relit her pipe.

After closing her purse, Jenny went back over to where clouds of tobacco smoke hung like a widow's veil around Gladys's head. Hoping the price would be within her means, she pasted on a friendly smile and gushed a comment.

'I love it so very much, but...' She heaved a huge sigh. 'It's a bit too good for Blue Bowl Alley.'

She was speaking the truth. The brass bedstead with its porcelain decals was far too glamorous for the vermin infested five-hundred-year-old house with flaking plaster and a leaky roof, where the stink of drains remained a problem even in winter.

She felt the full force of the old lady's piercing squint, as though working out how much she could afford – and how much she could get away with.

It was best not to meet the glassy glint, shining like a cluster of raindrops between the folds of loose skin. Jenny kept her eyes lowered; purse clutched in one hand.

Gladys's method of pricing was well known. First, she would test the water, work out how much Jenny had to spend based on what she knew of her life. This was the moment she feared.

In she came with her first move.

'Bear in mind it must 'ave cost a bit new. It ain't any old bed like the sort you'd buy from Sam Fowler. It's a good 'un.'

Wanting the bed at the right price, Jenny was willing to endure the praise and bidding game.

'Fifteen shillings.'

Jenny caught her breath. 'I can't.' She shook her head vigorously. Paying that would take most of the contents of her purse.

The price was daunting, but Gladys was a woman who liked to haggle. If she got top price right away, she would take it. However, when Jenny had run her fingers along the brass, they'd come back coated with dust. The bed had been here a while waiting for someone it suited or, more likely, someone who would pay the price. There had to be room for haggling if she was to take it back to Blue Bowl Alley.

Jenny shrugged helplessly. 'The price is beyond me.'

Sucking in her bottom lip, she took a step towards the shop door, determined to look as forlorn as possible. Acting or pretending had never come easy, but for the sake of her children, she had to play the game.

'I wish I could afford it, Mrs Hubert. If I paid you that, I'd have nothing left for a bit of liver and onions for our tea. On top of that, I've got to ditch the one I bought from Sam Fowler. Thanks anyway. If my mum was here, she'd be thanking you too, her being a friend of yours in the old days.'

They'd been close, still in touch when they were first married and had children. Gladys had given birth to a boy. Jenny was her mother's only offspring.

As Jenny had guessed, mention of her mother brought a change in the shopkeeper's manner. Gladys snorted. 'Your mother would be turning in her grave if she knew you'd done a deal with 'im. You should never 'ave gone there in the first place. Dirty sod, 'e is.' She leaned forward and tapped the side of her nose. 'And in more ways than one. A nice woman like you should keep away from the likes of 'im. How much did 'e charge you for that filthy bed?'

'Five shillings.'

She said it hesitantly. The very fact that she'd bought something so scruffy embarrassed her. The truth was that all she'd had in her purse to give Sam Fowler was seven shillings and sixpence. Five shillings had seemed a snip but had turned out not to be. Put it down to experience, her mother would have said. She was only thankful she hadn't paid the full seven shillings and sixpence.

Gladys tutted. 'Bloody disgusting. And only fit for burning.' The narrowed eyes narrowed some more. 'Did 'e try anything on while you were there?'

Jenny felt her cheeks blazing. 'I did have to step back a bit and keep my distance.'

'Hmm!' Gladys's head shot forward at a surprising speed seeing as it sat on top of a bloated body. 'So, you said no and 'e got 'is own back on you. Your poor little girl. But never mind. I'll get Robin to bring the brass one round in the 'orse and cart later. I'll do you a good price and take the single bedstead in part-exchange.'

Jenny waited apprehensively for Gladys to name her price. Her expectation sent her pulse racing. She dearly wanted that bed. With growing apprehension, she searched Gladys's crumpled face for any hint of what that price might be. At present, she had one eye closed. Jenny knew that once both Gladys's eyes were open, though one little more than a squint, she'd have her price.

Out it came. 'Ten bob.' Both eyes popped from deep wrinkles and then her brows furrowed. 'No.' She raised a finger, one eye closing again as she had a rethink.

Jenny held her breath.

A toothless grin ensued. 'Seeing as I likes you and taking yer iron bedstead in part-exchange, we'll call it seven and six.'

The price she'd been willing to pay Sam Fowler! This bed was so much better.

She almost clapped but settled to clasp her hands in front of her. She could afford to pay five shillings and sixpence from her housekeeping, plus the two shillings she'd received for the sack of moth-eaten woollens.

'Yes. Yes!'

She fumbled in her purse for the right amount and handed over two half-crowns, one florin and a sixpenny bit.

Gladys spat on her palm before picking up the coins. With greater energy than she'd so far exhibited, she lifted her skirt, exposing a pair of knee-length bloomers. The money disappeared into one of two pockets sewn into each bloomer leg. The skirt fell like a curtain over the secret stash, a secure cash register that few would attempt to rob.

A big puff of smoke rose into the air by way of celebration.

'I'll 'ave Robin bring it round this afternoon. He'll be there like a rat up a drain when he hears who it's for.'

Although taken slightly aback by Gladys's description of how Robin would react, Jenny left the shop with a spring in her step.

4

On the way home, Jenny bought one pound of pigs' liver and some bacon scraps from Reynolds the butchers at the bottom of Union Street.

Abe Reynolds was on top form, a twinkle in his eye for any woman under sixty who came into his shop.

'You look pleased with yourself,' he said.

She laughed. 'I didn't know I was.'

'Looking happy is the best way of staying happy,' he said.

'I feel happy. Yes. I feel happy.'

So true. The bed had brightened her day. And Robin Hubert would be delivering it. Even that seemed something of a bonus, taking her as it did back to old times before she was married, even before she'd met Roy Crawford. What a happy time that was, or at least from a distance it seemed that way.

The butcher wrapped her purchases up in white paper and was about to add another layer with a sheet of old newspaper but stopped. 'Whoops. Can't do that. Can't wrap a pound of pigs' liver in something with mention of the king's name on the front page. It wouldn't be right.'

With studied respectfulness, he folded the newspaper in four and laid it to one side.

For some, he was the only king they'd ever known. Some had been small children when he'd ascended the throne back in 1911. They were now in their twenties.

On the way home, she passed a board outside the newsagents and paused to read the headlines. She'd always liked reading. The books she'd brought to her marriage had been sold long ago, the money gone on things more necessary for a home, bedding, children's clothes. They grew so fast. Roy had sold the few books that had survived. Protesting had been useless. When Roy had decided they had to go, that was it. They were gone.

She stopped and considered buying a copy. Roy had specifically said that she wasn't to throw money away. Would he regard a newspaper as a luxury? Yes. Of course he would.

Even so, she hesitated. A quick glance at the headlines didn't tell her much. They mostly related to the royal family, preparations for the coronation and what the new king was up to.

On closer inspection, she espied an article and photo of a local march by Oswald Moseley sympathisers. Closer perusal revealed that fights had broken out between the Blackshirts as Moseley's followers were termed, and members of the communist party.

On a sudden urge, she pulled out a few coppers and bought the midday paper. Roy, who today had drawn the day shift, wouldn't arrive home until around six, so hopefully would be none the wiser. She certainly didn't want him there when Robin delivered the bed. He knew they'd been childhood friends and even though it was a long time ago, Roy wouldn't see it that way. *What was he doing in his house? Was something going on? What were they doing alone there together?*

She ran up the winding staircase to the top floor. The sooner Robin had been and gone, the better.

Hunger gripped her stomach, reminding her that she'd ate nothing since early that morning. On went the kettle, out came a loaf of bread and a bowl of beef dripping. Tea without sugar and a thick slice of bread scraped with dripping and dribbled with salt wasn't much of a meal but was all she had time for. She had a bedframe to take apart and once that was done all she needed was a pair of strong men to take it down the stairs. Isaac, with his bad legs, couldn't possibly make it. With Robin's help, she would manhandle it down the twisting stairs and broken treads.

Briefly, eyes fixed on the sky beyond the window, her thoughts went back to how it had been in the sweet years when Roy had first come to work for her father. He'd been the apple of her eye although at first he ignored her. Her mother had called it puppy love. Her father hadn't really noticed. He'd carried on with the business as best he could, though some days he just sat in the corner, noticing nothing including Roy not doing anything if he could help it. Not that Jenny had really noticed. She'd liked his rebellious nature, comments about the war and those that had been in charge.

'Donkeys leading lions – and from miles behind the front lines.'

The bedstead came apart easily giving her a little more time to put her feet up. Toast and tea hot and ready, she sat down in their one and only armchair, flicked the newspaper flat on her lap and began to read.

The headlines regarding the proposed coronation of the new king took precedence. There were pictures. Some were from his father's funeral. Others were more recent. To her mind, he didn't look very happy in any of them. In one of them, he was waving his hat at the crowds. Only in that picture did he show the trace of a smile. Perhaps the prospect of all that responsibility was too much to bear. Perhaps Roy was right. Everyone had thought him fun-loving though little was known except that reported in the press and on the wireless. Good-looking, fashionable, keen on golf and partying and 'caring for his people's welfare'. She wondered if that was true and then went on to wonder if there was a sweetheart in his life. None had been mentioned, but princes and kings were born to marry princesses whether they loved them or not. That must be hard, she thought and mused on her own marriage. Would things have been different if she hadn't married the man she'd thought herself in love with?

There were a few articles inside the paper that caught her eye. Pledges of loyalty from important people, suggestions about how best to celebrate the new king's ascension to the throne – after a suitable period of mourning of course.

She was about to throw the newspaper into the gate before Roy saw it when she spotted the headline and photo of a Blackshirt rally. Faces twisted with hatred had been caught by the photographer. Fists were flying as were hats and caps. The faces beneath them could have been of men she knew, working men of every description like those who'd marched in the General Strike in 1926. She'd been a new bride back then, had read about the working man's determination to fight for better wages for all.

She wasn't sure what Oswald Moseley's Blackshirts stood for but did know their opponents were socialists and communists.

As a child, she'd seen the hollow faces and sombre looks of her father's friends in the front parlour of their house in Berkeley Street, Eastville. She'd also overheard them saying that a quarter of the population were unemployed, that one hundred and fifty people a day were dying from malnutrition. Things had improved, but poverty was still widespread. Her mother had marched with others, including Gladys Hubert. They'd been vigorous campaigners against deprivation.

'Listen to me,' she'd said to the young Jenny. 'When money is scarce, love flies out of the window. Being poor brings nothing but heartache.'

Gladys had hinted at much the same.

Jenny's gaze returned to the photograph of the fighting Blackshirts. One face amongst the expressions of hatred stood out. She couldn't be sure. There was so much going on around it: gargoyles, not the faces of men, but still, was that Roy amid all that violence?

The prospect of him seeing it scared her. Page by page was screwed up into a tight ball and thrown onto the fire where it burned, blackened and was reduced to ashes.

* * *

It was around four in the afternoon, later than promised, when Robin arrived with the pony and cart, the brass bedframe glinting like gold in a sliver of sunlight that managed to pierce the leaden sky and touched its errant brightness.

After bringing the cart to a halt, the skewbald pony shook its head before hiding its muzzle in the nose bag Robin took from beneath the driver's seat.

Whilst he was thus occupied, she noted his broad shoulders and brimming confidence. Once the horse was taken care of, he turned his attention to Jenny. Their eyes met. Shared affection, a remnant left over from their childhood attraction, brought smiles to both their faces. His was so broad, it seemed to split his face in two.

'Mrs Crawford. How are you doing today?'

She touched her hair a little self-consciously, knew it was clean and glossy because she'd washed it only the night before.

'I'm fine. And how are you, Robin?'

He tipped her a wink. 'Jenny, if you weren't already married, I'd think I was in with a chance.'

'Saucy devil. Anyway, you're married yourself.'

His smile lessened and a haunted look came to his eyes. 'Aye. That I am.'

She wondered at the brief flash of something in his eyes. Disappointment?

'Is your family well?'

'My kids are growing up. Billy and Emily.'

She saw happiness at mention of his children. She didn't know his wife, Doreen, very well so didn't ask after her. Neither did he offer any information.

They bantered as old friends do. Some might call Robin brash, but his bright and breezy attitude was harmless enough, his banter welcome.

His shirtsleeves were rolled up to the elbows, exposing his hairy arms, his waistcoat hung open. Dark curls escaped from beneath a corduroy flat cap set at a jaunty angle. White teeth flashed when he smiled. As a child, he'd told her his grandfather was Italian. She was unsure whether it was true or not.

'I might need a hand getting this up that spiral staircase,' he said, giving the bedframe a slap. 'Nightmare they are. Could put a strong young bloke's back out.' He smiled as he rolled his shoulders to emphasise the point, when in fact it did precisely the opposite. Thanks to all the moving and lifting of furniture, it was unlikely to be the truth.

She laughed at his showing off. 'Not with them muscles, Robin Hubert.'

He glanced up at the crumbling façade of number five Blue Bowl Alley. 'The old man around to give me a hand?'

She shook her head and rolled up her sleeves. 'If you want a good man to do a job, get a woman. That's me. I can help you get it upstairs and the single bed you're to collect is already in pieces.'

He drew his chin into a disbelieving yet admiring look. 'You sure?'

She folded her arms across her chest. 'Robin Hubert, you should know me well enough to know that I'm far from being a weak and feeble woman and don't you forget it. Now come on. Let's get on with it.'

It took almost an hour to manoeuvre the head, foot, side frames and bedspring base of the new bed up the narrow twisting staircase. The mattress was the easy bit. The bedsprings, even though they folded up, were the bulkiest, therefore difficult to get round the sharp turns in the stairs.

Jenny heard Robin swearing under his breath as he tugged at one end and she pushed from the other.

Leaving flakes of plaster behind them where they'd bumped against the wall, they finally made it.

Once in the bedroom, Jenny paused to catch her breath, sweat on her forehead and hands resting on her waist.

Robin barely paused for breath but nodded at the bits of the single bed. 'That's 'andy. Thank your old man for doing that.'

Jenny folded her arms across her chest, cocked her head to one side and fixed Robin with a matter-of-fact look. 'Yeah. I would do, only he didn't,' she said. 'I did it. I've never been helpless you know.'

Shoving his cap back further on his thatch of dark hair, he grinned at her. 'Much appreciated. Old man too busy then?'

'He's been weighed on a lot of late. You know how it is down the docks. If you're in favour, milk it for all it's worth.'

'Good fer 'im. Some of them dock gaffers can be right... nasty.' Both he and she knew he'd been about to use the word that inferred gaffers were born out of wedlock.

She offered Robin a cup of tea. Would he know something that she didn't? Would he tell her?

He declined the tea. 'Too busy, love. I've strict instructions to get this bed frame back before seven thirty. There's a customer waitin' for it.'

He declined her help getting the bits down the stairs.

'It's only a single. I can do it in two trips.'

'Go carefully.'

'I will do,' he shouted back.

There was only emptiness once he was gone. It was a bit like seeing the past escape from before your very eyes.

She longed for that gap to be filled, for him to return and say he'd changed his mind about taking tea with her.

The bell in a nearby church chimed five. Tilly and Gloria came racing in, grabbed a slice of bread and dripping each then ran out again.

Alone again.

'Cooee!'

The clumping of footsteps accompanied the wavering cry.

Brenda Armitage cleaned the public bar of the Bunch of Grapes in King Street just off the city centre. She was around fifty years of age had no teeth and iron-grey hair. Her hands were red with hard work.

She smiled a snaggle toothed smile. 'The hens are laying. I brought you round three eggs. Thought you could make use of them.'

'Are you sure?'

Brenda kept chickens in old orange boxes with bits of wire over the front. Jenny reckoned she had a dozen at least. Some of them were cockerels that crowed first thing in the morning. Goodness knows what the neighbours must think.

'I got loads,' she said. 'They're laying well lately.'

Like her friends Grace and Polly, Jenny sometimes ran into Brenda down at Bakers buying bacon bones to make broth. She'd broadly confided a few pointers as to what men said when there were no women around.

'Jack Fudge reckons being a pub landlord behind that bar is like being a priest in a confessional. He gets to hear everything.'

Jack Fudge was a burly man with a thick moustache and bushy sideburns. A profusion of tattoos acquired during his days in the merchant navy ran up each arm.

Jenny wasn't a great one for going in pubs unless it was with Roy and that didn't happen much nowadays. Anyway, she was unlikely to hear much if she went in there asking questions. Jack Fudge favoured the ringing of his cash register. The last thing he was likely to do was upset his customers' secrets.

Jenny had pretended to be amused at Brenda's eavesdropping. She'd exclaimed, 'Some saucy stuff, I bet!'

They had been in the queue at Bakers corner store when Brenda had told her all this. She'd kept her voice low so low that Jenny had to urge her to speak up.

'I can't catch what you're saying.'

'Got to keep me voice low,' Brenda had replied. 'There's a lot of ears wagging in this queue.'

Brenda had leaned in close. Her breath was warm and wet against Jenny's ear.

'There's a bit of trading goes on in the Bunch of Grapes, I can tell you. Stuff that's fallen off a lorry – only there ain't any lorry. Nicked stuff straight from the docks.'

Jenny had arched one eyebrow in feigned surprise. Married to a docker, she knew full well what went on. Roy had once brought home a piece of meat carved from a frozen carcase and shared out between the gang working the ship that day. She guessed that thieving and sharing a bit with the gaffer was one of the reasons Roy had more regular work nowadays. Sometimes it was a bottle of spirits from a broken crate – bottles of port or sherry for a start.

Jenny and her daughters had tasted raw chocolate from West Africa. It had resembled brown stones, not like refined chocolate at all. She'd also watched as Roy had sat at the table and rolled out golden leaves of Virginia tobacco. She'd smelt the rich aroma as he'd sliced the fine leaf with a cut-throat razor or sharp carving knife. The resultant tobacco was stored in a tin along with a packet of cigarette papers.

'You tell no one,' he'd said to her when he'd caught her staring. That was the first time he'd brought home tobacco stolen from a broken crate.

'Won't you get into trouble,' she'd asked as she'd watched. 'What if somebody tells the police?'

'And who's going to tell them?'

He'd sprang so swiftly that the chair he'd been sitting in fell over backwards.

Jenny had stepped back and crossed her arms across her face. 'I was only watching. Hit me anywhere, but not my face. Please!'

Perhaps if Tilly hadn't suddenly appeared in the doorway, he might have slapped her around the head just because she'd asked him not to. He was contrary like that.

'Mum? Are you all right?'

Jenny's heart had lurched at the sight of her daughter's frightened expression.

The last thing Jenny wanted was for her daughters to be affected by her fractious marriage. She had a mask for such occasions, a bright smile meant to convey that everything in their world was lovely – when, of course, it was far from that. A bright voice too.

'I'm fine, love.'

To his credit, Roy never hit her when their daughters were present.

She had grasped the opportunity to escape, placed an arm

around her daughter's shoulder and gave her a reassuring hug. 'Are you hungry? Fancy some bread and jam?'

Tilly had eyed her father warily.

'Go on then, love,' he'd said to her. 'Get yerself some bread and jam.'

A tainted look of understanding had passed between them. The last thing she wanted was for Roy to take his temper out on either of their children. It hadn't happened so far, but Tilly was growing up. There'd always been defiance in those liquid brown eyes. As knowledge increased so would defiance.

Brenda was speaking now, bringing Jenny back to the moment. One comment struck a raw nerve and made her wonder.

'Had a right show the other week. A tart named Julie Giles came in mouthing about being owed money by one of the customers. "I gave 'im what 'e wanted and 'e scarpered without paying. I wants me money and I wants it now." Right hullabaloo it was. Turned out the bloke who owed 'er 'ad got on a ship and shoved off. Was a docker with a wife and four kids. Didn't stop 'im from paying for women though. Not that 'e's the only one. Far from it...'

Jenny swallowed before proclaiming, 'My Roy sometimes drinks at the Bunch of Grapes.' She said it in a slow, calm fashion, seeking disclosure, though unsure as to whether Brenda would confirm that Roy was amongst those who consorted with prostitutes. Could that be the reason he'd changed over the years because he was getting what he really wanted elsewhere?

'Life and soul of the party, your Roy – when he comes in.'

She felt Brenda studying her, discerning she was asking a question in not so many words.

'I've never seen your old man with a tart. He's always with the blokes, laughing and joking with the best of 'em. Always got a lot to say for 'imself 'as your Roy. Don't like foreigners for a start. Got a lot to say on that subject. So 'ave the blokes he 'angs around with. Some of 'em are them Blackshirts, smooth as you like but dangerous. I keeps away from them meself. Ain't got no time for politics – or for loudmouths, for that matter.'

Jenny had stopped listening. She remembered the time when she'd gone to the pub and heard him spouting about foreigners with a group of men who seemed to be hanging on his every word. Her mind turned to the report in the newspaper and the photo of men with cruelly distorted faces and one face in particular, the one that looked like Roy.

5

Rudimentary cooking at Blue Bowl Alley could be conducted on the small fireplace in each suite of rooms. Cooking a joint of meat or a big pan of stew or pan of something fried was done in the old-fashioned kitchen on the ground floor. It was next to the lean-to laundry and dominated by the huge Victorian coal-fired range that belched heat summer and winter.

Hidden by curtains made of sacking were two rooms with arched ceilings and no windows, each set with a full-size zinc bath. At one time, these rooms too had been occupied by large families too poor to pay rent for anything better. Following the families falling ill and a visit from the health department, the owner of the property had been served notice not to rent these out. He was further ordered to supply zinc baths for the tenants to keep clean and not fall ill like the previous tenants of these dank, cellar-like rooms.

'They'll be wanting me to provide them with running water before long,' he'd grumbled.

The kitchen was the best of these rooms, mainly because it was always warm, sometimes too hot. The tenants from all floors tended to congregate there whilst they waited for their food to cook.

Although grateful for its heat, Jenny considered the cast-iron range something of a monster squatting in its huge fireplace. Hot coals glowed at its heart like the entrance to hell. At either side were two large hobs above two identical ovens. Fire irons hung from hooks at the side along with old rags. The rags were necessary to prevent burnt flesh when meat was being retrieved.

Hair clinging damply to her head, Jenny lifted the lid of the saucepan, smelt what was cooking and dipped in a wooden spoon.

'Smells nice, Mrs Crawford. Fit for a king, I shouldn't wonder.'

Isaac was sitting at the big old pine table that occupied the centre of the room waiting for his own meal to cook. He had two plates ready, one for himself and one for his wife Ruth.

Tonight they were having meatballs. 'Thick with onions and gravy,' he'd said to her and licked his lips. It had only just gone in, so was likely to take some time.

After having a taste of the stew herself, she passed the spoon to Isaac. 'Here. See what you think.'

Despite his wide mouth, he sipped at the spoon daintily, the pinkie finger of his hand held aloft, more like a lady than a manual labourer.

He threw back his head and closed his eyes as he savoured the taste. 'Mmmm. Nectar.'

Jenny laughed. 'Hardly that. Pork bones, potatoes, carrots and onions. I only hope Roy thinks it's nectar.'

She turned back to the range so Isaac wouldn't see her expression. Roy had taken her by surprise and come home early that day, demanding hot water for a bath and a shave. Buckets were placed on the range and gradually she'd filled the bath.

He'd said nothing to Isaac as he'd stalked through the kitchen, merely ruffling Gloria's hair and tapping Tilly on the cheek. In fact, the look he'd thrown Isaac had been downright unfriendly. He'd also taken a brown paper carrier bag in with him.

'Fresh clothes,' he'd said when she asked what it was as she took his work clothes, shook them out and hung them over the back of a battered chair.

Isaac had already placed a vast cauldron of water on one of the hobs at the side of the range.

'You have it,' he'd whispered seeing her consternation. 'I can wait.'

If Roy had heard, he said nothing.

Thanks to Isaac's kindness, the bath didn't take too long to fill once she'd added her own pan of water.

She had smelled his sweat as she'd pulled off his underwear. Naked, he'd stepped into the hot water.

'Scrub me back.'

Taking a large block of Sunlight, she'd scrubbed his back and swilled it off with a face flannel, the warm water running down his back.

'And wash my hair. I want it looking decent tonight.'

As so many times before, she'd wondered if he was getting himself ready for a woman. Why else would he be doing all this? But she wouldn't ask. She'd prefer him to be out so she could have the house to herself. The stark truth was that she'd prefer him to be with someone else.

'That'll do. Give us the soap and flannel.'

'Your towel is on the chair.'

He hadn't answered. He'd frowned at the soap and flannel as he'd lathered one against the other, a signal that he wanted her to leave. She'd left him willingly with his clothes and a towel.

Isaac was telling her about somebody at the fruit and veg market, how they cut the sprouting roots off potatoes to take home and plant in their garden.

'He reckons he's grown loads of potatoes like that.' He shook his head. 'Makes me wish I had a garden, but then what with my legs, I can't see it would come to much.'

She turned to Isaac and asked after Ruth. 'How are her legs today?'

He made a so-so signal with his hand. 'Not so bad. A bit of dry weather makes all the difference.' He sighed and leaned against the back rail on the pine bench where he was sitting. 'This place will be the death of 'er, she says. Summer or winter, it's the damp.'

Holding up a ladle, she asked him if he'd like a drop more stew. 'There's plenty here.'

It was the least she could do.

He shook his head. 'I wouldn't want to leave you short. Anyway, I'd spoil me dinner. Ruth would cuss me uphill and down dell if I don't eat it all up. Takes her a lot of effort to put something on the table of a night, what with 'er joints being the way they are.'

Jenny smiled. She wasn't taking no for an answer. 'How about just a cupful?'

She held a ladleful of stew out of the saucepan, her pretty lips smiling enticement.

He nodded. 'All right then. Half a cup, but only of the gravy and no more.'

Isaac finished the rich broth Jenny had filtered from the thick stew and was voicing his appreciation just as Roy emerged from behind the sack curtain. She saw him stall, eyes glaring at Isaac, less so at her.

Isaac wished him good evening. Roy ignored him.

She didn't need him to say that he'd left the bath water for her to empty but had been about to ask him when he wanted his dinner.

Roy froze. His face was pink from the bath, but his look was cold. The glare he threw Isaac was one of contempt. The one he shot in her direction chilled her blood.

'I'll take my food upstairs,' he said. 'An Englishman's home is his castle and should be only for Englishmen.'

She felt embarrassed for both herself and for Isaac.

Another icy glare sped like an arrow in Isaac's direction before Roy headed for the stairs.

She called after him. 'Roy?'

He didn't look back. The sound of his tramping feet came from the narrow stairwell. Both she and Isaac raised their eyes to the ceiling. Dust puffed down from the ceiling plaster in time with her husband's heavy tread.

'It's nearly...'

He didn't give her chance but slammed the door behind him.

Hiding her fear, Jenny went back to her cooking, smiling at Isaac as though there was nothing wrong at all. As though she wouldn't bear the brunt of whatever it was Roy was angry about.

Isaac made a show of not noticing, though she knew beyond doubt that he had.

'My, Jenny, that was smashing and just enough. I won't be spoiling me dinner.'

'I'm sorry that Roy was so rude,' she said. She plastered on a smile. Always plaster on a smile. A fixed smile hid the hurt beneath it, a shield between the truth and the world. Roy was in a mood; she could tell but felt it her duty to make excuses. 'He's been working nights. It's made him tired.'

Isaac was silent. His eyes were downcast. One set of bony fingers stroked his silky beard.

'There. I'll leave you a bit more gravy...'

She was about to pour some from the saucepan and into the cup, but Isaac's hand, gnarled with a lifetime of work, covered the cup.

'You are very kind, but I have had enough.'

The sudden change in his manner confused and hurt her.

'Right. Then I'd better get going and give Roy his dinner.'

All the residents left their crockery and cutlery in the kitchen. The alternative was to take it up and down the stairs along with the prepared food. She certainly wasn't looking forward to traipsing upstairs, but Roy was in a mood. Lingering would only make matters worse.

Lid on the pot, dish and tea towel tucked beneath her arm, Jenny paused by the door. She looked back at Isaac. He'd pulled a newspaper from his pocket. His brows furrowed as he read it and his shoulders were hunched. She wondered what he was thinking about, possibly how rude her husband had been. His frown deepened; his eyes fixed on the front page of the newspaper. He sighed. Shook his head. Her overall conclusion was that he was feeling despair over something in the newspaper.

'Will I see you tomorrow?' she asked.

Isaac remained sitting stiffly, eyes downcast, skimming over the front page of the newspaper. Bony fingers forked over his forehead. He nodded in an oddly abstracted manner that made her think it was not entirely down to Roy's behaviour.

She felt it her duty to make amends, to apologise for something she had not said or done, but to cling to the excuse that he was tired. 'Don't worry about Roy. He'll be over it by tomorrow.'

Isaac came out from behind his hands. Unblinking, he gave her a look that made her feel naïve and fearful. At one moment, she interpreted it as sadness, but the next minute she changed her mind and thought it was fear – more than fear – outright terror. 'Your husband and others like him will never be over it. Never.' He shook his head and wrang his hands in front of him, one set of long bony fingers pulling on the other.

She didn't understand what he meant and that made *her* angry.

'Well, I can't stand here wasting time. He'll be wanting his dinner before going out.'

Isaac lifted his head and looked at her. 'He is going to a meeting.' It was a statement not a question, one that she thought he had no business making. How could he know more than she did?

She frowned. 'What makes you say that?' Her voice quivered.

Isaac sighed. 'He wears black. The Blackshirts wear black. That is where he is going.'

She vacated the kitchen swiftly. Her heart pounded. The brown paper carrier bag. Why hadn't his appearance struck her in the same manner as it had Isaac? Her mind went back to those awful photos on the front page of the newspaper. The riot. The fighting, the set jaws, curled lips, and hard angry faces.

She'd only read a few sentences before turning the page, too upset and disgusted to read the reasons why these men had been out for trouble. It was all about foreigners, colour, race and religion. These people, these Blackshirts led by a man named Oswald Mosley, went out looking for trouble, and if they couldn't find any, then they made it. That was what the newspaper had inferred. And it hadn't stopped if the despair etched on Isaac's face was anything to go by.

Her thoughts were in a greater stew than the one she carried in the saucepan. As she climbed the stairs, some of what she'd read came back to her. It was their aim to infiltrate trade unions and similar associations, to recruit working-class men, especially those who had fought in the Great War and felt passed over by their country, left without jobs, homes and the self-respect that came with it.

She raked over the article in her mind, trying hard to remember other details, principally the name of the organisation. She was almost at the door to her humble home when it came to her. The organisation was called the National Union of Fascists.

Trembling inside and out, she heaved her hip into the door of the top-floor rooms. Roy was standing at the window, his back to her, looking out. His broad frame dressed in black blocked out the light. Where had these new clothes come from?

She drew in her lips as she set the saucepan, plate and cutlery on the table.

Her heart was pounding and her throat too dry to speak, yet she had to say something.

She licked her lips and tried to sound normal, as though downstairs had never happened. 'Better eat your dinner before it gets cold.'

He spun round on her; his look as black as the new clothes he was wearing. Before she could make a move, he grabbed her hair.

'You are never again to feed that old Jew. I don't put food on the table for you to give away. Have you got that?'

She yelped. A fiery tingling broke out on her scalp, the feeling of a handful of hair being pulled out by the roots. What with downstairs and now this, a new realisation dawned. The fear she'd learned to live with was cracking. There had to be something better than this life she led. Live or go under. For the sake of her girls, she would not go under. The time had come to stand up for herself and in doing so, for them.

She grasped his hand and tried to pry his fingers from her hair. 'You didn't put the vegetables in that soup. Isaac gave them to me. Every week, he gives me vegetables. If he didn't, we'd starve to death.'

He flung her away from him, then grabbed her back, his eyes blazing. 'And what did you give him in return!'

'Pennies,' she shouted. 'Nothing but pennies.'

She knew what he meant. Had Isaac had his way with her. Isaac was disabled and gentle, a kind man who didn't deserve to be the subject of distorted truth.

In nightmares, she sometimes saw monsters, men whose features caught in light and shade made them look demonic. That's how Roy looked now, blotches of anger staining his cheeks.

'If he's laid a hand on you, I'll kill him. If you let him, I'll kill you too.'

Despite the pain from her tugged hair, she managed to shake her head. 'And I'd turn you in. I swear it, Roy. I swear it on my daughters' lives, you hurt the old man and I'll turn you in.'

The moment she saw the twitching of a pulse beneath his eye, she knew she'd said the wrong thing. Not only had she stuck up for Isaac, but she'd also threatened him. Dressed in his black shirt, his hair gleaming, muscles bursting against his sleeves, he was a new man, one opposed to anyone who didn't conform to the fascist model.

In an instant, he'd been demeaned because she had openly stated that some of the ingredients in the stew were not paid for by him but given her by Isaac Jacobs, a crippled Jew who was as poor as they were. Unfortunately to Roy's mind, and that of these people he was consorting with, Isaac was lower than them, less than a dog, less than anything living.

Without giving her chance to question what he was doing, or to say sorry, or to say anything, he grabbed her wrist. His glance went to the stew. She knew what he was going to do.

'Don't Roy. Please. Don't!'

She pleaded, dug in her heels, leaned backwards in an effort that he wouldn't succeed in his intention.

Smelling of shaving soap, his face was as a monstrous mask of the man he had become, eyes wild, mouth a twisted sneer.

'I'm master in this house. You do as I say. And don't you forget it.'

Although she resisted, crying out and only barely stopping

short of a scream, his grip tightened on her wrist. She tried to jerk back, but it was no use. Her hand went into the hot stew.

In order that her girls wouldn't hear and come running, Jenny's scream was muted. That's what she always did, although on this occasion another reason held sway. Roy wanted it to burn, to scald, to hurt enough to warrant a scream. The stew had been brought all the way upstairs so had had time to cool down. It was not scalding hot, but she made the right noises, just enough to massage his ego and reaffirm his superiority.

'Now just listen to me,' he hissed, his fingers tangled in her hair. 'You're not to 'ave anything to do with Isaac Jacobs. Is that clear?'

She eyed him silently. The change that had occurred earlier seethed in her belly. She was careful not to let it erupt in her eyes. In her heart of hearts, she wanted to defy him, but her fear for what might happen to her and the children – the workhouse, destitution – silenced her. Every married woman counted on a man's wage, but in time she would find a way out of this. There had to be something better and somehow, somewhere, she would find it.

He wagged a warning finger close to her face. 'And I don't want you 'aving anything to do with 'is missus. Got it?'

She neither nodded nor spoke but hung her head as though she was both beaten and obedient. She gritted her teeth when he squeezed her hand.

'I don't want you giving 'im any food, even a stale crust. I work bloody 'ard to put food on the table. If it weren't for the likes of 'im, there wouldn't be the unemployment there 'as been. Lucky for you the new gaffer thinks the same way that I do.'

But it isn't reflected in my housekeeping; that was what she wanted to say. Instead she pointed out that she'd only given Isaac a cup of stew whilst he waited for his own meal. 'And he gave me the vegetables. He always gives me a few bits and pieces from the market.'

'And that's what turned it into pigswill.' He bellowed it loudly into her ear. 'Giving any of it to a Jew is like giving it to a pig. Or a black. Anyone not proper British.'

'But he gave me—'

'No more,' he shouted.

For a moment, it looked as if he was going to hurl the lot through the window – saucepan and all. When he flung her into the corner, she found enough courage to shout that the girls hadn't eaten.

'Think of them, will you?'

Turning his back on her, he stood with parted legs in front of the mirror above the fireplace, eyeing himself full on, then in profile. He smoothed his hair, already glistening with Brylcreem. His hair glistened. He ran his hands along each side of his head. A grime-free finger, yellowed with nicotine, lovingly stroked his newly grown moustache. If Jenny could have read his mind, she would learn that he'd copied the one Oswald Moseley himself sported.

Her hand was only slightly red and felt better once she'd dipped it into a bucket of water.

Roy seemed not to notice.

Satisfied that his black uniform was immaculate, he threw her a warning look.

'Now just remember. Nothing to do with them downstairs. Right?'

She nodded, her eyes big with fear, her stomach taut and empty. She'd had nothing to eat and doubted she would eat anything tonight. Not after what had happened.

'If I didn't have an important meeting... I'll see you later.'

The door slammed and his feet thudded off down the wooden

staircase. Once the sound of his footsteps was no more, she got to her feet.

Despite everything, the girls must not know what had happened. She had to be their mother, there for them no matter what she had to go through herself.

Her girls were the world to her. No matter what, Tilly and Gloria came first. But how long before his brutality was turned in their direction? And how long could she tolerate living without love, without happiness? Only time would tell.

6

MARCH 1936

March blew in like a lion, tearing clothes from washing lines and cracking sheets like billowing sails. April was longed for when hopefully the March wind would go out like a lamb and the dripping dampness of Blue Bowl Alley would go with it.

The girls were growing out of their winter clothes. They needed bigger sizes of clothes that would take them through spring and summer.

Jenny met up with Brenda outside the Salvation Army Tabernacle where an auction of clothes and household goods was taking place. As they rummaged through what was about to be sold, Brenda excitedly told her the most wonderful news.

'I'll be chucking in me job at the Bunch of Grapes before long. Me and Harold's bin offered a council 'ouse in Southmead.' She placed a hand on her chest and breathed a huge sigh. 'We've 'ad our name put down fer ages. And now it's 'appened. I can't believe it, Jen, I really can't.'

Jenny couldn't help feeling envious as she offered her congratulations. 'You lucky thing. Wish they would offer one for us.'

Brenda touched her arm affectionately. 'Get your name down,

love. You won't get one unless you put yer name down. It's your old man that's got to do it. The head of the household, the man in the family 'as to do it.'

Jenny fingered a skirt that might just fit Tilly and sighed. It was a lovely shade of blue and in good condition. 'I have suggested moving to a house with a garden, but he doesn't want to leave the Pithay or Blue Bowl Alley. He was born in the Pithay. Reckons the only time he'll leave is in a box.'

Cigarette hanging from the corner of her mouth, Brenda nearly choked with laughter. 'Did you tell 'im you'd arrange it for 'im to go out in a box if that was what he wants? I bloody well would. Us women can cope without men – that's what I fink. Half the time they wear their brain in their pants – especially once they've sunk a few pints. I can't wait to move meself, and Harold is 'appy if I'm 'appy. Who wouldn't be? Your man is being daft. What's 'e got against a council estate anyway?'

Jenny handed over two coppers for the skirt, plus a threepenny bit for two dresses that would fit either of the girls. Less than sixpence for three items of clothing.

'Roy says that the council estates are too far out and he's got to think of getting to work at the docks.'

Brenda drew in her chin, cigarette now clenched in a different position. 'Don't he know they've got a bus service? Anyway, they've got their own shops, schools and everything! Even pubs. You got no need to go into town to shop.'

Jenny knew she was right and wished so much that it was her who was moving into a council house.

Brenda further extolled the virtues of the estate. 'Out by the aerodrome. And there's pubs nearby. I might be able to get a job there. Bags of fresh air though. That's what we want.'

Jenny sighed at the thought of gardens and wide-open spaces. Even the countryside was nearby. 'The girls would love it.'

'There you are then,' said Brenda, waving around the last half of her cigarette and sprinkling ash over the items piled on the counter in front of her. 'Never give in or give up, girl. Keep nagging until he gives in.'

The thought of Roy ever giving in to anything she wanted seemed remote. It wasn't as though she was asking for herself. She imagined Tilly and Gloria running around a garden. She imagined flowers growing. She imagined the sun on her face and being able to turn on tap above a kitchen sink rather than pump water from an ancient device that had stood in the yard for a hundred years or more.

'I might ask him again.'

'You should. For your kids' sake.'

* * *

No matter what, Jenny had every intention of keeping her children fed. This was why she was waiting at the pump this morning. The bucket was full and all she had to do now was to take it upstairs, but not yet. Despite her husband's aggressive behaviour, she had not curtailed her association with Mr and Mrs Jacobs. No matter what Roy said, Isaac was her lifeline.

The day was unseasonal, rain falling from clouds of mottled grey, puddles forming in the yard and clothes soaked through.

Wet and beginning to shiver, she hung around. Isaac was late and she began to worry. He should have been here by now.

The walkthrough linking the yard to Blue Bowl Alley was dark with damp and shadows. The cobblestones were slick with the rain that blew in from either end. In times past, its purpose had been to allow a horse and cart to come through into the yard. Only the milkman's horse and cart came through it nowadays. Apart from that it was little used except by Isaac. Someone had told her that it had also been used for bringing through animals for slaughter. People used to kill their own meat back then. One side of its length was in permanent darkness. The other a gloomy excuse for daylight.

Her eyes narrowed as she detected movement.

First there was one figure, short and moving fast on disfigured legs. Isaac was careering through the walkthrough faster than she'd ever seen him move before.

Behind him, moving from the gloom at the far end and into the shadows, three figures bore down on him. The sticks they were waving hit the low-hanging roof, their hobnailed boots clanged and clattered over the cobbles.

'Isaac!' her cry was breathless, lost in the wind and the rain.

Isaac ran as fast as he could, but his legs being the way they were, he had no hope of outdistancing his pursuers. They were catching up fast and she knew there would be dire consequences should they catch him.

In her eagerness to help him, she kicked over the bucket. The water spilled and the bucket drew her attention. Out of desperation and the belief that any kind of weapon was better than none, she picked up the empty bucket by its handle and headed to where Isaac was now a heap on the floor.

Sticks were raised and more than one blow fell on the old man. Screaming at the top of her voice, she launched herself at the three dark shapes swinging her bucket, crashing against one head and then another.

'Leave him alone! Leave him alone, you bullies.'

As her eyes adjusted, she saw the blackness of these men was not just down to the dim light in the alley. They were all attired in black. Even their faces were covered.

A strong hand grabbed her wrist with a familiar grip. A voice hissed close to her ear, 'Keep out of it.'

He swung her so that she tumbled out from the underpass and into Blue Bowl Alley itself. The bucket flew from her hand, rattling as it tumbled along the stone gutter despite the gushing water.

'Help,' she screamed hysterically, looking up and down the alley. 'Help. Someone is being murdered.'

The weather being bad and the time for returning for work not yet arrived, the alley was empty. Grey figures at the spot where the alley joined Union Street hurried along the wet pavements, heads hunched into the driving rain. Either they didn't hear her or didn't want to get involved. She kept shouting all the same, and finally somebody heard her.

They ran to her, three men, their boots clattering over the uneven ground.

It crossed her mind that they might be of the same persuasion as those in the walkthrough. Nevertheless, she had to chance it.

Pushing her hair from her eyes, she saw they looked like ordinary working men.

'What is it, love?'

She pointed into the underpass. 'They're killing him,' she sobbed, tears now running unchecked down her cheeks. 'They're killing him. And they're dressed in black,' she added.

They didn't hesitate. Swooping like eagles, they swept into the underpass. It was difficult to see what was happening. The men who had just arrived and those already there blended into one black mass, arms flailing, feet scruffling on the slippery ground.

It was hard to tell for sure, but she surmised that the rescuers were getting the better of Roy and his pals. She had no doubt it was him.

The black-clad men were big enough, but although she'd only had a fleeting glance, the new arrivals had seemed more lithe, more agile. She guessed them to be younger.

Her judgement began to be proved. One black-clad man

came running out, followed by a second, then a third. The first two got away. The third was detained and held against the wall by the three men who seemed very much in control of the situation.

'Right, mate. Let's see your face.'

Jenny didn't need to see the face of the third man. Roy had been at work last night and had gone out in black clothes soon after he had got up that day.

She heard a voice. 'Bloody fascist. That's what you are ain't it, old pal. Giving the poor old bloke a bit of bashing, was you?'

'None of your bleedin' business.'

Roy tried to resist, but the three men meant business. She wasn't quite so sure that they were younger than him but they were fit and just as fired up with what they believed in.

'It is our business, old pal. All three of us are members of the Labour Party and we ain't puttin' up with no bully boys round 'ere. I've got yer card marked, mate, and I'm close by. Me and my friends 'ere will be patrolling on a regular basis and we won't be putting up with you and your bully-boy tactics – especially attacking the likes of the old man here.'

'He's a Jew.'

'So what? I'm a Catholic. My mate here is a Methodist and my other mate...' He glanced at his third colleague. 'Well. Whatever he is, is his business. All muckers in. So, keep yer punches to yourself. I don't want to see you around here at all. Got that?'

Roy jerked his head in a single nod. Blood was pouring from his nose and from a wound at the corner of one eye. Bloodshot eyes swivelled in her direction. She saw something close to pleading in that look and at first it was difficult to work out what he was pleading for. And then it came to her. He didn't want her to tell these three tough young men that he lived here. He didn't want them catching up with him again. Not just because he didn't want any trouble. It was more than that. They scared him. These three young men who'd come to Isaac's rescue scared him.

'Isaac!'

She pushed past the group and into the gloom. Because of his legs more than anything else, Isaac was having trouble getting to his feet.

'Are you all right?'

He leaned against her when he stood up, the fingers of one hand digging into her upper arm. He dragged her close. 'They wanted to kill me.' Even in the gloomy tunnel, she could see his puzzled expression. 'Just because of what I am. Is that not crazy?'

She couldn't answer. The fact that one of those who'd injured Isaac was her husband sickened her.

'Is the old man all right?'

The speaker was the man she recognised as the first to have come to her frightened shouting.

Isaac answered before she could. 'Please. I am fine.'

The ringleader of the rescuers pushed through and insisted on escorting Jenny to her door.

'It's fine...'

'It isn't fine and I won't take no for an answer.'

The man had a powerful presence. He'd also aroused her curiosity, his face and voice somewhat familiar. Had she seen him before? Perhaps so.

He was forceful, yet in a gentle way. She couldn't say no.

Once out in the better-lit yard, Jenny saw the face of the man who had come to their rescue. He was blue-eyed and had a strong jaw. A tweed cap sat flat on a head of dark blonde hair. Creases lighter than the rest of his face made her think he'd spent time in sunny climes staring at the sun. He saw her appraising look, one that conveyed she would like to know more. To her surprise, he gave her the same enquiring look.

'Are you his daughter?'

She shook her head. 'No. Just a neighbour.'

They held Isaac between them, the other two men trailing along behind.

'My name's Charlie,' he said. 'Charlie Talbot.'

'Pleased to meet you, Charlie,' she said. 'We both are, aren't we, Isaac?'

'Very much so.'

As Isaac made to unlock the door, she saw Charlie's gaze absorbing the unrelenting gloom of the courtyard. At first, his look was one of alarm but in seconds became pity.

Although her surroundings were none of her fault, she felt shame. How dreary it looked, how antiquated and run-down. The ancient water pump, the glowering buildings and the mossy cobbles; the rain running in torrents from gutters choked with weeds coupled with the lack of decent daylight gave it a primeval, cave-like appearance.

Her husband's warnings that she was not to have anything to do with their neighbours, was shoved to one side. Fear diminished by a fierce feeling of defiance made her chance looking in his direction but he was gone. He'd intimated that she should not disclose that he lived here. That seemed good enough reason for why he'd disappeared. So be it. She would keep to that promise but wondered at what he would say when he did come home.

She swallowed the fear and concentrated on the here and now, thankful that all this had happened in daylight and her daughters were at school.

Isaac fiddled with the cast-iron handle of the door that opened to the stairs to his home.

'It's difficult to open,' she explained to Charlie. 'Isaac usually heaves into it with his shoulder.'

'And you?'

It meant nothing, but she didn't want him to know that she didn't live here. Not yet at least.

Isaac sighed, his shoulders sloping in consternation. He waved a hand at the pouring rain. 'All this wetness, the door has swollen.' He gave Charlie a direct look. 'Do you think you could oblige?'

'I dare say.'

One muscular shoulder thudded against the weather-worn oak and the door sprang open to expose the set of narrow stairs leading up to the first floor which were separate to the ones leading to the upper floors.

Led by Isaac, Charlie following at her back, Jenny entered the home of her friends, those very people that filled her family's bellies with food, the very same ones Roy seemed to regard as enemies.

The vision of Isaac being beaten refused to leave her mind. Should she have seen it coming? What could she have done to prevent it? Too many questions and all sprouting from her own guilt. Gladys's words came back to her about marriage. It was an ordeal not a permanent honeymoon. As for his violence, she'd never expected it to extend beyond her, beyond the four walls that was their home.

Ruth expressed a mew of surprise and shock at the sight of them. Using what little strength she had, she pushed down on the chair arms. If her aim was to get to her feet, she just couldn't. Her legs were even worse than those of her husband.

'Isaac! Isaac! What has happened to you?'

Isaac took hold of her hands and smiled through his bloodied lips.

'I am all right, Ruth. I am all right. This man, Charlie, rescued me.'

Between them, Jenny and the stranger settled Isaac into one of the two armchairs that normally sat to either side of the fireplace.

Jenny had moved the chair next to Ruth, allowing the old couple to reclasp their hands.

A kettle was boiling on the hob.

Whilst Ruth patted her husband's arms, chest and legs, as though checking for his wounds, Jenny made the tea.

She paused at one point when something strange occurred to her. Normally when she had a run-in with Roy her hands would be trembling; today they were not.

She asked Charlie if he would like a cup of tea.

He glanced at the clock on the mantelpiece as though it were allowing him time to consider. He smiled. Nodded. 'I think I could spare the time. My mates will wait for me.'

'Should I get them in for some tea too,' asked Jenny.

He shook his head. 'No. They'll be standing guard just in case the Blackshirt thugs come back.'

'Blackshirts?' The reference brought Ruth up short. She gasped and looked up at her husband. 'They were Blackshirts? Is that right, Isaac?'

Jenny saw an anguished look pass between them.

Her fingers brushed Charlie's as she handed him a cup of tea, and a tingle ran through her like an electric shock. Their eyes flickered when they met. She knew by his lingering look that he'd felt that same tingle.

She felt a need to take the conversation in another direction; to shy away from girlish feelings and the prospect of her face turning pink. 'Will they come back, do you think?'

After taking a sip of tea he seemed very much to relish, he shook his head.

'Not here perhaps, but you will need to be cautious. The British Union of Fascists are bullies. Small units like them will ambush people rather than face anyone who can fight back. My, but this tea is welcome.'

'So, you'll be safe; they won't seek revenge?' asked Jenny.

Charlie's smile though boyish brimmed with confidence and the blueness of his eyes held hers. 'I very much doubt it. It's to our advantage not to face them alone, but if one of us gets caught out and can't outrun them, then we will fight back. As I said, they prefer to attack those unable to do so.'

Ruth and Isaac still clung together, their looks flitting between each other. Rarely did they glance at either Charlie or Jenny.

Ruth upturned her face to Charlie and said, 'I can't thank you enough for bringing my Isaac home.'

'I was pleased to do so. Anyway, me and my friends couldn't possibly bypass the opportunity to give Moseley's yobs a good bashing.'

As nasty as the incident had been, none of them could resist a reserved chuckle, one that couldn't travel to the eyes where fear remained, though not for Charlie.

'You speak very nicely,' Ruth suddenly said to Charlie. 'You're not from around 'ere are you?'

He shook his head. 'No, Mrs...'

'Ruth Jacob,' she said. 'Call me Ruth.'

'Pleased to meet you, Ruth.'

Ruth untangled her hands from those of her husband before shaking Charlie's.

'My full name's Charlie. Charlie Talbot. Pleased to meet you both.' His smile widened when he turned to Jenny. 'You too, miss. Jenny, I think you told me earlier.'

'Yes. Jenny Crawford. I live up on the top floor.' She felt no guilt about not correcting his assumption that she was a miss rather than a Mrs. 'It was so lucky you were around, Mr Talbot. Are you here working?'

A hardness came to his eyes, but a smile blossomed on his lips.

'In a way. We're here to protest Oswald Moseley's marches and everything he stands for. As you've already experienced, they're bullies. Their way is not the only way.' The smile flew to his eyes as he extended his hand to her. 'And call me Charlie. It's what my friends call me.'

Earlier it had been their fingers touching. The shock of electricity turned warm with the clasping for their palms. They each held their look until Ruth burst into tears.

'This is all so terrible, and you are so good,' she said through floods of tears. 'I don't know what I would have done if anything had happened to my Isaac.'

There was both concern and reassurance in Charlie's engaging smile.

'Nothing did happen and with me around it won't. Look. I'll write down my address. If you feel scared, send for me. All right?'

Ruth nodded.

Isaac took hold of one of her hands with both his own. 'Don't worry, Ruth. I'll be careful.'

Ruth's worried brow remained. She shook her head.

Jenny rubbed the back of her neighbour's plump hand. 'You can send for me and if it warrants I'll go and fetch Charlie. How will that be?'

'Very kind of you,' said Isaac. 'But I wouldn't want to impose.'

'You wouldn't be imposing – not on me anyway.'

She sensed rather than saw Charlie's smile when he said to her, 'I know a kind nature when I see it. I don't think you'll feel put upon either, will you, Jenny?'

'Not at all. I'll do whatever has to be done.'

She took heed of what he'd said, most of all the fact that he'd called her Jenny. She liked the way he seemed to savour her name, spoke it slowly, unwilling to let it end too soon.

He tucked his hat more firmly onto his head, twisting it here and there until satisfied the fit was perfect. 'Right.' He took a deep breath. 'Better be going.'

'Me too,' echoed Jenny. 'Will you be all right now, Isaac? Ruth?'

Ruth's cheeks ballooned with a sunburst of a smile. 'We'll be fine, me duck. You get on. See this young man to the door for us if you will.'

Isaac nodded. The old pair continued to hold hands.

She couldn't be certain that a look that bordered on conspiracy flashed between the long-married pair.

'Then I'll be saying cheerio to you. Hopefully your attackers have learned their lesson. So don't worry. Good day to you.'

Jenny smiled at the Jacobs as Charlie stood aside to let her leave first.

She felt almost compelled to accompany Charlie out of the back door. The chill of the side alley made her shiver. She rubbed her arms. Charlie followed behind. The rain had stopped, but water continued to drip at either end of the walkthrough.

He began to whistle. The sound reverberated against the low ceiling, the damp walls. 'Echoes a bit.'

'Very.'

'Makes my whistling sound better than it is. Did you recognise the tune?'

'Danny Boy.'

'That's right. The Londonderry Air. Anyway, I think they were locals. Right time, right place. They knew he'd be on his way back from work at this time of the morning. Not guessed it. Knew it.'

Out of the side alley now, Jenny stopped at the battered façade of the overhanging building and her front door. Warped and battered with age, it hung askew in an opening that might once have been a perfect oblong. One side of the door was now longer than the other, the lintel lopsided and barely two inches above her head. Roy often complained of hitting his head on it.

'They're gone,' said Charlie in a surprised voice. He shoved his hat further back on his head. He was referring to his mates.

Jenny asked him where he thought they were.

'They won't be far away. Something must have attracted their attention.' He grinned at her. 'Don't worry. They can take care of themselves and they wouldn't have left without ensuring everything here was safe.'

He sounded so sure of both the situation and himself.

Feeling awkward and unwilling to enter the oppressive domain that was her home, Jenny hugged herself.

'This your door?'

She nodded. 'Yes. This is my door.'

The door led into the hallway. From there, it was a twisting climb up the narrow staircase to the rooms she currently called home. Home was a comforting word, a place of warmth and safety, even of happiness. Her home was not that to her, though she tried to ensure it was all those things to her daughters.

She felt the intensity of Charlie's blue eyes assessing her. What was he thinking? she wondered. What did he make of this thin-faced woman, scruffy cardigan held around herself, hair plastered to her head?

The silence that held them was punctured. A diversion back to the assault.

'I'm guessing them that attacked the old man live locally.'

'What makes you say that?' Her stomach churned. Had he guessed? Isaac certainly hadn't accused anyone and she'd kept her mouth shut.

Charlie wasn't to know it – or she hoped he didn't – but his conclusion was right. Roy knew what time Isaac came home. He also knew that Isaac helped feed them. She blamed herself for having mentioned it. Plainly it was a slight to his pride; that alone was enough for him to react violently. On top of that, there was this new crusade of his, mixing with the likes of those who hated anyone not British, anyone not of the same religion, the same race, the same colour. Even a woman was classed as lower than a man.

She saw Charlie look up at the crumbling building, the cracked windowpanes, the weeds growing in broken guttering. His Adam's apple moved in his stretched neck as his eyes roved over the timber-framed upper floors. At one time, they might have been straight and not looking close to collapse. But that was centuries ago. After all this time, they were twisted and likely to groan under the strain.

An odd feeling came to her, a need to reach out and stroke his voice box and stretched sinews. She didn't dare. Instead, she curled her fingers into the palms of her hands.

He faced her. 'You know, I thought the Great War would put an end to all this.' He took his hands out of his pockets, shrugged and adopted a helpless stance. 'Families deserve better. We were promised. Didn't happen though, did it.'

She'd heard much the same from Roy, his remarks delivered with bitterness and ire. He'd been a lad when he'd joined up in the last year of the war, but he'd served with older men. Some of those men had struggled to get a job. Driven by failure, they'd joined up. In a terrible way, the war had been their saviour, but it had also become recurring nightmares. Men of like mind had exchanged views, determined that they and their families would never want again. They had hoped for better times ahead. God knows they deserved it. But they'd been let down.

The sound of footsteps sounded from somewhere inside the house. Had Roy seen his way clear to getting back inside? He might be waiting for her. She had to ready herself and he mustn't see her with Charlie.

Dragging her woollen cardigan around herself, she said, 'I'd better go in.'

For a moment, their looks held. When that fixation broke, his gaze shifted around the narrow alley.

'I'm beginning to like it here – the people – or at least some of them,' he said a trifle ruefully. 'As for this time we're living in…' he shook his head disconsolately. 'Clouds are gathering.'

'Of war?'

His jaw tensed when he looked at her. 'I don't know. Troubles for certain. A war at home? A war between factions of your own is always a tragedy.'

Listening to him speaking of a very serious subject did not make her afraid. Perhaps because the timbre of his voice, as warming as a hug on a dark night, made her feel safe. No one had ever made her feel like that before.

Sighing, she said what she didn't want to say. 'I have to go.'

Roy might be waiting for her. She felt fear but also defiance. She'd disobeyed his instruction and if she could do so once, she could do it again.

She rested one hand on the door post, pausing a moment to look at him one more time. 'Thank you again for what you did.'

His hands were back in his pockets. His eyes shone in the gloom that was Blue Bowl Alley.

'It was my pleasure.' He grinned. 'Knocking the breath out of that bloke gave me great satisfaction.'

It was Roy he'd punched in the stomach. She felt neither pity nor guilt.

'Right. I'll see you around.'

'I should hope so.'

He tipped his cap at her. Even before his long legs were striding out of the alley, he was whistling another song she recognised. 'Early One Morning, just as the sun was rising, I heard a maiden singing…'

She stood in the cramped hall listening. The building creaked when anyone was on the upper floors. Nothing creaked, nothing groaned. No sound didn't necessarily mean no one was at home but was a good yardstick.

Climbing slowly might put off the dreaded moment of facing him, but for once she wanted to confront.

The door to the living room was only slightly ajar. With a flourish, she pushed open the door. It swung wide and knocked a few flakes of plaster off the wall. Then there was the room. No Roy. No anyone. It was totally empty.

The whistled tune of 'Early One Morning' faded. Now it wasn't morning she was thinking of but this evening when Roy came home. What would his mood be? Whatever it was, all she hoped for was that he'd save his muffled threats until the girls were in bed.

7

Roy Crawford was in awe. Trevor Collins, the local leader of the British Union of Fascists, looked every inch the kind of man favoured by Sir Oswald Moseley. He didn't have their leader's height or good looks, but he did look like a man of status. Roy had happily modelled himself on Moseley, from his glistening hair to his hairline moustache. And he did look like him, but Trevor had status and clean hands. He didn't get them dirty doing manual labour. He worked at a desk for the council.

Trevor noticed him, came over smiling and offered his hand to be shaken. 'Well,' he said, looking Roy up and down. 'You certainly look the part. At a distance, you could be Moseley himself.'

'Took a leaf out of your book, Mr Collins.'

'Trevor. All my friends call me Trevor.'

'Trevor. Good to see you again.'

Roy could barely contain his feeling of pride at Trevor comparing his appearance with the leader of the British Union of Fascists.

Trevor was wearing the requisite black, as was Roy, but as if to elevate his status, he was also wearing a black leather belt, jodhpurs and knee-length leather boots. Even Moseley didn't wear jodhpurs.

It was only after a few more friendly words that Mr Collins's attention turned to Roy's cut lip and eye. He frowned. 'What happened?'

Roy took a deep breath. He'd fully accepted that his injuries would be questioned and had thought about what he would say. 'Local roughnecks. I got set upon. They were foreign. I could tell by their accents.' He shook his head dolefully. 'Where I live 'as always been a bit rough, but it's getting worse. Luckily I can handle meself, but it's the missus and the kids I worry about.'

Trevor frowned. 'Am I right in thinking that you live in the Pithay?'

Roy found his face warming when he had to confirm that, yes, he did indeed live in the Pithay. He'd lived there all his life, had even been proud to admit it. Not so much now though, the tenements were in a worse state than ever. The centuries had taken their toll.

He shook his head as if to emphasise how worried he was. There was no way he was going to admit the truth, that three of them had been set upon and all because they were beating up Isaac, his Jewish neighbour.

'Terrible place it's gettin' to be.'

He'd lived there even before he'd married Jenny. She'd been vulnerable when he'd first met her, but then women did fall easily for his dark good looks and boyish shyness. He'd found most women too forceful for his tastes but having met Jenny when she was just sixteen, he'd been less uncomfortable. On marrying Jenny he'd expected to gain the best of her father's business, a bit of money if not the premises, but that hadn't happened. The old man had lost his marbles in the war and run the business into the ground. There had been barely enough to pay for the funerals of the pair of them, one following quickly after the other.

There were times when he strolled around the Pithay as though he owned it. He was the local hard man and liked being respected. Everything had changed when his attack on Isaac Jacobs had been thwarted by strangers who'd proved stronger than him.

Trevor's hand lay gently on his shoulder. His expression was one of great sympathy.

'Roy, you've come to my attention as someone who can grow as British fascism grows.' Trevor shook his head disconsolately. 'You need to move. A man like you should be living in something better. Leave the filthy places in the city centre to those not of our blood or our beliefs. Best they were all gathered in one place so we can keep an eye on them. You deserve something better.'

Roy beamed. He felt warm all over that a man of such lofty status in the organisation was his friend, but also because he'd got away with telling a lie. Being beaten on his own patch was a blow to his ego. What was more his wife had been there to witness it and he'd seen the look in her eyes. Not love. Not respect, but triumph.

'If you say so, Mr... Trevor... It's time I looked around for something better.' He felt favoured. Not everyone was allowed to call Trevor Collins by his first name.

The hand that had lain gently on his shoulder now gave him a reassuring squeeze. A fatherly gesture. That was what Roy told himself and he liked it. He felt privileged indeed to have Trevor show him such affection.

Trevor winked. 'Leave it with me, my boy. 'Me and my colleagues in the housing department at the council want good tenants in our properties, people who would be an asset and would look after their houses. You shall have one, my boy,' he said, giving Roy's shoulder another squeeze, another friendly pat. 'As soon as the right house comes along, it's yours. I promise you.'

8

APRIL 1936

Roy stood in front of the ornate mirror hanging above the cast-iron fireplace. *The only thing they ever gave us,* he thought to himself. He'd expected more from Jenny's parents but had got less. Far less.

He smoothed back his hair with both hands, pleased no grey showed in its dark glossiness, admiring the pencil line moustache, his aquiline nose, the proudness in his brow.

He turned this way and that, admiring himself from every angle. His hands went from smoothing back his hair to running them over the black polo-neck sweater stretched across his chest.

He'd just arrived home from yet another meeting of the local fascists and was feeling very pleased with himself. Pride burst with his words.

'Mr Collins thinks very highly of me,' he boasted. 'Reckons I look every inch one of the British Fascists foot soldiers; that's what he said to me. He's promised me that I'll reap the benefits. As a veteran of the Great War, he reckons I deserve that.'

Jenny watched him with mixed feelings. He'd never spent so much time looking at his reflection, cinching in his waist, holding back his shoulders.

He looked at her over his shoulder. 'Did you hear a word I said?'

'Yes. It's nice.'

'Nice?' he said, his eyes glittering with pride, triumph and even joy. 'It's more than nice.' He turned back to the mirror, head held high and beaming from ear to ear.

'Mr Collins – Trevor – values my support. He's very good to me. Said he'll be calling on my services more and more.'

'What kind of services?'

'*What kind*? Political services. Guarding the door when he or someone important in the organisation is giving a talk. Marching beside the important people in the party. Ready to protect 'im against all-comers.' A whole week had passed since Charlie and his friends had given her husband the beating he'd deserved. Roy had not mentioned anything about it and neither did she. As he went on and on about his position in the party, she kept her head bowed over her knitting whilst her fingers continued to fly. She didn't want to raise her head. She didn't want him to see her slightly triumphant expression.

She'd been with her daughters the last time she'd seen Charlie and hadn't dared acknowledge him. Yet she knew he'd seen her. For a while, their eyes had locked. It was only fleeting, but in those few seconds it felt like she was walking on spring grass, not the pavements of Union Street.

'So he'll be asking you to do more.'

'That's right, and I don't want to 'ear any moans and groans from you about me being out all the time. Got it?'

'It's very important. You must go.'

'I'm glad you think that.'

On the one hand, she welcomed being alone with only the children of an evening. On the other hand, she feared where his membership of this questionable organisation was going and what it was doing to him. She'd read the newspapers and listened to the wireless, which she had managed to get fixed, and it filled her with dread. Was there any way she could communicate her fears? Express her opinion? She dared not. The one thing that did occur to her was to take advantage of his sudden joy and exuberance.

'Do you fancy taking me out for a drink one night?'

It sounded trivial, but she said it brightly.

'It's been a long time,' she added. 'I just thought we might—'

He turned swiftly around, shoulders back, head held high. 'I'm not taking you anywhere. Your place is in the home, keeping house, taking care of the girls. You're going to get the benefit of my membership before very long. So do as I say and know your place.'

His expression was as hard as cement, but suddenly his eyes glittered as though some secret that only he knew had set them on fire.

Jenny swallowed the dryness in her throat. Was there going to be a scene? She hoped not. The girls hadn't long gone to bed.

She swapped her knitting for a bundle of sewing. Thinking of something else helped her block him out. In her mind, a warm smile and a pair of blue eyes were locked with hers. Since that first meeting, Charlie Talbot had lived in her head. Fear lessened when she thought of him. What might have happened the other day if Tilly and Gloria hadn't been with her? It was nice to dream, but consequently her concentration lapsed and she stabbed the needle into a finger.

'Ouch.'

The droplet of blood she sucked was warm on her tongue, but still she kept her eyes downcast.

Roy took her by surprise when he placed his fingers beneath her chin and raised her head. Unsure what would happen next, she looked up. A rapturous smile flickered around his lips.

'As I was telling you, Mr Collins, our local leader, thinks well of me. He thinks it's time we moved out of this dump and I do too.'

'He does?'

Jenny's eyes opened wide. She could hardly believe what she was hearing. Roy had always resisted moving away from a place he'd lived in all his life. This Mr Collins, the local Blackshirt leader, had successfully persuaded him where she had failed. 'Where will we go? Does he have somewhere in mind?'

The neat black moustache, as thin and fine as though it had been drawn with a graphite pencil, spread with Roy's smile.

'Mr Collins – Trevor.' He rolled the name over his tongue savouring both it and the feeling of privilege it bestowed. 'Trevor works for the council. In the housing department, as a matter of fact. And guess what?'

'What?' Her voice was small, no more than a whisper.

'He's going to see to it that we get something better.'

'My goodness. You've been doing well at the docks and now this! It's all happening at once.'

It occurred to her that Roy had got involved with the fascists when he'd first curried favour at the docks. Had the gaffer also been a member of this dark and violent organisation that marched and did battle with those who didn't agree with their views?

'Don't look so bloody scared,' he said, cupping her face between his hands, smiling down at her as a cat might a blackbird. 'You've always wanted a house with a garden, well, we'll be getting one. A three-bedroom house with a garden out on the new estate.'

His words were music to her ears. 'A council house. You mean it? You really mean it?' All the fear she'd felt overwhelmed with excitement at the prospect of acquiring her dream.

He confirmed that it was a council house on the Knowle West estate.

Everything she'd always wanted, that's what he was telling her.

'You'll be the queen of yer own house. There's shops, a school and a pub nearby. Everything you could want in fact, so no need to catch the bus into town. No need to wander at all,' he said, his bright expression turning dark. 'You can stay at 'ome and just look after me. And the girls of course.'

Despite everything, despite his bad temper and almost keeping her prisoner, she gasped with delight. 'The girls will love it.'

'Ssh,' he said, placing a finger on her lips. 'Keep yer voice down. Don't want to disturb them, do we.'

That certain look came to his eyes. When they were younger and she was more naïve, she'd welcomed that look. Since then, she'd sometimes feared it, loathed his touch and the feel of his hot body against hers.

His lips were soft but demanding as his mouth moved down her face. His hands cupped her breasts, slid to her waist, still trim despite having had two children. From there, without preamble, they moved down over her belly and between her legs.

There was no turning back. It had to happen. She made a move to go to bed.

His chunky fingers gripped her wrist, preventing her from going into the next room.

A knot of apprehension gripped her. She breathed in the intensity of his hair oil, the mix of cigarette smoke and sweat. Not just his sweat, but that of others with whom he'd been in proximity. The smell of men, excited, violent, drinking and making plans.

Distaste was swallowed along with those smells but she dared not show it.

'You can thank me out here. Over the sofa. That's what I want. Show me you're grateful. You bloody well should be.'

* * *

Feeling sore and used was nothing unusual after enduring Roy's idea of lovemaking. They were now in their bed in the low-ceilinged room at the front of the house. As Roy snored beside her, she thought through the news he'd so proudly imparted.

There was gladness of course, excitement that Tilly and Gloria were going to live in a decent home with a garden, not the cramped rooms and poor amenities of a building long past its prime.

Alongside that gladness, though, was a nagging question. She understood that he'd made powerful friends in that terrible fascist party. Even so, he'd loved this place. The Pithay was at the heart of the city and he'd lived here all his life. What had helped sway him to move away?

The events of the last few weeks ran through her mind. Living close to the likes of Isaac and Ruth Jacobs was a possible factor. She thought of the look in Roy's eyes tonight bordering on excitement; and something else that she construed as relief. Relief for what? Was he relieved to be moving away? It seemed strange.

She thought it through. There was only one possible answer.

It was just a short while ago that he and his Blackshirt friends had laid about poor old Isaac, but things hadn't gone to plan. She remembered how fascinated she'd been to see the fear in his eyes, no sign of his usual arrogance, the veneer of the bully he'd grown into. She'd watched and he'd seen her watching. She also recalled that warning in his eyes not to divulge to the rescuers where he lived.

Roy never referred to what had happened on that filthy, rain-soaked day. He'd been sheepish that evening after the event, hadn't mentioned it but ate his evening meal in silence. Then he'd gone out to meet friends, he'd said. His silence had halted her asking any questions, but she knew what she had seen. Violence on his part, but when attacked in turn she'd seen fear in his eyes.

Charlie and the others lived close by. The undeniable – and

rather surprising truth – hit her like a thunderbolt. Roy had met his match. It had very much surprised him and he couldn't live with such a threat nearby. He had to move. He had to put space between them.

Suddenly the prospect of moving filled her with regret. Leaving these cramped rooms would be welcome, but it meant she was unlikely to see Charlie Talbot again.

Having her girls housed decently had to be her main concern. Flights of fancy regarding a man she'd met just once was silly. She was a married woman, and as Gladys Hubert had said, for better or worse.

'Might take a while for Trevor to sort something out,' Roy had said to her as they'd got ready for bed.

'Rome wasn't built in a day,' Jenny said laughingly.

Roy frowned. 'It ain't in Rome. It's a council 'ouse.'

'I don't care where it is as long as we have a real house. The girls will love having their own bed in their own bedroom.'

'All down to me,' he said proudly tapping his chest.

She didn't hesitate to agree with him and hoped fervently that it wouldn't be too long before her dream came true.

9

JUNE 1936

Jenny felt as though she was walking on air and Roy was looking pleased with himself. The summer air was warm and although her best dress was too warm for this weather, she didn't care. She wanted this house and so had to make an impression.

'This is all down to me,' he'd told her repeatedly when the offer of a council house had come through.

Mr Collins had arranged for a dour-looking woman in a tweed suit and permed hair to show them around the house they hoped would be theirs – providing they met the criteria of course. A tenant must be able to prove income, keep a clean house and not be a nuisance to others. They had a form from the council which Roy had signed and posted. The woman had come on receipt of that form.

She introduced herself as Miss Venables and arrived on a bicycle. The would-be new council tenants, Roy and Jenny, had come by bus.

'Mr and Mrs Crawford?'

'Yes. That's us.'

Roy offered his hand to be shaken. Jenny felt a trifle embarrassed when Miss Venables turned abruptly away as if such an action was beneath her.

The smell of new paint puffed out from the hallway as two council decorators in paint-splattered dungarees whistled their way to a handcart outside the front gate. They nodded and said good morning. Jenny and Roy returned their greeting. Miss Venables did not.

Three pots of distemper sat next to the front door, along with two stepladders that they had to get round.

Keys in hand, Miss Venables led the way. 'Follow me please.'

Jenny didn't care about her offhand manner or sharp tone. The red-brick house filled her eyes.

'The garden's a bit overgrown. You will need to keep it tidy,' said Miss Venables, her needle-like look aimed directly at Roy.

'I'll get a pair of shears,' he said nonchalantly, hands buried in his pockets. 'I'm grateful to Mr Collins for this house and I promised I would look after it. You might say that I'm his right-hand man.'

Mention of Mr Collins seemed to pull Miss Venables up short. 'Oh. I was unaware you were acquainted. You've already discussed the house with him?'

Roy's chest puffed out. 'Yes. We've been acquainted for some time; in fact, we meet up on a regular basis.'

Miss Venables nodded. She looked intrigued but was not so impolite as to ask how they were acquainted or how come they frequently met.

Perhaps she guessed, thought Jenny glimpsing what seemed like a lighter touch in the woman's disposition.

The smell of newly applied paint was stronger as they ventured into the living room.

'Watch your clothes,' said Miss Venables, her elbows bent, her hands somewhere near shoulder level. 'Some of the paint is still wet.'

Jenny didn't care about the paint. She loved the smell and didn't mind that each room was painted the same colour.

The living room was square and bright, daylight streaming through the window. Doors, floorboards and fitted dresser were of wood and heavily varnished. Although there was no furniture in the room, there was no empty echo from their footsteps or their voices. A warm room, a warm house, thought Jenny and felt even more elated than when she'd first passed through the front door.

On entering the kitchen, Miss Venables pointed out the coal hole to the right of the gas stove. 'Behind this door. It's beneath the stairs which we passed out in the hallway.'

Jenny walked across the kitchen to the pale green and cream gas stove. She thought of the range back at Blue Bowl Alley. It was so much cleaner and gas was far more efficient than coal. She traced her fingertips above the gas taps – three for the gas rings and one for the oven.

'You're lucky. You won't have to buy a stove,' said Miss Venables on seeing Jenny looking so enthralled by the gas stove. 'The last tenant left it behind. The boiler too for your laundry.' She indicated the zinc boiler sitting in the corner of the kitchen. A boiler stick lay on top of it. 'And there's a mangle outside.'

Roy peered out of the garden window. 'It's got a tree.'

'An apple, I should think,' said Miss Venables as Jenny joined her husband to look out of the window. 'This used to be orchards.'

Without asking for permission, Jenny opened the back door. Behind her, Miss Venables was showing Roy the bathroom.

'You have a pull chain, a sink with a tap and the water for the bath comes from the zinc boiler in the kitchen. You light the gas beneath it and open the stopcock so it flows into the tap on the bath. Let it warm up and you will have hot water.'

Jenny went out the back door. A mangle of Victorian vintage sat beneath the kitchen window, its rollers a little yellow with age, its ornate ironwork a trifle rusty in places. Her eyes skirted over that and went to the garden. It was the garden she had wanted above all else.

Long grass whispered as it bent to the breeze, its seed heads waving like lace wands. Butterflies flitted in and around the heads of grass and gathered in clouds on the yellow blooms of a straggly rose clambering up a drainpipe.

Jenny thought how lovely it was, when the feeling of being watched made her turn sharply to her left and the garden of the house next door.

A sharp-faced woman stared from the other side of the privet hedge; arms folded shield like across her chest. There was no sign of friendliness in her expression, but Jenny smiled at her anyway as Roy and Miss Venables stepped outside.

'Hello. I'm Jenny and this is my husband Roy. We're hoping to move in shortly.'

'Do you have children?' The question was sharply delivered.

'Yes. Two,' returned Jenny, smiling in appreciation, thinking her new neighbour had expressed interest because she liked children.

To her surprise, the woman's expression, already sharp, turned as sour as a gooseberry. Without saying a word, she disappeared into the house, the door slamming behind her.

'Upset someone, 'ave we?' said Roy, hands in trouser pockets and a smirk on his face.

Miss Venables was dismissive. 'You'll come across all sorts on this estate. Now come on. I don't have time to waste. Let me show you the bedrooms.'

Feeling confused rather than disappointed at what she

perceived as hostility in her neighbour, Jenny followed Miss Venables and Roy back inside.

Like the rest of the house, the three bedrooms were painted cream, the doors varnished in the same colour as the downstairs doors and floorboards. Linoleum covered the bedroom floorboards, a diametric design. It struck her that whoever had chosen it had not wanted to be cheerful. Her choice would have been a pale green background sprinkled with rose buds. She vowed that in time her choice would replace it.

As she surveyed the second bedroom, a shaft of sunlight sent dust motes dancing with life. The room itself seemed made of sunshine and almost made Jenny burst into tears. It was so different to the three rooms they lived in at Blue Bowl Alley, full of fresh air and with every modern amenity.

Roy too was impressed.

'No more going to the lavatory in the dark. No more dragging the zinc bath in from out back,' he chortled.

It was a rare thing indeed to hear her husband amused. Would he laugh more and be less bad-tempered once they'd moved in? She sincerely hoped so. A marriage was for life and they had more years ahead than they had behind them.

* * *

Dorothy Partridge peered out from behind the living-room curtain in time to see the young couple and woman from the council leave.

She hissed through her teeth before proclaiming her view on the new neighbours to Harriet who was really Harry, her husband who had deserted during the war and lived in disguise. He couldn't bear the thought of going to prison and had cried like a child at the prospect. He'd hated the war, hated the army and preferred to live as a woman rather than a man. 'They look to be in their thirties. Can't tell for sure.'

'Do they have children?'

Dorothy glowered. 'They didn't have children with them, but I asked. Best to be forewarned, I thought. And it seems they do.'

'They might be very nice, well-behaved children.'

'They might be little monsters. Children can be so noisy and destructive. Not that I'll let them get away with anything. They needn't think that! Oh no.'

Harry's attention went back to his newspaper but he didn't read a word. If only she'd be easier going, he thought. If only she could be as cheerful and bouncy as Thelma Dawson across the road. He could almost be happy then, as happy as anyone can be when they're living a lie. In time, things might change. Deserters from the Great War might finally be pardoned. Until then, it was a case of grin and bear it as best one could.

* * *

Thelma, who lived at number twelve Coronation Close, which because it was a cul-de-sac was right opposite number one, was told of the young couple by her friend Cath Lockhart, who lived at number eight.

'They looked a lovely young couple. He was very upright, a military type, and she was very pretty. I hope they get the house.

Thelma shook her head and tutted sadly. 'No matter who moves in, nobody's good enough for old Mother Partridge. She'll make their lives a misery. You just see if she don't.'

10

JULY

Jenny felt the eyes of the neighbours watching as the horse and cart carrying her furniture turned into Coronation Close.

A small group of women were gathered around the gate of the house she and her family were moving into.

One at a time, other women headed out from other houses and joined the original three. Why were they staring? Would they be friendly? As yet, there was no chance to find out. Having so many eyes trained on her was discomforting. She couldn't hear what they were saying but imagined their low whispers discussing her sparse amount of furniture, her looks, her clothes, her husband and her children.

The horse had his nosebag and Robin was keen to get her moved in. He'd confided in her that he had a darts match that night and was first on the oche. Robin always had been keen on darts.

Roy had bristled when told who was moving them in. Begrudgingly he calmed down once he found out he was cheaper than everyone else.

'It's because he still uses a horse and cart. Removal firms who use a van cost twice as much.' Jenny had told him.

Roy had arranged with his gaffer to have the night shift so he could oversee the moving in. His request was reasonable enough, but he'd assured her he would have got it anyway.

'Griff Rowlands is one of the members. Trevor 'ad a word with 'im. Made it clear that he'd gone out of 'is way with the council, that he knew people – and 'e does. Trevor pulled rank and Griff 'ad no choice.'

She knew he'd been referring to membership of the Blackshirts.

The sound of the horse's hooves had echoed between the frowning buildings of Blue Bowl Lane, she had taken one look back and one only. Isaac and Ruth had said their goodbyes earlier that morning when Roy had still been in bed. The alley itself would not be missed. But she would miss Isaac and Ruth very much.

Roy had purposefully sat silently beside Robin, not speaking to him, not looking at him. If Robin noticed he gave no sign, but whistled merrily, Tilly and Gloria singing along with some of the tunes from their place beside their mother squashed in amongst the furniture.

The sound of her daughters' laughter pierced Jenny's wandering thoughts.

'We're here,' she told them as the horse and cart came to a standstill.

The girls leapt off the back of the cart, Jenny following behind. She surveyed the houses, the width of the sky no longer a thin ribbon between towering tenements.

Brimming with excitement, the girls carried smaller items into the house, then promptly disappeared, eager to be exploring, claiming their bedrooms, arguments between them yet to be overcome.

Two women standing either side of a garden gate stopped gossiping and turned to watch. Jenny felt their eyes upon her but felt too shy to say anything.

Two boys having a mock fight with wooden swords and dustbin lid shields also paid attention, though not to her.

'That's a nice 'orse, mate,' one of them called out. 'What's 'is name?'

'Laurel,' Robin called back. 'And he's got a mate named Hardy. Just like Laurel and Hardy.'

With gruff resignation Roy helped Robin with the heavier things. Jenny lugged the battered old suitcases, which were bursting at the seams with bedding and clothes. Once they were inside, she came back for pillows, eiderdowns and boxes of pots, pans, kettle and teapot.

Roy never once looked in the direction of the women, with their crossover pinnies, metal curlers and toothless mouths. He was offloading their possessions as fast as he could. Back at Blue Bowl Alley, he'd carried pieces of furniture down the stairs at lightning speed, leaving Robin, Jenny and the girls, trailing in his wake. He'd been adamant it had to be done as swiftly as possible.

'I ain't got time to waste. I'm a working man and I need to work. This new 'ouse is going to cost more rent than the old one. You do know that don't you?'

Jenny had said that she did. She'd also thanked him profusely for thinking of his family and wasn't he clever to have made a friend of Mr Collins. She said this aloud to the children. 'Isn't Daddy clever, darlings, that Mr Collins considers him his right-hand man.'

Gloria, always willing to curry favour – a trait she'd no doubt inherited from her father – agreed and offered up praise. 'My daddy is very clever. Aren't you, Daddy?' She had clung onto his arm as she said it, smiling up at him with fluttering eyelids. *One day that fluttering might be your undoing young lady*, thought Jenny. She had grimaced at the prospect before pushing it from her mind.

Tilly, more incisive, more aware of the situation between her parents, had been less enthused and stayed silent.

The idea that he was doing this for his family was utter nonsense, of course; Roy was doing this for himself. For now, at least, Mr Collins was the centre of his universe, a shining example of everything he wanted to be.

Over the years, she'd learned what made Roy tick. In the beginning, he had been the centre of her universe and she'd been foolish enough to think that she'd been the apple of his eye. Poverty and the passing of the years had diminished everything they might once have been or were ever likely to be. Poverty was the worst. Terrible living conditions and bone breaking, muscle straining work – when it was available. Hunger marches were still going on. The heroes returned from a bloody war had been short-changed. In one way, she could understand why the fascists had come into being. But where would it go? Could it be possible that without reparation, better living conditions and the availability of jobs, their aims could become a means to a different end? A darker and harder place?

Not concentrating as she should, she tripped over a kerb. Pans and pots clattered onto the pavement and into the gutter.

''Ere. Let me give you a 'and.'

The woman had a merry smile, dark eyes and dark hair swept up into a topknot. Loose tendrils floated like scraps of lace around her face. She helped Jenny gather up the pots and pans, placing them back in the cardboard box they'd fallen out from.

'Thank you,' said Jenny.

'Glad to help, love. I'm Thelma Dawson from number twelve,

almost opposite,' she said jerking her finger at the house across the road. 'If you want anything, just pop across and see me. I know everything that goes on around here. I gave a hand in getting it renamed. I love the new king, don't you?'

'Jenny Crawford,' Jenny said, immediately warming to the friendly smile and deeply expressive eyes. Like pools of chocolate, she thought.

If Jenny thought she was going to get away without making any pronouncement on the new king, she was very much mistaken.

Thelma's face fell. She pressed her question again. 'The king? Don't you think he looks like a film star?'

'Yes. Yes... I suppose he does,' she stammered.

Conversation about the new king was unexpected. In fact, she hadn't considered having any conversation with anyone on the first day of moving in – except perhaps to be offered a cup of tea by a neighbour who already had a pot brewing.

Just as she thought it, Thelma said, 'Soon as you're a bit sorted, pop over for a cup of tea. It don't take two minutes to put the gas on.'

'That would be lovely.'

She could see from Thelma's expression that the fact that she was well spoken had been noticed.

'Not from 'round here are you.'

It was a statement. She had no choice but to tell the truth.

'I grew up in Montpelier.'

She didn't go on to say that she'd won a scholarship to Red Maids' School where the boarders still wore the old-fashioned cape and bonnet and expressed their thanks on founders' day to one John Whitson, a former mayor of Bristol and responsible for funding its foundation. Not that she'd stayed there very long. It was still expensive. Her mother had gone into service at fourteen straight from the workhouse. It was her beauty that had snared her father. All would have been well, but her sojourn at Redmaids School was short lived. Money had been in short supply.

'Oh. That's nice.'

There was something questioning in the look that Thelma gave her. She guessed what it meant. *How come someone from your background has their furniture delivered on a horse and cart? How come you don't live on the north side of the river?*

By choice, she told herself. My father made a choice to marry the maid and the family never forgave him. Her entry into the oldest girls' school in the country had been won on merit – and every penny her father had. Until it had run out.

'I'm glad I've moved here though,' she said, looking appreciatively around her. 'There's so much greenery and fresh air.'

Thelma placed hands that looked silky white, tips red with nail varnish onto her hips. Her smile seemed to brighten the day. 'There is. I hope you'll be happy here.'

'I'm sure I will.'

She caught Jenny unawares when she leaned forward and whispered into her ear, 'Just one word of warning...' She jerked her chin at number one. 'Careful how you go with old Mother Partridge next door. She hates kids, hates neighbours and hates just about everybody else. Reckons she just keeps herself to herself, but don't be fooled. If she can make trouble, Dot Partridge will make trouble.'

Jenny watched as the rolling hips proceeded across the road. So provocative were those hips that both Robin and Roy watched her sashay along to the other women.

The neighbours listened to whatever Thelma said to them, then looked across to her, their expressions less grim, opinions influenced in a good way by a woman who looked likely to be a very good neighbour.

Every stick of furniture was moved in by five o'clock that

evening. Robin was paid and after the beds were put together, the heavy horsehair mattresses placed on the springs, Roy began to make himself ready for work.

Whilst he went to the bathroom which was adjacent to the kitchen, Jenny made him cheese sandwiches and a flask of tea.

The fact that the kitchen was next to the bathroom and on the ground floor struck her as the height of luxury, absolute bliss in fact. No more venturing out on a freezing night to a lavatory at the end of the yard.

As for having a bath, back at Blue Bowl Alley, it had meant having a daily wash. Water had been heated up on the old iron cooking range and poured into an enamel bowl. Having a bath was necessarily a once-a-week affair.

Her only regret was that she'd left behind two of the kindest people she'd ever known. Whilst Roy was out of the way, she'd told Isaac and Ruth how much she'd miss them. All three had hugged until it seemed they would squeeze the breath out of each other. There'd been moist eyes and promises to visit.

'And I will. I promise,' she told them.

If Roy had his way, it might not happen. Roy had stressed that Melvin Square had all the shops she would ever need, plus the school and a pub.

'You don't need to get a bus into the centre,' he'd said to her. His tone and the hard set of his jaw conveyed to her that this was a command not a statement. Disobey at her peril.

She treasured that last meeting with Isaac and Ruth, but the look in their eyes had pained her. However, their parting statement had helped ease the pain.

'Great news, my dear, great news,' Isaac had said with glowing enthusiasm. 'It won't be long before we'll be moved out. The landlord's said the council want to pull it down. We might end up moving in next to you.' The bright joy in his face had lessened as he'd considered what this would mean. 'Though I can't be too far away from the market. Not with my legs.'

'You'll get a bus in,' Ruth had announced more hopefully.

Jenny knew there was no guarantee that they'd end up on the same estate as her. The alternatives were Southmead or Fishponds, both on bus routes, but on the other side of the city to where they were going to make their new home.

Who knew when she might see them again? Or him, the one whose lips smiled when she smiled, whose eyes caught hers with the same longing.

She shook the thought away and began placing plates and cups and saucers on the dresser in the living room and the pots on the high shelf in the kitchen. The sink was deep, the wooden draining board scrubbed. She peered into the coal house, very conveniently placed beneath the stairs though accessed from the kitchen. Whoever had designed this aspect had not considered the amount of coal dust that would circulate when the coalman emptied his sacks in there.

Roy was still in the bathroom and the girls had been allotted their bedrooms. Gloria had bagged the biggest one. Tilly had ended up with the box room. Both rooms overlooked the back garden, the windows open to fresh air, high-growing privet hedges and hazelnut trees nodding at the far end beyond the lone apple tree.

A bright-faced Gloria came bounding into the kitchen. 'I'm going to show Dolly to my new friends,' she stated with a confidence that belied her youth. She held up her favourite doll foraged from one of the boxes waiting to be unpacked. 'Are you coming?' she asked her sister.

Tilly shook her head, eyed her mother, and expressed her willingness to help unpack.

'There's no need, darling. I can manage,' said Jenny. 'You go out and make new friends.'

Gloria had already disappeared. Jenny glimpsed her out on the green, holding Dolly high for inspection by two girls of roughly her own age. It was obvious from her stance that she was only showing them the doll, nobody was allowed to touch.

Tilly maintained a nervous look. Funnily enough, Jenny had expected her to adapt to their new surroundings first. It appeared not to be the case and worried her. Give it time, she told herself, just give it time. She stroked her daughter's hair and smiled at her lovingly. Parents weren't supposed to have favourites, but Tilly was her firstborn. They were also more alike, Gloria being more like her father.

'Don't you want to go out and make new friends, sweetheart?'

'I'd like to put things away in my bedroom.'

Jenny smiled at her and agreed that she could. There was a cosiness to the smallest bedroom. Tilly had meekly accepted it; Jenny suspected to save any argument with her sister. Gloria had also bagged the brass three-quarter bed. Because they were to have a bedroom each, Jenny had managed to acquire a single bed from Gladys. By further way of compensation, Jenny had bought a cream-coloured chest of drawers for Tilly. Gloria had to make do with a pine blanket box.

From the bathroom came the sound of whistling. Shaving in the evening was a strange phenomenon. Few labourers, including her father who'd laboured all his life, shaved before going to work, preferring to do so after coming home. But Roy had a meeting before work.

She was sorting out the last of the saucepans in the kitchen when he finally emerged clean-shaven, washed and smelling of soap.

Without saying a word, he went upstairs to change. He'd

already laid out his black clothes on the bed.

'I don't want you touching them. I'm perfectly capable of getting them ready me self.'

It was as though he was afraid of her spoiling them in some way. She gave him a carrier bag in which to pack his work trousers, waistcoat, cap and shirt. For convenience he had to wear his hobnail boots, though she knew he coveted a pair of high black boots, just like his mentor Trevor Collins wore.

When he came back down he wore an overcoat over his dark clothes, clothes that reminded her of Hollywood gangsters on film, their clothes adding to their inbuilt menace.

He took one last look at himself in the old mirror from Blue Bowl Alley. He'd hunted out a hammer and nail specifically for that one item. She could have asked him to hammer in a few more for the few pictures she'd brought with her. But she hadn't wanted to. She wanted him gone. She wanted this house to herself.

'I'm off.'

'I'll see you later then,' said Jenny. Some wives would have resented a husband going out on the day they'd moved into a new house, unpacking to be done, furniture to be placed around. Even if he was going to work, they'd expect him to wait until he really had to go, not attend a meeting in which they played no part.

She didn't ask what time he would be home. He might come home after his shift had finished: or he might not. Either way, she dared not ask him and, if she was deeply honest, didn't care. She was head over heels in love, but not with him. She was in love with this house.

Frowning, he waved one arm around the kitchen. 'Get all this sorted and put away. No drinking tea with that… that…'

'Thelma. Her name is Thelma.'

'Right. No going over there drinking tea and leaving everything unsorted. I don't want to come 'ome to it. Do you hear?

She said that she did and that she wouldn't be taking up Thelma's invitation. Though in time she would, regardless of what he said. This was her new beginning, a new house in a different place.

She wanted to be alone in the house, to breathe its smell of fresh paint, to place furniture and other possessions around at her own leisure. She wanted to walk in the garden, flick her fingers over the feathery tips of overgrown grass, touch the bare branches of what looked like an apple tree.

It was an odd feeling, this fresh view of things growing like a seed inside. Everything seemed so new, so bright and so full of hope.

To her mind, she too would grow in many ways in this house, just like that old apple tree that had so far survived and thrived despite the changes going on around it.

She wondered at the lightness that now touched her soul. It was as though the fresh air and greenery of this place had provided fertile earth in which courage might grow.

She sighed deeply as her eyes swept around the room, lovingly touching on things that added the comfort of home. Two armchairs had come with them, plus the green velvet Victorian settee. There was little else, not that it mattered. The inbuilt dresser held all the crockery and cutlery that she owned. Above the door in the kitchen, a saucepan shelf ran to one corner. With a bit of stretching, she placed the last of her cast-iron cooking pots in a row, stood back and looked at them. Black with age and use, they beckoned to be used, to yet again provide a good meal. Many a good stew and suet pudding would be made in those saucepans. Many a roast joint of meat or pie or cake would be cooked in the oven. Instead of roasting, boiling or baking on the range, they would be cooked in and on a proper gas stove.

She eyed it with something close to the kind of attraction that passes between people. The gas cooker had released her from topping up a cranky old range with coal. The cold-water tap hanging over the sink had alleviated the need to crank the handle of the water pump out in the yard.

'This is wonderful,' she whispered to herself.

In a moment of gazing at the falling dusk out in the back garden, it came to her that she had escaped both Roy and Blue Bowl Alley. Everything about their old home and the Pithay had been related to him but this place... Her happiness made her feel as though she'd sprouted wings. Her world was changing. Her husband had some way to travel to work and to his meetings. It was no mere leap of faith that she would see less of him, that he was no longer at the centre of her world.

After the gate had slammed shut behind him, she had watched him stalk off towards the end of the close. There had been many times she'd asked herself when things had changed between them. There had also been many times when she'd cried herself to sleep at night, her face bruised after she'd dared to ask him if he had another woman.

'One's enough,' he'd snapped. Her head had jolted to one side with the force of his blow. 'Why would I swap one stupid woman for another? None of you are worth it. Not one of you!

This evening she didn't care. Coronation Close had come into her life. She would make a home for herself and her children and cope as best she could with a man who no longer cared.

The children fed and in bed, it was close to eight o'clock when she saw from the window Thelma Dawson, done up to the nines, sashaying off down the road. That was when she realised that her new neighbour lived alone with her children.

At times, she felt the same. She was married but lived a solitary existence with only the briefest interaction with women of her own age. Perhaps here, on the edge of the city, things might be different.

11

Thelma had waited until seven thirty for Jenny to respond to her invitation, then, deciding she was still unpacking and sorting herself out, went out to meet Bert.

No lights showed from any of the shop windows lining one side of Melvin Square which formed the heart of the Knowle West estate. Like the houses, the buildings housing the co-op, the newsagents and the greengrocer had been built after the Great War. Facing the shops on the other side of the grassy square were the dark green railings of the school playground. Dominating the corner to the right of that stood The Venture Inn, dark and vast at one end of the square. Oblongs of amber light fell from its windows. The sound of music could be heard despite it being at the opposite end of the square to the chemist shop. It was in the direction of the chemist shop that Thelma headed, away from the lights and into Daventry Road, where Cuthbert Throgmorton would be waiting for her.

Daventry Road was wider than most of the surrounding streets, where the red-brick council houses were mainly semi-detached and looked as though they'd been given the space they deserved.

To obtain a tenancy of one of these houses was very much sought after. Thelma believed you had to know someone high up in the council to get one. You had to have the kind of job that could pay the slightly higher rents.

To her right where the road left the square was a piece of scrubland separating the chemist from the first of the houses. Even though it was mid-July, it was like entering a black pool continuing for a dozen steps before the next streetlamp.

It was a cool evening with a threat of rain and her breath steamed on the air, but she didn't feel cold. A night out helped her forget her lack of money and companionship.

In the gathering gloom, Thelma knew he was there, the car a more solid metal blackness than the night.

She slid into the front seat beside him. Inside was relatively warm and his breath had steamed up the windows. She shivered her appreciation.

'Warmer in here. Brass monkeys out there, it is.'

He patted her knee. 'Never mind, pet. I'll warm you up.'

He leaned into her shoulder, kissed her cheek and would have gone further, but she pushed him off.

'Mine's a brandy,' she stated in a no-nonsense way. 'That'll warm me up.'

He chuckled. 'You always know what you want, don't you, Thelma.'

She sniffed, got out a cigarette and lit it. 'And I don't come cheap. Never said I did. Right. Are you going to take me for this drink or are we going to sit here all night?'

He used a cloth to wipe the condensation from the windscreen, then did the same to the window on his side. 'I never give a promise I don't intend keeping.'

'I'll hold you to that.'

A blast of night air came in as he got out of the car, starting handle at the ready. Through a fug of cigarette smoke from her newly lit cigarette, she watched his head bobbing up and down as he tried to start the car. Half a dozen turns of the handle, and the engine begrudgingly sprang into life.

He slid back into the front and tossed the handle onto the rear seat and rubbed his hands together before placing them on the wheel.

'Bert, you're a genius,' Thelma laughed.

Bert grinned. 'My mother would have a fit if she heard you calling me Bert. "I named you Cuthbert," she's fond of saying, "and not Bert." Lays down the law does my mother.'

'Tell 'er I think Cuthbert's too much of a mouthful.'

Bert was a rent man. Not just a rent collector knocking on the front door every week on behalf of the council. He was the rent collection inspector and oversaw all the rent collectors in the city.

They'd first met in a professional capacity – when she'd fallen behind with the rent after losing her job at the Bounty and Pippin sweet factory. If she was honest with herself, the writing had been on the wall. It wasn't the first time she'd pushed her luck.

A few months before being given her cards, both her girls, Alice and Mary, had gone down with scarlet fever, and she'd taken time off work. Mr Osborne, the manager, had not been sympathetic. He'd told her, after the kids had only been ill for five days, that if she didn't return the following week there'd be no job to come back to.

More caring of her children than her job, she'd told him in no uncertain terms that she could get a job anywhere and he'd be losing a valuable employee. Unfortunately, Mr Osborne was true to his word, and she'd been given her cards.

She'd exploded with anger and defiantly told him what to do with his boiled sweets. 'You ain't Fry's Chocolate factory, Mr bloody Osborne. They treats people right. You bloody well don't.

And you're too free with your hands. My bottom's black with bruises.'

Wincing at the attack he hadn't seen coming, he'd given her a second chance. That was before management had received a letter accusing her of leading an immoral life. Of going out with men.

'I'm a widow,' she'd screamed and laughed all at the same time. 'I ain't a bleedin' nun.'

Her anger had fallen on deaf ears. Luckily, she had her widow's pension, but that was hardly enough to survive on. Besides, she liked working.

In a letter to her son, George, who was currently away at sea, she outlined her most treasured hope.

'I don't like factory work. What I'd like is to get a job in a shop selling lovely dresses. I'd quite like that, but then you probably know that already. You know how I like to dress up and look good. Not for me going around wearing curlers and slippers all day. It might suit Cath, bless her heart, but it don't suit me. Anyway, brazen as ever I walked into Bertrams in Castle Street, put on a posh accent and my best clothes. Told them I used to work for Lady Bountiful. They weren't to know it was a brand of boiled sweet and weren't too worried about a reference. It seemed one of their sales ladies had left their employ in a hurry. No reason was given, but I guessed she'd got herself in the family way. So there you are. I've got a new job and I'm loving it.

Take care son,

Your loving mother. Xxx

She knew she'd been lying about working for a titled lady who featured on a caramel, but Mr Philip Bertram had been suitably impressed. The poor chap wasn't to know that her only experience in selling women's fashion were altering the old-fashioned items she bought from jumble sales, recutting, redesigning and selling on to a host of delighted customers.

Besides a new job, she'd become friendly with Cuthbert Throgmorton, the senior rent collector who'd come calling after she'd got a bit behind with her rent.

The moment he'd entered her house, she knew she would overcome the problem. His eyes were everywhere. Most red-blooded blokes would have concentrated on the creamy cleavage poking above her gaping neckline. Instead, he'd gaped at her collection of royal memorabilia and told her that his mother was also a firm royalist and collected too.

Once they'd become friends, he'd told her that Truro Close was about to be renamed Coronation Close. The new king had ascended the throne in January. The change of name happened in May when the close was looking at its best, the sycamores lime green and the smell of flowering privet hedges and May blossom filling the air. She'd claimed some influence in the name change, principally because Bert had seen her collection of royal memorabilia.

Everyone had turned out to see the Lord Mayor make the declaration. A reporter and a photographer had taken pictures of the momentous event. Thelma had felt a great surge of pride. She was the only one in the street who had turned up for the event wearing a revamped dress of red, white and blue. Her neighbours had made do with Union Jack flags provided by the newspaper for the photo opportunity, then taken back when the event was over to use on other coronation-themed scenarios.

Now, inside a pub up on the Wells Road with an alcoholic drink inside her, Thelma told Bert of her concerns for the young family who'd moved into number two Coronation Close.

'The looks on their faces – over the moon they were. The trouble is they don't know who they've got living next door.

Friendly neighbours they are not. In fact...' Her artfully made-up eyebrows beetled into a frown. She considered whether she should tell Bert about the accusations in the letter sent to the sweet factory and, more so, who she suspected – no, knew – who'd sent them.

His fingers gave her hand a gentle squeeze. 'Thelma, you should know by now that you can tell me anything.'

As she considered this, her breasts heaved in a heavy sigh. She took a quick sip of her brandy – not too much, although Bert wouldn't hesitate to refill her glass. But she didn't want him to do that. No matter what else people might think of her, she wasn't one to take advantage.

Keeping her eyes fixed on her drink, she told him. 'Somebody sent a poison pen letter to my old employer saying I carried on with men all the time.' She couldn't help her blush and the bashful way she looked at him from beneath fluttering eyelashes. 'It more or less accused me of being a tart... you know, a woman who takes money for... you know what.'

Bert took out his man-size handkerchief and gave his nose a good blow. 'Nasty,' he said before putting it away again.

Thelma sipped at her drink and sighed; her gaze fixed on the picture of the new king hanging above the bar. He was so handsome. She'd be his queen any day of the week. As for Bert, well, he was no prince, but he made her feel good. What with the shop and him, she'd refined the way she spoke – not so much as to be posh but just a bit more polished.

He hadn't asked her who she thought was responsible for the poison pen letter, but she enlightened him anyway.

'It's them in number one.'

'Never mind, darling.' He patted her hand again. 'All's well that ends well. You're at the ladies' dress shop now. More suited to you, I should think. You're a smartly dressed woman, Thelma. I might be biased, but to my mind you could be a mannequin in a shop window. You're a smart woman, inside and out.'

'That's lovely of you to say so, Bert. And thanks for understanding.'

'Accusing someone to your face is one thing. Sending an anonymous letter is cowardly. Now,' he said, looking tellingly at the wall clock, its brass pendulum dulled by years of nicotine, 'time I was going. I told Mother I would be home by ten.'

He swallowed the last of the alcohol he'd told his mother that he never drank. The pint of beer had been superseded with a measure of whisky, which went down a treat when he was out with Thelma. She fascinated him but remained a secret he kept from his mother.

'Where does she think you are tonight?'

He paused and for a moment she wondered whether he was going to tell her the truth or – like his mother – be told a lie.

'Out with a friend.'

'It's not exactly a lie, is it?'

'A friend from schooldays who also happens to be in the masons. She has hopes of them letting me join.'

'Do you think your friend will ask you to join?'

There was a quiet satisfaction in the way he smiled. 'He already has. I said no.'

They shared the same smile. Some people might regard Bert as a bit of an old fuddy-duddy – still living with his mother at his age. Thelma herself had thought so too at first. But things had moved on a bit since then. She was growing to like him. He didn't pounce on her and try to rip her clothes off. He talked to her and when he kissed or touched her, there was only affection, the softness of fingertips, the shared smile that said all was well between them.

Marriage might be a possibility, once his mother was gone, that is. He said little about her. Thelma had no idea what she looked like or any indication of character. Bert kept family and personal information close to his chest, like a man playing poker who is loath to show his hand.

In the meantime, they crept around in a dark and secret world, afraid of being seen and reported back to her – or to the council. Officials at the city council didn't approve of liaisons between employees and those who paid them rent. A conflict of interests; that's what Bert had told her.

On leaving the pub, a wind driven drizzle whipped Thelma's hair across her face.

They almost sprinted back to the car, Thelma hobbled by her high heels, Bert holding onto her elbow with one hand and his hat with the other.

Once inside the car, they sat there wiping the wetness from their faces, their warm breath steaming up the windows.

They hugged. He rubbed at her arms and she reciprocated.

She drew in her chin and eyed him quizzically. 'Do you think your mother really believes you?'

'She looks at me funny sometimes and makes comment about the smell of cigarette smoke.

Thelma laughed. 'Crikey, these fags give me a bad enough cough as it is, though I'll start smoking cigars if you think it might put her off the scent.'

He threw back his head and snorted a laugh. 'My mother! I'm forty-five years old and she still treats me as if I'm fourteen.'

'Oh Bert!'

He glowered. 'It isn't funny.'

* * *

Bert watched as she walked away, gave a little wave, then disappeared in the direction of Coronation Close.

Thelma made him feel good. Full of fun she might be, but she was also a strong person, one who faced the world head on and wouldn't give up without a fight.

Hidden behind the car windscreen, nobody could see the happiness drain from his face. He'd taken on her concerns about how the occupants of number one Coronation Close would behave towards the young family who'd moved into number two. The council had previously received letters complaining about the old man who'd lived in number two. Unsigned of course. Thelma's suspicions, plus the fact that someone had sent an unsigned letter to her employer resulting in her losing her job, jarred with him. He'd read those letters about the old man, a Mr Clark, who'd lived in number two. He'd died and now a young family had moved in. It was a matter of time before letters were received about them and like Thelma, he couldn't help but be concerned.

12

It was late on the Sunday morning after moving in and Jenny was still alight with happiness. Somewhere, a bell called the faithful to church. The house was quiet, peaceful and bright with light. So different to the shabby rooms in Blue Bowl Alley, no smell of drains or drifts of falling plaster.

Tilly and Gloria had been persuaded by a boy in the street to attend Sunday school and Roy had not returned from the night shift. If recent behaviour was anything to go by, he might not get home until teatime.

The fact that he had further to travel had something to do with it, but on top of that was his obsession with Moseley's organisation.

'I can stay at Trevor's place if I must. There're important things to discuss besides fitting in the job at the docks.' He'd sounded both pleased and slightly apprehensive about so doing.

'You do what you must,' she'd said to him.

She didn't mind one little bit. She had her house and the more Roy was absent from it, the happier she would be.

Even though it was Sunday, she had no intention of going to church. She'd got out of that habit a long time ago. For the children, it was something to occupy them and help them make friends. The same children they were with for Sunday school would also be at their new school. It made sense to get them acquainted.

Jenny tingled with delight as she wandered from room to room, straightening things, putting things away, deciding that a cushion looked better in the centre of the sofa rather than against one of the arms.

Upstairs, she made beds and opened windows to let in the fresh air. In the kitchen, she checked the stone base of the larder where a bullock's heart, already stuffed with sage and onion, awaited transfer to the oven. A gas oven! She laughed out loud. She might have missed some of her neighbours at Blue Bowl Alley, but she certainly didn't miss that temperamental old range.

In a way, she felt like a child playing at house, making a home from bits and pieces that had seen better days. The house deserved something better, but for now it would have to do.

A breeze ruffled at her hair as she took a bundle of washing out to peg onto the line. Whilst doing so, she heard clattering pans from the house next door.

The lid of a dustbin clanged as the woman she'd seen on the day she'd moved in placed rubbish into the bin and slammed the lid.

'Good morning,' she said brightly. 'I'm Jenny Crawford. We met the day I moved here.'

The woman ignored her and went inside. The back door slammed.

It was disappointing. Perhaps she hadn't heard, though Jenny couldn't quite believe that.

The day was too bright and the house was too exciting to dent her spirits. Besides, she had so much to do.

The curtains she was hanging at the living-room window had been a moving-in 'present' from Gladys Hubert.

'Seeing as I knew yer mother, I'll let you have them cheap. The neighbours will judge on how good a housewife you are by the quality of your curtains. They're a snip at two shillings though I should charge five.'

As Jenny stepped up onto a chair to hang them, her attention was drawn to a strident figure who looked to be heading her way.

Dressed in a summery dress of blue flowers with a crisp Peter Pan collar and cuffs, Thelma was marching out from her house across the road. At the same time, another slight movement drew her attention to another woman exiting number seven at the end of the road.

There was purpose in the way both smiling women walked towards each other then came to a halt outside her garden gate. She knew at once that at least two of her neighbours were coming to make friends, recompense for the woman next door ignoring her.

Thank God Roy wasn't in.

Thelma waved one hand. The other held a teapot. The other woman, mousier than Thelma and nowhere near as well dressed despite it being Sunday, held a plate covered with a tea towel.

The garden gate squeaked on metal hinges as it was pushed open.

'Oh my,' breathed Jenny as she carefully stepped down from the chair. She felt a little guilty she hadn't taken her new neighbour up on her invitation.

A ready excuse on her tongue and a new joy in her heart, she rushed to the front door.

Thelma's teeth beamed ultra-white against her bright red lips. 'Brought you a brew. Thought you could do with it after yer busy day,' said Thelma. Without waiting for an invite, Thelma stepped over the threshold and into the hallway, her mate following in behind her.

Jenny began her apology. 'I'm sorry about that, but I got so caught up with the unpacking and everything.'

'My fault,' said Thelma. 'I should 'ave known you'd be whacked. Besides which I 'ad to be out by seven thirty.'

A small head swathed in a halo of metal curlers tipped sideways behind her. 'I'm Cath Lockhart. I lives up the far end at number seven.'

On getting a better look at her, Jenny saw that Cath wasn't very mousy at all. Blonde hair gleamed from around the steel curlers. Her eyes were blue and she had a pert nose. Perhaps it was just her being alongside the more vibrant and dark-haired Thelma that lessened her impact.

Without waiting for an invitation, Thelma barged into the living room, pulled out a dining chair and plonked herself on it. At the same time she set the teapot down on the scratched and scuffed surface of the dining table. 'Me mate Cath's brought you biscuits. Thought you might need something a bit sweet to boost your energy.'

Cath jerked her chin at her companion. 'Thelma Dawkins. Widow of this parish, three kids and two cats named Albert and Victoria.'

Jenny smiled. 'I know. We've already met.'

'Oh yes. Of course.'

Thelma laughed. 'Seen enough of me to know that she's likely to see me big bosom coming round the corner before she sees me.'

They laughed as though they'd known each other for years.

Cath set the plate of biscuits she'd brought with her in the middle of the table. 'Do you want us to use tea plates?' she asked. 'Wouldn't want to scatter crumbs all over the floor.'

Jenny fetched three from the pile on the dresser waiting to be put away.

'I'll fetch milk and sugar from the kitchen,' said Thelma. 'Don't bother to tell me where it is. I can guess.'

She came back with both sugar and milk and put them beside the teapot whilst Jenny laid out cups, saucers and spoons.

'Right. We've got everything now,' Thelma declared, returning to her chair with a contented sigh.

Cath pushed the plate of biscuits in Jenny's direction, leaned over them and whispered. 'We thought you could do with making new friends.'

Thelma added, 'Are we right, or are we right?'

'You're right. You cannot imagine how pleased I am to be here. It's so different to the place we lived before. I feel so grateful to have this house.'

'And new friends to go with it,' said Cath with a soft sigh. Everything about Cath was soft, except for the curlers jangling like a brace of teaspoons suspended in her hair. Jenny couldn't help liking her.

Thelma was bouncy, brazen and larger than life. Her hair was shoulder length, her face powdered, and the buttons of her green satin blouse barely restrained her voluptuous breasts.

Jenny had liked her on first meeting and now decided that she liked her even more.

'So where did you live before you came yer?' asked Cath.

Feeling a blush come to her face, Jenny's hair swiped around her face as she looked down into her teacup. 'The Pithay. We had rooms.'

Cath said nothing and sipped at her tea.

Thelma nodded knowingly. 'Well, you ain't living there now. You'll soon settle in.'

'I already have.'

'Lot to do though.'

Recovered from embarrassment, Jenny laughed lightly. 'I haven't even put the curtains up yet.'

'Don't you worry about that,' said Thelma. 'We'll give you a hand.'

'Tea first though,' said Cath, 'or it'll get cold.'

Over the cuppa and biscuits, they told Jenny all about themselves, that Cath's husband's name was Bill, that she had three children and that she'd lived in Coronation Close for ten years.

'Course, it was called Truro Close back at the beginning of the year before the old king died. A lot of the roads around yer are named after places in Cornwall or Ireland. So you 'ave Newquay Road, Kildare Road and what 'ave you. Then, a few weeks back, the council decided to rename Truro Close in time for the coronation next year. The Lord Mayor came along to rename it. We 'ad a lot of clapping and people from the newspaper, but nobody brought cake or anything. I thought they would 'ave'

'Cath does love a bit of cake,' said Thelma. 'But never mind that. That weren't what counted. I can't tell you how pleased I was,' gushed Thelma, patting her chest as though she might faint away with the excitement of it all. She heaved a huge sigh and, in doing so, a button came undone and yet more pale flesh, as wobbly as blancmange, was exposed to view. 'Mind you,' she said with a hint of pride. 'It was partly down to me. I mentioned it to a certain friend of mine. He thought it was a good idea and put it to those whose job it is to decide these things. Chuffed to bits I was when they agreed. Ain't that bloody marvellous!'

Jenny agreed that it was. Never in her wildest dreams would she have any idea of how to contact somebody in the know to make things like that happen. She might have done at one time, but that time was long past. It seemed that knowing people in power was something both Thelma and Roy had in common.

She spotted Cath rolling her eyes.

Thelma appeared not to notice and carried on with her story. 'A bloke from the newspaper came round to ask me where I got the idea. Well, course, I showed him me knick-knacks and photos and that. Cath knows about me collection. I've got coronation mugs from the last coronation, George the Fifth, God bless his soul. And I've got one for Edward the Seventh and the diamond jubilee of Queen Victoria. Pictures too. I cuts out everything about the royal family.' She shrugged her shoulders in another satisfied sigh and said, 'I can't get enough of royalty. I've got quite a collection. I'll show them to you sometime once you're settled in.'

Cath Lockhart had been sitting quietly munching biscuits and leaving Thelma to do the talking. Now she butted in.

'It's about the coronation that we're 'ere. We want to arrange a street party and wondered if you'd like to join our committee.'

'But that won't be until next year.'

'May the twelfth to be exact,' said Thelma. 'I can't wait meself. Flags everywhere, loads of food and drink. No obligation of course, but we thought you might like to. It might help you getting to know the neighbours. You'll find them a friendly lot – overall,' she added.

An unfathomable look passed between the two women. She guessed they assumed she might refuse. It was the last thing she was likely to do even though Roy might have a fit if he found out. She was so happy to have good neighbours so openly offering her friendship.

'That's a lovely bit of grass out there,' Jenny said, nodding towards the window.

'It belongs to all of us,' stated Cath. 'Though there's some that thinks otherwise.' Cath grimaced. Again, a look passed between her and Thelma.

'She's the problem,' said Thelma, gritting her teeth and jerking her chin to sudden activity at the end of the close. 'Old Mother Partridge next door to you. She thinks she bloody owns it!'

Cath craned her neck so she could better see out of the living-room window. 'She's out there now. Washing the street sign.'

'Washing what?' exclaimed Jenny.

'The street sign,' said Thelma. 'You come and see.'

The legs of three dining chairs scraped across the floorboards.

Together all three women stood at the living-room window eyeing the oval of green grass. Two women stood at the bottom of the sign which was wooden and perched on top a concrete post.

'Fancy. On a Sunday too.'

'They go to the evening service. They're sisters,' Thelma added. 'Mrs Dorothy Partridge and Miss Harriet Smith. Or at least I think she's a Miss. Hard to tell, though my guess is that she is. Dot Partridge lost her old man in the war, so I hear. I think her sister was engaged but her man never came back. Just like me.'

Three heads together, they continued to peer at what was going on. One woman, the thinnest, climbed a rickety-looking stepladder. The other stood at the bottom, a heavy foot placed on the bottom step to prevent it from toppling.

With great deliberation, the woman on the top step of the ladder began washing the newly erected sign stating that the name of the cul-de-sac was Coronation Close.

'Thinks even that is her private property,' growled Thelma.

'But it ain't.' Cath shook her head, an action that sent her curlers singing.

'Of course it isn't.' Thelma sounded as though the very idea was heresy. 'She tells the boys they've got no business playing football on the grass and the girls not to run around like gypsies. I can tell you now, I've had a few run-ins with the old sow. Cath too.'

Up until now Jenny had truly believed she'd landed on her feet. Now it seemed that the woman next door might be a fly in the ointment. Her new house meant everything to her. She vowed there and then to avoid the woman at all costs. It was all she could do. 'Sounds a right old dragon.'

Thelma grimaced. 'She is. And Welsh at that.'

'Is she likely to join in the coronation celebrations?

'We'll be celebrating the coronation of our new king. If she don't want to take part, then that's up to her. But I'm telling you now, there'll be repercussions. She'll be a traitor! Unpatriotic! Never mind hanging her at the Tower of London if she comes out with any of her nonsense. I'll 'ang – sorry – hang her meself.' Thelma's voice rang around the room. Arched eyebrows furrowed above her eyes. The cheery expression had turned dark with indignation.

Jenny had noticed every so often she slipped into a strong Bristol accent dropping her aitches and rolling her 'r's. Jenny guessed that working in a dress shop had made her change her ways. She'd heard Bertrams were a bit posh. All the same hanging a neighbour seemed a bit far fetched.

Cath saw Jenny's puzzled look and smiled. 'If she protests, Thelma will be round there accusing 'er of being disloyal. Ain't that right, Thelma?'

'Too right I will,' said Thelma.

'You'll 'ave to see her collection of mugs and cups and suchlike. Wonderful they are. Already got one for the new king, ain't you, Thelma.'

Thelma beamed. 'Two mugs so far and one tile. And pictures. I cut out a picture from the newspaper the other day of the king visiting the mines in South Wales. Saw the same thing at the pictures. Everyone was cheering him.' She sighed. 'I reckon he'll be the best king we've ever had.'

Cath threw Jenny a rueful grin. 'Sounds as if you're in love with 'im.'

'Don't be daft,' Thelma bristled. 'I'm just patriotic and aching for a bit of change in this world. You mark my words; he'll be like a breath of fresh air.'

Cath and Jenny finished off their tea without saying anything.

Thelma resumed. 'We don't need to sort out food just yet. Let's get Christmas over first before we start doing that, but we could start making things such as fancy dress and bunting.'

'I look forward to it,' said Jenny. She found herself getting quite excited about becoming involved. 'Will this party be just for Coronation Close or for everyone else around here?'

'Coronation Close only,' said Thelma, stressing the name with a superior sniff and a queenly tossing of her head. She slapped a curvaceous thigh. 'We've been singled out to be royal, you might say, so let's keep it to ourselves. I've counted. There should be over thirty of us, including the kids and invited grannies, uncles, aunts and suchlike. That's more than enough. We can dress up and run games and give prizes to the kids. P'raps we can get hold of a gramophone so we can have a dance.'

'Mrs Partridge 'as got a gramophone. Doubt she'll lend it though.'

Thelma grimaced. 'We'll get hold of one somehow.'

Jenny positively glowed with enthusiasm. She had friends close at hand. She'd done so at the old place, but Roy had forbidden her to meet up with them. Something told her that he'd be hard pushed to keep Thelma Dawson at bay.

Her spirit soared. 'It sounds wonderful. I'd really like to help. Just ask and I'll do what I can.'

'Any good with a sewing machine?'

Jenny shook her head. 'I haven't got one. I only wish I did. I sew by hand. Only small things, taking down the hems on the girls' dresses – they grow so quickly.'

'I was thinking about fancy dress costumes. You'll need a sewing machine for that.'

'I wish,' said Jenny with a heartfelt sigh. 'I would love to make the girls some new clothes – and myself for that matter.' No smoothing or altering could make the clothes she wore less shabby. She'd had them for years. She felt Thelma's eyes scrutinising the faded dress she wore, the darns and patches that held it together.

'Well, that's sorted,' said Thelma, getting to her feet and picking up the teapot. She smoothed her skirt down over her ample hips. 'I'll give you a hand with them curtains before I go.'

'Me too,' said Cath, returning her plate to the table. 'I'll take the plates and stuff out into the kitchen and get the washing-up done.'

It didn't take long for the three of them to put the curtains up. Afterwards, they took a moment to admire their handiwork.

Thelma declared it a job well done.

'Them curtains look nice there. If you want some more help with anything, come and knock.'

Jenny noticed that although Thelma had ample hips and bosom, her waist was narrow, the classic hourglass figure. Edwardian ladies came to mind, tightly corseted, bosoms held high and a bustle making their hips and bottoms look twice the size they really were.

Jenny's new friends paused at the door before leaving and looked to where Gloria and Tilly, still in their best clothes after Sunday School, were playing on the green.

'Your girls look as though they've settled in all right,' Thelma remarked and nodded to where Tilly and Gloria were throwing a ball between themselves and two other young girls of their age. One of the girls had copper-coloured hair, the other whitish blonde.

Jenny smiled. 'It looks that way.'

'How about yer old man?'

An excuse fell easily from her tongue. 'Oh, you won't see too much of him. He's a docker. They've got him working nights.'

'My Bill's a docker. They might know each other,' said Cath and looked quite delighted that it might be so. 'Ask 'im if he knows Bill Lockhart. Everyone knows my Bill,' she proclaimed, not without a smidgen of pride.

'Roy doesn't mention work that much. I'll ask him though.' The fact was that she had no intention of asking him. These women were her new friends. She wouldn't be telling him anything about them. He occupied one compartment of her life, these new friends another.

Thelma laughed as she stepped from the front step onto the garden path. Her breasts jiggled when she laughed. 'At least you got a man in your life.'

'Oh. I'm sorry,' said Jenny and made an instant assumption.

Thelma threw back her head and laughed a big throaty laugh that must have been heard the entire length of the close. 'Well, you know what they say, love. Better to have loved and lost than not to have loved at all.' She winked. 'And believe me, sweetheart, I've loved a lot since that silly bugger got himself killed.'

With that, she followed Cath to the garden gate, hips swaying seductively, the heels of her shoes beating a tempo all the way down the path. High heels! At this time of day? Jenny was amazed.

The kids on the green were yelling and laughing, a ball tossed between them.

'I can throw it over the tree,' shouted one of them.

True to their word, the ball sailed high into the air, through the mid-level branches of a sycamore and into the garden of her neighbour in number one.

Suddenly, all hell let lose. Mrs Partridge, the stringy woman from number one came racing out, face screwed up like a dried apple, fist clenched and held high.

'Sunday is the Lord's Day. No ball games should be played on the Lord's Day.' Her voice was strident and her tone harsh.

'Mum,' shouted Gloria, running panic-stricken across the grass. 'I didn't mean to do it. I just wanted it to go high. I didn't mean for it to go into her garden.'

Before Jenny had chance to do something about it, Thelma came bursting out of her front door, her heels clattering like gunfire down the garden path.

'Oi!' Thelma shouted. 'Give them kids back their ball or I'll be over that fence and giving you a bloody good kick.'

Thelma's loud bellow brought other women out into their front gardens, some leaning on their gates, keen to see what would happen next.

Cath came running from the other end of the cul-de-sac. One side of her head was a mass of bouncing curls. The other was still spiked with curlers that she hadn't yet had chance to take out.

The garden gate of number one swung on its hinges and crashed against the privet hedge. Thelma stormed up the path, Cath close behind her.

Jenny patted her daughter on the head. 'Wait here. I'll get your ball back.'

On seeing Thelma and Cath storming up her garden path, Mother Partridge – who seemed far from motherly threw the ball, dashed into her house and slammed the front door.

Gloria ran back to join her friends who were all smiling. Thelma's daughters didn't so much look smug as proud of their mother.

'Your mother don't stand no messing,' Jenny heard her daughter say.

'Nope,' responded Mary, who seemed totally unsurprised and unconcerned – as though this was quite normal behaviour on behalf of her mother – which it probably was. As a widow, she would be used to fighting for everything she had.

Thelma gave the ball an almighty throw, sending it back to the four girls playing on the green. 'If she does that again, you come and get me. Right?'

'Right, Ma,' said Mary, the girl with the very red unruly hair. 'You gonna whack 'er if she does it again?'

She sounded as though she looked forward to the prospect.

'We'll cross that bridge when we come to it.'

The girls went back to playing catch, throwing the ball from one to the other.

Thelma and Cath congregated with Jenny at her gate.

'Now listen,' said Thelma, leaning in close, her eyes dark and compelling. 'You be careful of that old bat next door. Don't let her shove you around and don't tell her anything she can use against you.'

Jenny took on board the seriousness in Thelma's eyes and nodded. 'I'll be careful.'

* * *

Later, in the glow of the evening light, the smell of privet hedge, cooking and wildflowers permeating the air, Jenny eyed the long expanse of garden, the insects flying around the vegetables planted by Mr Clark, the previous tenant , the birds rustling the leaves of the apple tree. She had the garden she wanted. She had the house she wanted. On top of all that, and a distinct bonus, her new friends had taken her to their hearts in double quick time. Things could not have been better, except...

Her gaze transferred to the house next door. No light fell from its tightly shut windows, not a chink showed from the dark, drawn curtains.

She'd felt so light these past few days, so happy to be here. Meeting Thelma and Cath had made her happier than she'd been for years.

Would that happiness continue? Mrs Partridge's reaction to the ball had been trivial. That's what she told herself. It was hard to believe that this oasis of calm viewed on such a lovely evening was not her little slice of heaven. She hoped it would remain so, but only time would tell.

13

AUGUST 1936

Before going to work, Thelma hooked out a very pretty dress she'd bought at a jumble sale the previous week. It had been of a style harking back to the twenties when a straight up, straight down figure was lauded. A tuck here and a tuck there and she could bring it right up to date.

'Is that a new frock for you, Ma,' asked Alice as she hooked two slices of bacon out of the pan and slapped each onto a slice of bread – one for her, one for her sister. At just nine years of age, she took pride in getting breakfast for the pair of them before setting off for school. Thelma never had the time, seeing as she had to get the bus at eight to get into town on time.

Thelma laughed. 'No, darling. I never did dance the Charleston.'

Alice and Mary exchanged frowns. 'What's a Charleston?'

'Da, da, da, da,' she sang and did a pretty good attempt at the dance, and giggling, the girls joined in.

The face of the clock on the mantelpiece grabbed her attention.

'Oh crikey. Just look at the time. Must get going.'

She loved working for Bertrams, so as usual set off to work with a spring in her step. It was the best job she'd ever had and regular customers were beginning to ask for her. Fashion was her thing. She loved clothes and was always well presented, plus she knew how to flatter.

'I think your husband will fall in love with you all over again,' said a smiling Thelma later that morning as she folded and wrapped the royal blue dress for the middle-aged customer who had bought it.

'Do you really think so?'

Even though the top half of the woman's face was covered by a net veil, Thelma saw a pink flush creeping up her and heard the almost girlish laugh.

'I'm absolutely certain. Here you are. Do come in again and tell us how many people at the Masonic dance thought you were the belle of the ball.'

Clutching the string handles of the stiff white carrier bag, the name *Bertrams Modes and Millinery* printed on the sides, black patent handbag under her arm, the satisfied customer left the store. Thelma remained at the counter.

She'd always been told she had the gift of the gab. Serving the discerning customers of Bertrams had given her the opportunity to prove it true.

'Mrs Dawkins?'

Her employer, Mr Gilbert Bertram, was bearing down on her; Mrs Apsley, Thelma's senior, walking close at his elbow.

Thelma took a deep breath, hands clasped in front of her, a ready smile on her face. Hopefully she presented a picture of humility, or as close as she could get to it.

'Mr Bertram,' she nodded a greeting to Mr Bertram first. 'Mrs Apsley.' Another nod was returned, though less freely given. From the very first, there'd been a wariness on her senior's part. Thelma had sometimes caught her staring at her. It could have stemmed from the fact that she'd been less than honest at her interview. Stating she was a widow with three children to look after was far more likely to get her a job than the truth. She was indeed a widow, but there had only been one child from that marriage to a man who'd never come back from the Great War. The other two were the issue of two different lovers, both of whom had promised to marry her. She'd been caught out twice but swore she would not be caught again.

Women who'd never married but had children rarely got took on if there were other applicants. War widows, on the other hand, received sympathy, along with preferential treatment. Nobody in authority knew that two of her children had been conceived and born outside of marriage. She admitted to being a war widow and that was all that really counted.

'Please come to my office, Mrs Dawkins. Mrs Apsley will take over.'

Unsure what was going on but holding her head high, Thelma followed him. Behind her, she heard the crisp voice of Mrs Apsley fawning over a customer enquiring about leather gloves. A small sale as far as Thelma was concerned. Her sales figures were already high this month and it pleased her.

Mr Bertram closed the door behind her and invited her to sit down. Dark wood lined the walls of his office. A filing cabinet as dark as the walls blended into one corner. The smell of pipe tobacco was strong. So was that of whisky.

Looking a trifle awkward, he shifted a pile of paper from in front of him. 'It's like this,' he said, keeping his gaze fixed on the blotting pad revealed by his moving of the paper. It was very pink and splattered with ink spots. 'You've been with us three months now...'

'Yes. A very happy three months, Mr Bertram.'

'Yes.' He coughed into his hand and didn't meet her eyes. She could see he was nervous and it worried her.

Right, she thought, *put your cards on the table Thelma old girl.*

She did just that. 'I'm hoping the reason for this meeting is that you're going to congratulate me on my sales figures for this week. In fact, for the whole month. I do believe I'm Bertrams best. I put it down to one thing above all others. The customers like me.'

Taken by surprise, Mr Bertram's mouth opened and shut like a fish out of water.

It couldn't be about the sales figures. But Thelma was nothing if not persistent. 'Is that why you asked me in here? To congratulate me?'

She could see he'd been taken off guard. In her mind, she was already cursing Mrs Apsley. She'd seen the way she'd eyed her enviously when ringing up a sale. On some occasions, Mrs Aspley had checked the till after Thelma had rung in a particularly high-value sale from their upper range of ladies' fashion. Fastidious to the letter, she'd always stayed behind to balance the takings for the day. She'd also insisted Thelma stayed until she'd finished. 'In case there is any shortfall we might need to check together.' There never was of course, but all the same, Thelma was on edge until the cashing up was over.

Mr Bertram remained looking like a goldfish, mouth gulping for words and ending up with only air.

Thelma leaned into the desk. 'Can I get you a glass of water?'

'No.' His response was abrupt. He swallowed and composed himself, then checked through the pile of papers he'd moved to one side. 'Mrs Apsley reported the sales to me. I'm a man who believes in rewarding hard work. To that end, I'm increasing your wage by two shillings and sixpence a week. I would like to give you more, but in these challenging times, I'm inclined towards frugality. I'm sure you would agree?'

Now it was her whose mouth hung open. She'd been taken completely by surprise. So, Mrs Apsley was not quite the harridan she'd thought her to be. Best of all, nobody was sacking her because she'd loved three men and had children by all three. These things happened, but it appeared nobody at Bertrams had found out her little secret – or rather her two little secrets. For now, at least she was in the clear. She had her job and she had her family and for that she was grateful.

* * *

Although it was August and the days were getting shorter, she reckoned there was time before bed to do what she'd planned that morning.

The girls had warmed up the stew they'd made from Sunday leftovers.

'What would I do without you girls, looking after yer old mum as you do.'

'We like cooking,' said Alice.

'You only sliced the bread,' said Mary accusingly. 'I lit the gas under the stew and gave it a good stir.'

'It ain't all your work. We both cooked it up yesterday.'

Thelma smiled. 'You girls are better cooks than I ever was.'

The girls exchanged giggling glances. 'Yep. You're right. But you are good with the sewing machine.'

They were right. In fact, her feet were already working the foot-plate of the treadle, feeding through the pale blue Charleston dress. It had needed the waist nipped in a bit and darts on each side to give shape to the bosom.

'There. I think that should fit nicely,' she said, holding it up against the light, satisfied that it was updated and exactly the right size for Jenny, her new neighbour.

Nobody made comment. Without a word to her, Alice and Mary had gone outside to meet up with their friends. She could hear shrieks of laughter coming from the green.

After a quick ironing of the new seams, she folded up the silky dress and tucked it under her arm.

Jenny looked surprised to see her. 'Put the kettle on, love,' said Thelma, barging in yet again without being asked. 'I'm choking for a cuppa.'

'Thelma...'

'I've got something for you.'

She stopped dead in the living room. The light from a standard lamp fell onto the dark good looks of Roy Crawford, Jenny's husband. He was reading a paper.

'Mr Crawford,' Thelma exclaimed, never one to be taken aback for long. 'I didn't know you were home.' She pasted on a smile.

For his part, he looked back at her with antagonism which surprised her. Most men gave her a good once-over, noting her curvaceous figure and happy face. It struck her as strange that he did not.

'I didn't know I had to inform you.' His voice was curt and his expression unsmiling.

'You don't,' said Thelma, just about clinging onto a lukewarm smile and keeping her voice level. 'Anyway, I didn't come in to see you. I came to see Jenny.' She turned abruptly from him to his wife. 'I brought you a present. Although it was some time ago, call it a moving-in present if you like. How about we go into the kitchen and you can make me that cuppa in there and we can talk women's talk?'

For a fleeting moment, she saw a flash of fear in Jenny's eyes, a glance at her husband, a glower in return.

Well, she thought, *this is a woman cowed. That ain't right.*

'Well, come on then. Let's leave the old man in peace with his paper.'

Jenny's face brightened; fear replaced by defiance.

'Come on through.'

Out of the corner of her eye, Thelma spotted the look of pure hatred he threw at her and what seemed a trickle of icy water ran down her back. Not many men scared her, but Roy did. There was something else too, something she couldn't quite put her finger on, but all in all, he was a wrong 'un. Her heart went out to Jenny.

Jenny gasped at sight of the pale blue dress. 'It's beautiful.'

'Will it fit?'

Jenny held the dress against her and did a little twirl.

'Oh yes. It's so kind of you. Let me give you something...'

'No!' Thelma's response was sharper than it might have been. She told Jenny how she'd bought the dress at a jumble sale. 'Old but beautifully made. I can imagine the woman dancing the Charleston in it.'

Jenny laughed. 'So can I.'

'I put in a couple of darts here and there.'

'It's beautiful.'

It gladdened Thelma's heart to see the pleasure glowing in Jenny's eyes, so much so that she resolved to alter other suitable items. Never mind that she bought from jumble sales and second-hand shops, she was good with her sewing machine. The dress Jenny was currently wearing looked only fit for the ragbag. *But that's just me*, thought Thelma. *I have standards. High standards.*

Over cups of tea, they talked about their children – always the priority. Thelma told Jenny about her eldest, George, who was presently at sea.

'I named him after King George the V. I named my girls after Queen Mary and Princess Alice.'

'I named my girls after my mother and an aunt. They're both passed,' Jenny said a little sadly.

When they'd finally finished their tea, Thelma made her excuses to go. As she reached for the door between kitchen and living room, she saw Jenny's shoulders tense.

'Rather than disturb your old man, I'll go out the back door. Good friends always use the back door around here.'

14

OCTOBER 1936

Roy continued be away from home not just for work but also doing things with his new Black shirt organisation that she just didn't want to know about. Jenny had got used to him not being around but he hadn't been home for three days now and money was short. It wouldn't be long before they were down to eating only bread and marge.

Thelma was a regular visitor on a weekend or after a day working at Bertrams. She was always bringing Jenny something old replenished with flair on her ever-busy sewing machine.

'I can offer you tea but forgot to buy any sugar. If you don't mind drinking it without?'

'Then I've got no choice,' said Thelma, a knowing smile on her face and her fists resting on her hips.

Jenny smiled vaguely and busied herself with the kettle.

Making no comment, Thelma pulled up a chair and sat down. Jenny felt her eyes following her, though nothing was said until the teacups were sitting on the table.

'I haven't seen your Roy for a while. Working away from home, is he?'

'He does sometimes.'

Jenny could feel Thelma's incisive look across the table. She sipped her tea, not minding it being sugarless.

Thelma leaned over the table, her breasts almost colliding with her teacup. 'Jenny, if you're short of a few bob, I can lend you some.'

Jenny shook her head vehemently. 'I'm fine. Anyway, neither a borrower nor a lender be. I won't borrow.'

Thelma chewed her lips as though thinking something over. 'What are you going to do?'

Jenny looked up, surprised. 'I don't know what you mean.'

'Yes you do.'

For a moment, both women held a look, understanding in one set of eyes, resignation in the other set.

Lying to Thelma was useless. She had a knack of getting to the truth.

Jenny sighed. 'You might as well know. He hasn't been home for three days and I'm running short of money.'

'I can lend you some.'

'No. I won't borrow...'

Thelma looked at her. 'Then what will you do?'

Jenny took a deep breath. 'I've got to go into town. I'll go along to the docks office and find out where he is.'

'I'd go with you if I didn't have to work.'

'That's a kind offer, Thelma, but I must do this myself. Anyway, there's a couple of old friends I want to look up.'

'Then that's what you must do,' said Thelma, slapping her palm hard on the tabletop. 'And don't worry about rushing back for the kids. They can have their tea with my girls.'

'Thelma, I do not want charity,' Jenny responded, her eyes blazing. 'I can look after my own. They can have...' Her head fell forward onto her hand. The look in her eyes was hidden, but she could do nothing to stop her lips quivering.

'Bread and marge?'

Thelma had hit the nail on the head and knew it.

Jenny looked away, ashamed there was so little in her larder but she was unwilling to admit anything. Raising her head high, she resolved to face this.

'I won't take advantage of your friendship.'

'You won't be. My girls always cook the evening meal. Besides, they'd love your girls to come for tea. They just love cooking for people.'

When Jenny opened her mouth to protest, Thelma held up a warning finger.

'My girls would be disappointed if you said no. Let them have a little tea party to themselves. They'd love it. Anyway, they've already made a big pot of mutton stew – too much for just three of us.'

Jenny caved in. Thelma was one of the kindest people she'd ever met. On top of that, there was a serious necessity for her to go into the city centre and find out where Roy had got to. Whilst there, she would also take the opportunity to visit Isaac and Ruth. 'Thanks, Thelma.'

Thelma shrugged. 'What are friends for?' She peered more closely at Jenny's flawless complexion before looking her up and down.

'You know, I've got a lovely sea green dress that will suit you. I was going to wear it myself, but it's too small.' She pushed her breasts together and laughed. 'Couldn't find room for these beauties could I. Shall I bring it over?'

'Oh yes. As long as you're sure you can't make use of it, or perhaps Cath might like it? She's slim.'

'She's skinny and a bit of a scruff in case you haven't noticed.

Though the colour might match one of her headscarves. She's got enough of them.'

Jenny laughed with her. No matter what Thelma did, Cath went her own way, comfortable in being herself.

Thelma eyed her questioningly, head cocked to one side. 'Ain't seen you in that other dress I gave you a while back. Still got it?'

'Yes. Yes, of course I have. I've hung it up in the wardrobe for best. Don't want to muck it up doing housework, do I?'

Her smile was as sincere as she could make it. The lie had rolled easily enough off her tongue. After all the time and effort Thelma had put into the dress, she couldn't bear to tell her of Roy's anger, shouting at her that his family didn't take handouts from tarts like Thelma Dawson.

In a fit of temper, he'd torn the dress from her, rolled it into a bowl and slung it into the pig bin. Once he'd set off to work, she'd retrieved it and put it into the wash. The stiches had held and it had taken a bit of scrubbing but it had proved almost impossible to get the stains out. She'd done her best but couldn't tell Thelma the truth – not after all the effort and kindness she'd put into it. Her new friend deserved nothing but praise and she was glad they had met.

'How long's your old man away this time,' Thelma asked.

'I never know. I wish I did though. I could organise my life better if I had some idea.'

Thelma picked up on it.

'Wishful thinking?'

Jenny tossed her head. 'I don't know what you mean.'

'I think you do.'

Thelma adopted an incisive look that made Jenny feel as though her thoughts were written on her forehead.

Jenny shrugged. 'I have to take it as it comes and take my chances where I can.'

15

The day was cold and a thick fog plus the smoke from thousands of coal fires threatened to become impenetrable but despite its menace, Jenny was desperate to visit the Jacobs. It had been so long since she'd seen them.

The sound of her footsteps echoed against the roof and walls of the cut-through at Blue Bowl Alley. In a strange way, the fog softened the grim lines of the old buildings, making it seem as though they were vanishing into the past, the place they truly belonged.

A light thrown from indoors assured her that they were at home. There being no door knocker, she rapped hard with her fist. Nobody came, so she rapped a second time.

'Hold yer horses,' shouted someone from inside.

The voice was loud and rough and sounded nothing like Isaac or his wife.

She stepped back as the door opened and a woman she recognised as the landlord's wife filled the gap.

'What do want?' Mrs Smith's tone was surly. She'd never been one for sounding pleasant.

'The Jacobs family. Are they in?' Jenny asked nervously.

'They ain't yer any more.'

'They've moved?'

The woman had been about to close the door but held it halfway.

'What do you want 'em for?'

'I used to live here. Mrs Crawford's my name. You might remember me.'

'Oh yeah.'

The surly tone failed to improve. Jenny recalled her as a shrew of a woman who'd pass you on the stairs without speaking.

'Why did they move?' she asked hopefully, thinking they too might have realised a dream and moved to somewhere better.

Mrs Smith let go the door, folded her arms across her meagre chest and eyed her inquisitively. 'I 'ad to give 'em notice. My husband Jack dropped dead and I needed these rooms. Not that it's any concern of yours.'

'No. Of course not. Do you know where they've gone?'

Mrs Smith sniffed. 'Pie Lane up behind St James's Church.'

Jenny nodded. She'd heard of it but had rarely gone there. From what she did know it was an old area of grim looking houses and few streetlights, thus she had reservations about Isaac and Ruth living there. Such kind people needed someone to enquire after them. She steeled herself to go there.

'Do you have the number of the house?'

'That's all I know.'

Before she could ask anything else, the door had slammed in her face.

She turned away feeling both dejected and concerned. Poor Isaac and Ruth. They'd been happy enough here, simply because they were both together. She hoped their strong partnership would sustain them in their new home. It felt now even more important to see them to make sure they were coping.

Thanks to the fog, the day was getting darker, the air on her tongue tasting gritty and sulphurous.

St James's Church was on the other side of the Horse Fair, so named because in medieval times it had indeed been a place where horses and other beasts of burden were bought and sold.

Pie Lane was as ancient as she'd heard it was and none of the houses had numbers. Jenny decided to go by instinct. One of these houses would shout out to her, or at least, that's what she hoped.

The overhanging gables of houses, old even back in the time of Queen Elizabeth the First, leaned against each other, like old men seeking support for crooked limbs. Overall there was an air of menace which reminded her of Blue Bowl Alley, though perhaps marginally worse.

It was harder to tell than she thought. She began to feel disheartened, until she came to one displaying a sign in the window: no children and no pets.

It was an incongruous beginning but seemed likely, seeing as Isaac and Ruth had neither children nor pets.

The house was as old as those around it, its timber-framed upper floor jutting out over the ground floor. The crooked front door was low and the windows grubby. The knocker was heavy, rusty and stiff obliging her to use both hands. The sound reverberated in the thick fog. She eyed the fog despairingly hoping it would dissipate enough to see her way home.

As she waited, a long black shape slunk from one dank drain to another.

Finally, after a few more raps, the door was wrenched open, the man who opened it lifting it slightly so it would clear the step.

The step went down into a dark void from where the man had emerged.

'Yeah?'

'I'm looking for Mr and Mrs Jacobs.'

'Well, I ain't 'im. I'm Fred Baker.' He laughed as though he'd cracked a big joke.

Besides his perpetual smile, he had oiled hair and a very fine moustache. Both hair and moustache were glossy.

'No. Mrs Smith, the landlord in Blue Bowl Alley said my old friends had moved here.'

He looked her up and down. 'That's a shame. I thought you might want some rooms. I'd like a better class of tenant, especially a woman.'

'I'm sorry, no, I don't want a room. I'm just trying to find my friends.'

'My dear lady, do come in,' he said with a flourish of his hand, pulling the door back as far as it would go. 'I'll take you up to the second floor myself.'

The fact that he'd said that Isaac and Ruth lived on the second floor worried her. Neither of them was good on their feet. Filled with apprehension, she followed him up the narrow twisting staircase to the second floor. The building smelt of damp plaster. There was no stair carpet, just rough floorboards dark grained enough to be oak.

After the last twist in direction, she stepped onto the landing. Sunshine fell through an arched window at one end. All the same, she wondered how on earth Isaac and Ruth were managing.

'I wouldn't have thought my friends would manage those stairs.'

'I know it's a lot,' he said, 'but because it's on the second floor, there's a lovely view over the city. I'm sure you'll be taken with it.' That said, he bashed on the door. 'Mr Jacobs. Are you in there?'

Before Isaac on his wobbly legs could have made the door, Fred Baker was hammering again.

'Come on, Isaac. You got a visitor.'

The door was a misshapen oblong that had twisted over the years. Isaac was obliged to draw it open.

The tired greyness of his face lit up when he saw her. 'Jenny!'

She could tell just how thrilled he was to see her by the fact that he had called her by her first name. He rarely had. It had always been Mrs Crawford.

Rather than greeting her, he shouted over his shoulder, 'Ruth. It's Jenny Crawford come to visit. Our old neighbour Jenny Crawford!'

'I'll leave you to it then,' said Fred, who had lingered too long at her shoulder, perhaps waiting for an invitation to join them.

Isaac ignored him and closed the door as she stepped inside. 'Come in, my girl. Come in.'

He sounded and looked ecstatic, taking hold of her elbow and drawing her into his new home.

'Ruth! Ruth! Did you hear what I said?'

Bright sunlight would have lifted the grimy paintwork and crumbling plaster but today was far from sunny. Two twisted beams held up the ceiling of the first room. A stove, a deep white sink with draining boards, plus ancient cupboards and a free-standing dresser comprised the kitchen set at one end of the room. The furniture from the old place was instantly recognisable: an old-fashioned windup gramophone, a chaise lounge and chairs with springs threatening to burst through the faded red upholstery.

She'd expected Ruth to be in her usual chair and was surprised when she wasn't.

'In here,' said Isaac and took her into the bedroom.

Ruth lay propped up in bed, looking as pale as the pillow her grey head rested upon. Nevertheless, her face brightened.

'Jenny! It is so good to see you. Isaac. Help me sit up straighter. Puff up these pillows.'

'Let me help.' Jenny wound an arm around her old friend. She was shocked to feel the lack of muscles, the prominence of shoulder bones.

Isaac did as he was told, bashing at the pillows, straightening them and asking her whether she was comfortable.

Concerned by Ruth's appearance, Jenny helped him get her propped up better with an assortment of cushions and pillows.

'Ruth.' She took both wrinkled hands in hers. They felt as light as the claws of a bird. 'Have you not been well?'

'No. I haven't.'

'But she's getting better now,' Isaac said. 'She'll get better even quicker now you're here, Jenny.'

Ruth's eyes held hers. The look in them told her things were far from well. Jenny guessed that she was agreeing with Isaac that she would recover to keep his spirits up.

Isaac offered to make tea and she accepted.

Cups and saucers rattled in the other room. Jenny sat on the bed and smiled. 'It's so good to see you, Ruth. I've often thought about you, but what with settling in and... other things...'

'I can guess why. He wouldn't let you see us – that husband of yours – he wouldn't let you come.'

At first, Jenny was going to lie but thought better of it. Why should she? They knew what he was like. She nodded. 'He's away a lot nowadays, what with work and out with his friends.'

An awkward silence followed. They all knew these friends he was out with, but none dared say their name.

Ruth began coughing, her chest shaking with the effort. She pointed at a piece of white cloth on the washstand. Jenny grabbed it and handed it to her.

A profuse amount of coughing ensued. Even before she handed it back, Jenny knew that red would have stained the whiteness.

Not wanting to admit to having seen the blood Ruth had brought up and Isaac entering the bedroom with tea, Jenny steered the conversation elsewhere.

'I read in the paper that these houses are coming down along with others in this area. Do you know when?'

He chuckled. 'I can't really say and Fred Baker is clueless, but...' He winked. 'We have a friend who's fighting our corner.'

Jenny frowned. That wink had been meant to convey something to her.

She took a sip of tea and eyed him over the rim of her cup. 'Are you going to tell me more?'

Isaac's smile lit up his face. 'That young man, Charlie, who saved me from being beat up. He pops in now and again to see how we are. He's been asking questions, seeing if he can get the housing department to do something even before they tear this lot down. He knows a few of the councillors. Once he's got a date for the demolition, he's going to get us put at the front of the queue.'

She exclaimed how wonderful it was that someone was doing something. Inside she thrilled at the mention of Charlie. Moving out of the city centre had its advantages but also its drawbacks. Charlie Talbot was one of those drawbacks.

'He's such a nice young man,' said Ruth, hand resting on her chest each time another cough threatened.

Jenny agreed with her. Even thinking about him sent her blood racing.

It was no good telling herself that she was a married woman. Charlie's smile was a permanent fixture in her head. No matter how hard she tried to dismiss his image, it was there, fixed in her mind.

Isaac poked at a patch of dry, flaky plaster around the window. Pieces the size of a postage stamp fluttered to the floor. 'It can't come soon enough,' he said and gave it another jab.

If what she'd heard was right, anyone still living in the last of these old properties – deemed unfit for human habitation – would be rehoused.

She looked around, noting the doors, the sloping floor, the meagre daylight coming through the windows. A central gas candelabra provided lighting. Heating was by way of a small fireplace and the stove which had just about enough room for two saucepans and no oven.

'How much rent do you pay?'

'It was seven and six a week, but then Charlie had a word with the landlord and he reduced it to five shillings. We're very grateful for that. It's made things a bit easier. I'm not good with the stairs, but I tell myself I won't be here for ever.'

'That includes gas, mind you,' Ruth added. 'There's no electricity. But them gas lights warms a room as well as lighting it. Fred brings up the bath from the back wall if I ask him to. I suppose it's better than nothing.'

Jenny doubted that the gas lights warmed the room that much. She would shiver if she took her coat off.

More tea was offered, but Jenny declined. She knew they'd been glad to see her and promised to call again.

On her way back down the twisting staircase, very similar to the one back at Blue Bowl Alley, she checked the contents of her purse. There wasn't much in there.

The thick fog was further diminishing late-afternoon light, moving like a living thing around the amber glow of streetlights. Footsteps and the sound of vehicles, horse-drawn and mechanical, were heard but not seen.

The bus stop was on the other side of the tramway centre where roads circled the greenery of the central reservation. The docks offices were off to her right in Princes Street.

She crossed the roads with care, the misted light from vehicle and bus headlights like cats' eyes in the gloom.

Taking a right into Princes Street, she headed for the square brick building where men were taken on and paid for their labour. Figures moved about in the light behind the windows.

Heart racing, she watched as she sought the courage to enter. A big man was eating something. It looked like a pie. He held it in one hand, a piece of paper in the other. Another man bent over a desk, pencil or pen in hand, looked up and laughed, presumably at something the other man had said.

For a moment, it felt as though he was laughing at her for being so stupid as to hang about outside in this terrible weather.

The courage she'd entertained earlier melted away. There was no way she could enter that office and ask for her husband's wages. There was no way they would hand them over. A man's wages were his concern and nobody else's. How could she have been so stupid.

The big fat man sauntered to the window, his bulk almost obliterating the light within.

Was he looking at her? Fearing that he might be, she stepped back into the road. A bicycle bell sounded a warning. Startled, she stepped sideways, her heel caught between the cobblestones and she fell over.

'Damn!'

She lay full length, resting on one elbow, her stockings and coat wet with the slick from the cobbles.

'Are you hurt?'

The rider of the bicycle that had almost hit her propped it against one of the cast-iron bollards that had lined the road since Victorian times. The faint glow of a bicycle lamp fluttered as he readjusted the bike so it wouldn't fall over.

As he knelt, his face almost level with hers, the light from the lamp caught his features. The gloom failed to dim the blueness of his eyes, the warmth of his smile. The real Charlie Talbot compared favourably with the one in her dreams.

She attempted to explain. 'I came here to—'

'No need to explain. Let's get you to your feet. Now, where do you want to go?'

He lifted her up as if she were as light as a feather, though she knew that wasn't true. She'd put on weight of late and she feared the reason for it.

'Thank you so much, Mr Talbot.'

'Charlie. Remember? I said to call me Charlie.'

She brushed at the grit that had adhered to her coat.

'Charlie,' she said, once she'd raised her head. 'Oh, just look at my skirt.'

'It won't notice in this weather.'

'I suppose not. Do you know if there are any buses running?'

'I believe there are.'

She took another look at the office windows. She could still see the two men inside, oblivious to what was happening out here.

'I need to go in there and ask where my husband is. He hasn't been home for three days.'

She sensed raised eyebrows. 'You want to go in and ask where he is. And?'

'I've got no money. I need his wages.'

To her own ears, she sounded pathetic and weak. She also knew it was hopeless.

Charlie confirmed it. 'They won't hand over his wages. It's the man that earned the money and if the wife and family don't get the benefits, that's no concern of theirs.'

There was anger in her heart and its bitter taste was on her tongue.

She felt his eyes boring into her, looked up and saw a thoughtful expression.

One hand brought out a fistful of coins from his pocket. 'Here,' he said. 'Take this. Ten shillings. That should see you over.'

'No.' She shook her head, hair damp and flinging around her face. First Thelma feeding her kids and now this. 'No. I can't do that.'

She turned half away.

'Take it.'

'I won't borrow.'

'I'm not lending it. It's a present. A birthday present.'

'It's not my birthday.'

He laughed. She could have drowned in that laughter. He shook his head. 'It's my birthday.'

'I don't believe you.'

'It gives me pleasure to give to you. That's a present to me.'

Hesitantly, she accepted the money. It would cover the rent. The few coppers she had at home would go into the gas and electric meters. A little for food. A shilling perhaps to pay Thelma for her kindness in giving her children a meal.

'Thank you.' The whispered word floated off into the fog, along with her breath.

'No need to thank me. What are you going to do now?'

'I need to go home. My daughters will be waiting. I was heading for the bus stop.'

'Let me take you there. This weather is getting worse. We don't want you getting run over by something bigger than a bicycle now, do we.'

As they made their way across to the bus stop, their conversation mostly involved Isaac and Ruth.

'I hear you've been pushing the council to get them rehoused. They certainly can't go on with all those stairs where they are now. Their legs won't stand it. Plus Ruth is not very well.'

'Isaac told me she hasn't got long, but a short time somewhere nice might help her hang on.'

'I didn't think Isaac knew how sick she is. Ruth seems to think he doesn't know. She doesn't want him worrying.'

'And he doesn't want her to know just how ill she is. That's how close they are. Wedded for life.'

Jenny wondered at the fortune that had brought them together on this foul afternoon. At the same time, she yet again felt the electricity flowing between them, saw the fervent glances, the secretive smile and the way his eyes lit up when her dark eyes met his.

There was a queue at the bus stop, a line of people trying to get home from shopping or work. When they joined the end of the queue, Charlie stood his bicycle in the gutter.

'That was very kind of you to accompany me across the centre.'

'Just to make sure you're safe, I'll wait with you until the bus comes.'

'There's no need.'

'I reckon there's every need.'

'Honestly, there's not...'

He leaned close to her and whispered in her ear. 'I've dreamed of a moment like this, us meeting up purely by coincidence. And now it's happened. I'm not going to let the opportunity of being with you slip away too easily – even if it's only waiting for a bus!'

The faceless people in the queue remained without form and without comment. Even if they had heard what was said – though she doubted it – they kept facing forward, keen to escape the dampness, the world the fog had obscured.

Twin circles of light blearily pierced the thick soup of greyness.

'My bus,' Jenny whispered. 'I have to go.'

His hand caught hold of her arm. 'Shall we meet up sometime – for a drink? To talk?'

This was the moment when the reality of her feelings for him could go no further. He was just a dream and she had to tell him the reason for saying no, she could not meet up with him.

'The Bunch of Grapes in King Street. Next Wednesday. Around seven o'clock.'

She shook her head vehemently. 'No. I can't. I can't.'

'I'm attracted to you and you're attracted to me. We're made for each other. I know it. You know it.'

She half closed her eyes. Her mouth was dry and her heart was beating like a drum. But she had to break this. Had to stop it right now.

'I'm married,' she said. 'I have to go home to my children.'

Though she ached inside, she forced her voice to be cold and determined.

Such was her vehemence that he let go her arm. The queue ahead of her shuffled forward onto the bus. Slowly, she did the same, fiercely facing straight ahead, determined not to glance back – until she had one foot on the platform of the bus. She looked back then and kept looking until he was swallowed up in the evening gloom.

Dizzy with emotion, she stepped onto the bus, found a seat, paid her fare and took the ticket. Home was some way off. She didn't expect Roy to appear. She didn't want him to, prayed that he would not.

16

A FEW DAYS LATER

Four women with scissors in their hands sat around Jenny's dining table where they could get the full benefit of the overhead electric light. Piled in the centre were scraps of material – old shirts, skirts, dresses and blouses, all in shades of red, white and blue.

It was four o'clock on a Saturday afternoon and this was the meeting of the coronation committee. Thelma had directed the cutting down of the old clothes into triangles for bunting and items that with a bit of redesigning would come in for fancy dress outfits.

Jenny had made tea, plus bread pudding cut into squares small enough to sit on a saucer. Cath, just for once with her hair out of curlers, which seemed to happen mostly on a weekend, was unpicking a large pair of white cotton bloomers. Maude, from number seven was peering over the top of her glasses at stitching on a tray cloth that was proving particularly obstinate.

Half the pile remained by the time they'd decided to call it a day.

Jenny glanced out of the living-room window. The light was

fading but her two and Thelma's daughters were still bounding around the trees playing catch me if you can.

A lone figure watched them from the gate of number one. Mrs Partridge stood like a sentry to attention behind her gate. No leaning on it for her. Figure poker-straight, she stood there as though daring them to run her way, dash into her garden and trample her grass – as if they would.

Jenny watched her thoughtfully.

'Do you think she's lonely?' she asked.

Guffaws of laughter sounded from behind her.

'Well, she ain't the sort to make friends easily, that's for sure,' said Cath.

'One neighbour we could well do without,' Maude added. 'As for that sister of hers... strange she is. Scurries away if you dares speak to 'er.' Maude, a woman in her late forties, sniffed, blew her nose in one of the rags, sniffed again and put it back on the pile.

A look passed between Jenny and Thelma, both noting where the snotty piece had been placed so they could throw it out once Maude had left.

'Off out tonight, are you, Thelma?'

'You know I am, Cath. And why shouldn't I? I'm footloose and fancy-free. I've told the girls if they're stuck for anything to come to you.'

'I'll keep an eye on them.'

'There's a lot of widows,' said Maude. 'Mind you, if I was one, I wouldn't bother again.'

'I didn't say I was going to get married again,' said Thelma sternly. 'I just like male company and Bert is a very nice man. No hanky-panky and lives with his mother.'

'He's the rent man,' Cath said to Jenny.

'No,' Thelma said stridently. 'He's the *senior* rent man. Comes out to speak to them who gets behind in their rent. Sorts things out for them.'

A fleeting silence fell as Maude put on her coat and Cath tied on a headscarf.

'Better be off.'

Jenny had the distinct impression that something was being left unsaid.

Thelma offered to stay behind and help Jenny put the rags away and wash the dishes. Thelma suggested they had another cuppa.

'Just you and me.'

Once the rags were put away and the tea had brewed, Thelma began telling Jenny about Bert.

'It was like this...'

She went on to explain how she'd lost her job thanks to a nasty letter someone had sent to her employers telling them that her children were all illegitimate.

Jenny gasped. 'How terrible. But it's not true... is it?'

'Not exactly. I had George with my husband. He got himself killed in the trenches.' She smiled a little ruefully, almost with girlish innocence. 'I had my girls with blokes I fell in love with. One of them wanted to marry me, the other did a runner when I told him I was like it.'

'I see.'

Thelma sighed, sipped at her tea and carried on, 'It all started when my Alice got scarlet fever so I couldn't go back to work until she'd got better. Then Mary got it.' She shook her head. 'Sod's law. The letter came after that. Her in number one of course. Can't be anyone else.'

'You must have been worried.'

'Out of my mind with worry.'

'You didn't tackle Mrs Partridge about it?'

'Oh I did, but the moment she saw me coming, she slammed the door in my face. Horrible time it was. I got a bit behind with the rent but got round that.' She smiled. 'Funny how life can spring surprises, how bad things can lead to some really good ones.'

Jenny began to put the pieces together before Thelma got round to telling her the details about how she'd met Bert.

'I got behind with the rent and he came calling. Well, his eyes were out on stalks.'

'I'm not surprised. You're a handsome woman.'

'No. Not with me,' laughed Thelma. 'With my collection. You've seen it.'

'Ah! The crockery.'

'Not just any crockery. Crockery with royal connections. I actually swore to their majesties – my cups and saucers, that is – that I would never sell any of them no matter how short I got. And I didn't. Just as well. Bert couldn't take his eyes off it. You see his mother collects as well. Absolutely worships the royal family. So that's how me and Bert got together.'

'And you're off out with him tonight?'

Thelma nodded and a dreamy look came to her eyes. 'He's a funny old stick but wouldn't hurt a fly. You can't say that about some blokes. Some are far too free with their fists.'

Jenny flinched and knew Thelma had seen it.

She shook her head. 'I won't ask any questions, darling. What goes on between man and wife is nobody else's business – unless you want to talk about it, that is.'

Jenny fondled the handle of her cup, turning it on its saucer. The saucer was of a different pattern to the cup. She recalled that the cup had smashed on her forehead when Roy had thrown it at her. She pressed her lips together tightly as she considered what to say next.

'The more he goes away, the happier I am, even if it does mean

I run short of money.' She frowned as she thought of what she meant and what she wanted to say. So many new things were occurring to her that both filled her with excitement and trepidation. 'I'm going to do something that will mean I'm less reliant on him so I can survive when he's not around. As yet, I don't know what.'

A comfortable silence ensued. Jenny felt Thelma regarding her.

At last, Thelma said what was on her mind. 'I think you need more than money. You need someone to love you.'

'I don't need romance,' Jenny snapped, though inside she still thrilled when she thought of Charlie's face and the sound of his voice.

Thelma sat back in her chair; arms folded beneath her ample breasts. 'You're a good-looking woman, Jenny. You deserve better than you've got. And you speak well too. You didn't come from the Pithay, did you. You're certainly a bit posher than I am.'

'It's all water under the bridge,' said Jenny, shaking her head. 'I made the wrong decisions. As they say, it's a case of making your bed and lying on it. I've two girls. I've no other choice, and before you say that it doesn't matter, it does to me. And that's final.'

There was no give in that last look, but Thelma smiled anyway as though she understood.

'I don't know why, but I don't quite believe you. In time, you might care to tell me more, but not yet obviously, not until something happens that makes you judge that the time is ripe.'

Jenny said nothing, but that night she dreamed of Charlie – or thought she did. It seemed like him, though she fancied he was driving a horse and cart, not a bicycle.

17

During the following days a strong wind was plucking the last of the leaves from the trees, sending them scurrying over the ground like a herd of frightened mice.

Whole pages of newspapers, bits of paper from tied-up bundles were torn away from beneath the string holding them together.

The kids in the close were making impromptu kites and aeroplanes from scraps of paper, sending them up into the air, chasing them, laughing when one landed high up in a tree only for the wind to snatch it back and send it flying again.

Clutching her hair to her head to stop it flicking around her face, Jenny went out to call her girls into tea. Again and again, she shouted, the wind taking her voice so she had no option but to go out of the garden gate and across the road.

'Tilly. Gloria.' She waved once she had their attention. 'Tea's ready.'

It was always hard to get them in for their tea, especially when they were having such fun.

Leaves rustled and scattered around her feet, pages from newspapers flew up into the air and raced along the pavement. One piece landed on her shoulder, another – a small, blue piece of paper – covered her face.

Annoyed with it, she screwed it up and, keen to get back inside, shoved it into her cardigan pocket.

Back in the house, the children rushed to the bathroom, jostling and sniping at each other as they fought to wash their hands.

The smell of cottage pie and the living-room fire were very welcome.

Jenny rubbed her hands together. 'Come on. Sit up and get something warm inside you.'

The girls fell to the food in super quick time.

'Don't gobble. You'll be sick. Take it a bit slowly.'

She said the same thing at most meals, especially midday on a weekend when they were desperate to get back out and play.

'Nice,' she said, after finishing her own meal, placing her cutlery neatly on her plate.

Suet pudding draped in treacle followed. She only ate a small piece herself, but the girls devoured theirs and somehow still had room for more.

'Can we go out again?' asked Gloria.

'Not tonight. It's getting windier. I wouldn't be surprised if it blew a few tiles off the roof or brought down a tree. It's school tomorrow. Read or draw. I'll clear the table.'

'Alice and Mary clear their own dishes away. And they cook. Can we learn to cook, Ma?'

'I'll think about it.'

She left the girls, picked up a magazine – one Thelma had bequeathed to her – and began to read.

Before she'd hardly got going, she prodded in her pocket for a handkerchief, fumbling in one cardigan pocket and then in another. In doing so, her fingertips touched the screwed-up piece of paper that had flown into her face.

The paper was blue and likely from a Basildon Bond writing pad. The right thing would be to throw it onto the fire but she didn't. Old words spoken by her mother popped into mind.

Curiosity killed the cat.

Something about that made her smile, even made her defiant. She just *had* to read it.

She unfurled the paper and laid it on her thigh. Crinkles were smoothed out. To her eyes, it seemed someone had begun writing a letter, then stopped halfway. Words were crossed out, a line scrawled through the rest. She could imagine whoever it was, pen tapping against teeth as they thought about what they'd written and decided it wasn't right.

It's a private letter, she thought. *I've got no right reading it.*

Then and there she might have thrown it into the fire if her gaze hadn't landed on the first words.

Dear Mr Bertram,

Although Mrs Thelma Dawson is a very good friend of mine, I do feel you should be aware that not only is she unmarried, but all three of her children were born out of wedlock. She also likes men too much and I think...

The ink trailed off into a series of scratches.

A very good friend of mine...

Thelma believed that Mrs Partridge had sent the accusing letters, but would she really describe herself as a friend? It didn't seem likely.

Placing the crumpled piece of paper between the pages of the magazine, she went out into the kitchen to make a cup of tea. She needed to think about this and decide what to do. Cath Lockhart was Thelma's closest friend. Was it possible that Thelma had been barking up the wrong tree?

Cath and Thelma had always struck her as complete opposites. Whereas Thelma resembled a mannequin from a shop window, Cath was casual in the extreme. Rarely was she seen without her hair being in curlers and scuffing along in her slippers. She'd also seen her curling her lip in a surly manner when Thelma had altered yet another item of clothing to suit Jenny's trimmer figure.

As she sipped her last cup of tea of the day, Jenny thought long and hard. Should she mention it to Thelma or not?

'No,' she said softly to herself. 'I can't.'

With that, she screwed the letter back up and consigned it to the glowing coals of the fire.

Let sleeping dogs lie. Another one of her mother's old sayings. On this occasion, she would take her advice until one way or another she knew for sure.

18

Around two in the afternoon on Wednesday, half-day closing for most shops, Thelma came dashing across to Jenny's house, scuttling round to the back door and letting herself in.

'Look,' she said, buzzing with excitement and waving an envelope and a piece of paper above her head. 'I've got a letter from my boy George.'

In response to Thelma's infectious joy, Jenny grabbed the kettle. 'That calls for a cuppa and a digestive biscuit.'

'Calls for two. Calls for something a bit stronger too, but I'll leave that until later.'

There was a girlish blush to her face when she said it. Jenny guessed she had a date with Bert that evening.

Before the kettle had chance to boil, Cath also entered the kitchen. As usual, she was dressed in slopping slippers, headscarf and rattling metal curlers.

'Saw you cross the road in a hurry, so thought something must be up,' she said to Thelma.

'There'll be enough in the pot for three,' said Jenny.

It had become noticeable that whenever Thelma entered

Jenny's house, Cath was not far behind her. She wondered whether Thelma had noticed but assumed that she had.

'I've got a letter from George,' said Thelma once she'd got her breath. 'Short and to the point. But then that's my boy. He never did have much to say for himself.'

'I'll make the tea. Read it out. I can hear well enough in the kitchen.'

A clatter at the back door heralded the arrival of Tilly and Gloria accompanied by Thelma's two girls.

A hammering at the front door was answered by Tilly.

'It's Fred and Paul,' she called over her shoulder to her sister and her friends. 'They want to know if we're coming out to play knock out ginger.'

Thelma nearly choked. 'Just don't go knocking at next door. I don't want that old bat spoiling my evening.'

The girls disappeared, leaving Thelma still breathless and patting her chest.

'Well read it out,' Jenny shouted from the kitchen.

'I'm too breathless. I'll be needing that tea.'

'Well, Cath can read it out for you.'

There was a pause, then a shout of, 'I'll wait for you to come back in. You can read it.'

As Jenny placed the tea things on the table, Thelma explained that being at sea, George had little time to post letters. 'Let alone write them,' she added with a chesty chuckle.

As she took her teacup and saucer from Jenny, she passed her the letter. 'Read it for me, will you, my lover?'

Jenny glanced at Cath, the prospect of seeing envy on her face. There was none, but there was a look she couldn't quite make out. Surprisingly, she thought she detected embarrassment.

After a good swig of tea, Thelma said, 'I'm all ears.'

'I thought you'd already read it?'

Thelma chuckled. 'I have but would love to hear you read it out. You've got a good voice for reading.'

Sighing, Thelma settled back in her chair, cup and saucer balanced on her belly.

'Right.'

Jenny took a deep breath:

Dear Ma, hope you are well. I am fine. Be home in New Year. Have my room shipshape and Bristol fashion. See you then. Love, George.

Jenny passed her back the letter. 'You're right about him being short on words, Thelma.'

Yet another bout of banging at the front door knocker was accompanied by a boyish voice ringing out.

'Ma! Our dad's 'ome and wants 'is dinner.'

Cath swigged back the rest of her tea. 'I'd better be off. He was on the early morning shift so gets 'ome early for 'is dinner.'

'Lunch?' Jenny queried.

'Yeah. Lunch. That's it.'

The living-room door slammed behind her.

'I bet you're over the moon,' Jenny said.

In response, Thelma reached for another biscuit. 'I can't wait.'

Jenny laughed. 'I like his comment about making his room shipshape and Bristol fashion.'

Thelma frowned. 'The old chest of drawers in his room's got a touch of woodworm. It needs a new one, but I can't take the time off work to find one. On top of that, I haven't much money to buy one. Paying off the rent arrears a while back didn't help, plus the girls needing new clothes. Not that I buy new dresses. You know me, buy cheap at the jumbles and wave my magic wand.'

Jenny laughed. 'The magic wand being your sewing machine.'

They laughed in unison, reaching for another biscuit as they did so.

Although Jenny smiled, serious thoughts were going on behind her happy face. She'd been thinking for a while how best to pay Thelma back for all she'd done. Mention of sourcing an inexpensive chest of drawers got her thinking. She now had three new outfits hanging in the wardrobe, all of them given to her by Thelma. The woman was a wonder with the sewing machine and everything Jenny had been given was eminently wearable – even the one Roy had thrown into the pig bin. After three washes, she'd managed to get out all the stains.

'Thelma, I know where I can get you a chest of drawers and they'll deliver. I can guarantee it will have no woodworm.'

Thelma looked deeply interested. 'Before the New Year?'

'Easily. It'll probably come by horse and cart, the same chap who moved me in.'

Thelma beamed. 'I saw the bloke. Nice-looking with dark curly hair and more muscles than the horse.'

'I'm not sure Robin would like to be compared to a horse.'

'Jenny, my love if you could do me that favour, I'll be in your debt forever.'

'Nonsense. I'm already in yours. Those clothes you made for me. I can't thank you enough.'

'They cost pennies.'

'Pennies make pounds.'

'If you could do that, Jenny... do you have the time? And what about Roy?'

She shrugged. 'He's here less and less. I can fit it in easily.'

'How much do you think I need to pay?'

'Hard to say. How about ten shillings or did you want to pay a bit more?'

'I'll pay that and a bit more willingly. We'll settle that and I'll leave you to it. Oh well.' She got up from the chair and stretched, arms bent, hands above her head. 'Better get on home. My girls have promised me jam tarts to go with a cuppa – as if I haven't drank enough,' she laughed. 'They are so good you know.'

'They're a credit to you.'

Mention of Thelma's daughters brought the letter that had flown into her face to mind.

'I'd better get going. I'll get you the money for the new chest of drawers. And make sure it's that handsome bloke who delivers on his horse and cart. It'll make my day.'

'I'll let you out the front way. It's getting dark out there.'

'Don't worry about that,' said Thelma, already yanking open the back door. 'I know my way. You didn't mind reading that letter for me, did you? Only I couldn't catch my breath. I was that excited.'

'Of course not. You could have let Cath read it though. It didn't have to be me.'

Thelma paused before stepping out into the night. 'Of course you did, Jen. Cath can't read or write. Best not to mention it though. Don't want to embarrass the poor girl, do we.'

Jenny was dumbstruck. 'No. Of course we don't.'

She didn't mention the letter. It was burned to ashes and anyway she knew for sure that Cath had not written it. Thelma was right in accusing Dorothy Partridge. She should have known she would be.

19

Roy had arrived home from work early and told her he was going to have a bath.

'Make sure the girls are yer when I come out of there,' he said. 'I've got something important to tell the lot of you.'

Long before he emerged from the bathroom she went outside to call the girls in and told them that their father wanted to speak to them.

Tilly scowled but Gloria bubbled with joy. 'I bet he's bought me a present. My dad knows I like presents.'

Tilly rolled her eyes and Jenny thought yet again that one daughter was chalk and the other cheese. So different, but still loveable. She would always love her daughters. She just couldn't help herself.

A daughter standing either side of her, Jenny stood frozen to the spot. Roy was home and he had news to tell.

He'd shaved and had a bath. Now he stood before her wearing a black polo neck, matching trousers and polished black boots – just like his hero, Sir Oswald Moseley.

A packed suitcase nudged against his leg, not the old battered one that had held some of their clothes when they'd moved in. This one was brown and glossy, not exactly brand new but far nicer than the old thing with one broken clasp, scraped and scratched from age and wear. She guessed it was recently bought. Roy was out to make an impression.

'I ain't working on the docks any more. I've got a new job. No more heaving heavy stuff around off the ships or loading stuff onto them. I've got a job working for the party. It's in London. Everything important 'appens in London. Trevor put my name forward.'

'They'll pay you?'

He scowled at her as though she was stupid. 'Of course they'll bloody pay me, and more than I was getting at the docks, and I don't have to wait around for work. It's regular. I get paid weekly. I'll send you housekeepin' and rent money by postal order for you to cash at the Post Office. I'll be getting paid a bit more so you can 'ave a bit more, though I 'ave to allow for accommodation and transport. You won't go short though. And my girls won't go short, especially my darling Gloria.'

His thin black moustache stretched along with a smile that held more pride than warmth. He reached out one arm to their youngest daughter, inviting her to fit herself beneath it.

Jenny knew he was waiting for her to applaud his success. A fixed smile remained on her face. 'That's wonderful, and if it's what you want then I'm pleased for you. What exactly will you be doing?'

'I'll be a kind of policeman, there to protect the party's integrity.'

Jenny's heart sank. Integrity. Like the attack on Isaac? She swallowed her revulsion and kept her mouth tightly shut, still smiling a faint, pleasant smile, oddly sincere. In her heart of hearts, she would be glad to see him go.

For some strange reason, and quite unlike him, he couldn't

seem to look directly into her eyes. It struck her as odd. He'd never had any problem beating her down with a look before. It was as though he feared she might read the look in his eyes, a look that might betray his inner thoughts, something he didn't want her to know.

He hugged and kissed Gloria on the top of her head. Tilly leaned stiffly into him when he belatedly wrapped an arm around her and repeated the act.

A peck on the cheek was all Jenny received. Not that she wanted more. Intimacy between them had become negligible since moving here and for that she was thankful. A dream had come true. She had a new house with a garden. She also had her girls to herself.

He gave her a five-pound note before leaving with instructions to make it last.

That crisp white note held her attention long after he'd left. She stared at it. Never had he given her so much before. It was like giving her a flag of surrender – his surrender. He was off to carry out more important matters than keep his wife in check. He was out to keep the country, and perhaps even the world at large, in check.

Arms around her daughters' shoulders, she watched him go. Gloria was tearful, her bottom lip pouting as she swiped at the wetness in her eyes. Tilly showed no emotion in her expression, but her eyes looked brighter.

It surprised Jenny when she saw him pause outside next door, where Mrs Partridge was deadheading the roses growing just behind the privet hedge. Out of everyone else in the street, number one was the house with the most immaculate garden front and rear. Everything was about flowers, a riot of colour and not a vegetable in sight. Beans, potatoes, cabbages and carrots were lovingly tended in most back gardens when in season, a few flowers or just lawn at the front. Several of her neighbours kept chickens. Maude kept a pair of goats – a billy and a nanny.

Whatever her husband said to her next-door neighbour, Dorothy Partridge paused in her task. Jenny saw Mrs Partridge's sour expression soften and for one fleeting moment she was almost certain a smile had appeared.

And then he was gone. She drew back from the window with mixed feelings. She wouldn't miss him and neither would he miss her. He was going where he wanted to go and she would be content staying behind, keeping house, enjoying both it and her children without fear or reprimand.

The slamming of the front door had possessed the same air of finality as closing a book and she felt satisfied that this particular story was over. In time, other stories would emerge, but already the house seemed lighter without him.

'It'll be all right, darling,' she said, wiping Gloria's tears away. 'Daddy has just gone away to work. He has a very important job now. You should be proud of him.'

Though I won't, she thought. *I know the kinds of things he'll do in the name of new work, new horizons.*

'Are you all right, darling?' she asked, smoothing Tilly's glossy brown hair back from her face.

Tilly beamed. Her eyes sparkled, then darkened as she voiced a thought that had surfaced. 'Will he come home for Christmas?'

'I expect so.'

Tilly's face dropped. 'Dad spoils things.'

'No, he does not,' chirped Gloria, her sobs diminished.

'He does for me,' said Tilly. 'And for Mum. You were his favourite. He didn't hit you.'

Jenny felt a lump in her throat. Tilly implied that her father had hit her. She had witnessed a few occasions of a quick slap, but on the whole Tilly had kept out of his way.

She wrapped her arms around both her children, held them close and whispered wonders into their clean, soft hair. 'No matter what, we'll have great fun together, just the three of us. There are all kinds of fun we can fill our time with whilst he's away. How about we begin making paper chains for Christmas? And how about thinking about fancy dress for the coronation next year? There are so many things we can do whilst your father is away. We'll be too busy to notice he's gone and the time will fly.'

Gloria perked up at this. Tilly liked the idea of making paper chains and fancy dress. The fact was that she didn't like her father and it showed.

Jenny shook Robin from her mind, though felt him lingering there. Like her, he was married, unhappily, she decided. Vows do not a marriage make! Who was it had said that? She didn't know who had said it, only that it was the truth.

An odd thought suddenly occurred to her. How did Roy feel about their marriage? Could it be that he was as unhappy as she was? Was she wrong in assuming he accepted his lot just as she did?

The thought surprised her and made her wonder if he was unhappy what sort of circumstances would make him happier?

She had no answer to that.

'Ooow, look at this,' she said, picking up a lacy doyley that Thelma had given her. 'I think I can make a fairy for the top of the tree with this. There's plenty enough time between now and Christmas.'

'Can we put the tree and the decorations up on the 1st of December,' asked Gloria.

'Much too early. The needles will have dropped off the tree by Christmas. Let's get everything ready first then decide. Lots of things can happen between now and then.

20

It was the middle of the following week when Jenny found the time to keep her promise to Thelma about a new chest of drawers for George's room.

Over the weekend, she'd helped Thelma wallpaper over the distempered walls. Between them, they'd made a pretty good job of it. The wallpaper chosen by Thelma was pale blue scattered with tiny red berries.

'Don't think it's too plain, do you?' Thelma had asked her.

'Seeing as it's for your son's room, I don't think roses or daffs would have suited, do you?'

After they'd had a giggle and yet another cup of tea, they'd gone over the basic details of the chest of drawers.

Thelma handed over two ten-shilling notes. 'I'll leave the price to your discretion.'

So here she was on a Wednesday morning standing outside Huberts Furniture and Pawnbroking Emporium. Jenny smiled at the familiar sign stating in no uncertain words that items on display were free of bugs and fleas.

A brass bell jangled as she pushed open the door. She looked to where Gladys usually sat on the two-seater settee. It was empty.

A voice rang out from the back of the store where wire netting protected the more valuable items of the pawnbroking business. 'Won't be a minute, love.'

She recognised Robin's voice.

Two children came out ahead of him. They looked a bit down in the mouth as Robin herded them towards the shop door. He glanced at Jenny, looked surprised, then continued escorting the two children, a boy and a girl, both of whom looked like him.

'Now go on. Back to yer mother. And here's a threepenny bit each to buy some sweets.'

He looked thoughtful as he shut the door behind them before throwing Jenny a smile.

'Well, that's made my day.'

'I take it they're your children.'

He shoved his hands in his pockets and smiled. 'Simon and Susan. They're twins.'

'I thought they might be. They look a lot like you, though I might be wrong. I can't quite recall what your wife looks like.'

Or her character, thought Jenny. On the few times she had seen her, she'd thought her flash and loud, an unrelenting flirt, a bit like Thelma but without the warmth.

There were a few things Gladys and Robin had said that made her suspect things were not perfect. She hadn't pried but let it go over her head. She'd been concentrating on her own problems at the time.

'My wife is attractive. Draws blokes to 'er like moths to a flame.'

Jenny sensed there was more, but she wasn't here to pry. She was here to buy a chest of drawers. All the same, she couldn't help feeling sorry for him.

She looked tellingly around the shop, which felt somewhat

empty without Gladys's bulk and character. 'Where's your mother? I thought she never missed a day...'

The moment she'd said it and saw the look on Robin's face, she knew what had happened.

'Oh, Robin, I'm so sorry.'

He looked at her then at the floor. 'Fancy a cuppa?'

She hadn't planned to stay but never had she seen Robin look so down.

'Yes. That would be nice.'

Before taking her into the back kitchen beyond the pawn shop, he bolted the shop door top and bottom.

'Can't help it. Mum would skin me alive if I didn't bolt up when there was nobody in the shop.'

Jenny smiled. 'I can hear her now.'

She didn't ask what had happened until he was filling the kettle and setting out the tea things. The cups and saucers were of the finest bone china porcelain. No doubt an item that somebody had pledged but never came back for. Gladys had certainly been the winner.

Once the hot water was in the pot – another handsome piece decorated with jade-coloured dragons – Robin told her about his mother.

'One minute she was puffing on her pipe; next she was coughing her lungs up. She died that night. That was about six weeks ago.'

Jenny digested the sad news, unable to believe that big, blithe Gladys had passed so quickly.

'There's a big gap in the world without her.'

Robin stirred the tea and shook his head. 'You can say that again. She left everything to me, but...'

He set a cup of scalding hot tea in front of her and, at her direction, added just milk, no sugar.

'It's a good business.'

He shook his head. 'It would be, but not to run all by meself. I've got a young lad willing to help but I can't cover furniture and the pawn shop. The pawn shop makes the most money, but then I like selling the furniture. It 'elps people out, people without the money to buy new. I'm struggling to keep everything going.'

Jenny's thoughts turned to the two children he'd seen to the door. 'Well, the children might be young, but they'd probably enjoy giving you a hand – and your wife of course.'

The moment she saw the expression on his face, she knew this would not be the case.

'She's left me. Took the kids with her. They only stay with me for a few days now and again.'

She sucked in her breath. 'Oh, Robin, I'm so sorry.'

He shook his head. 'In a way, I welcome it. We were married, but she never did stop fishing for compliments. One man will never be enough for 'er. Growing old gracefully don't sit well with her either.'

Pinched between finger and thumb, he let a sugar lump fall into his tea. A second one followed.

The tea went down well enough but seeing Robin in such despair brought a lump to her throat.

'I need time to think about what I'll do. I need to talk things through with someone I trust – not my wife,' he added with heartfelt vehemence.

She declined a second cup of tea and at the same time noticed that he'd barely sipped at his. For now at least, he needed a distraction, something else to think or talk about.

Buying a chest of drawers would appear mundane to some, but she'd been looking forward to it. Hearing of Gladys's passing and Robin having split with his wife had dampened some of the joy – though not quite all. She'd been looking forward to helping

Thelma out. After all, Thelma had been kind to her. It was no skin off her nose to be kind back. In the interim, it might take Robin's mind off things.

'I came here to buy a chest of drawers for a new friend of mine, but if now is not the right time, I can call back another day.'

She looked for an uplift in his countenance and got it.

He smiled a wan smile, nodded and got to his feet. 'I'm sure I can find something for your friend. How are you doing out there on that estate anyway?'

She told him of her new friends, of how they helped each other out even though they had little themselves.

'Apart from Thelma, that is. She's got a job in a dress shop. She dresses the part too. Never a hair out of place. Never sloppy. At times, she makes me feel quite dowdy.'

'You!' Robin stopped in his tracks in front of a very nice but large Victorian chest. He remained facing the chest of drawers when he said, 'You've never been dowdy. Not ever and not now.'

She refrained from blushing, though his compliment did make her feel like a young girl again. He used to say things like that back then. And now here was history repeating itself.

The conversation returning to more general matters, they stopped in front of several likely candidates for George Dawson's bedroom. She settled for a four-drawer affair with white porcelain knobs and bun feet. He told her it was made of pine and she could have it cheap.

She asked if he could deliver.

'How else would it get there? It ain't going to fly that's for sure.'

Jenny grinned, a mischievous look in her eyes. 'On the bus?'

'You'd be charged for two seats and more.'

They laughed. She fancied that laughter could be the first step to healing Robin's fractured feelings. Early days yet, she thought as she handed him ten shillings for the chest of drawers.

'Saturday afternoon, but not this Saturday afternoon. I'm already booked,' he said, before she could ask when he intended delivering. 'I close Saturday afternoons so have to fit all my deliveries in then...' He hesitated. 'But as it's for you I'll make an exception and bring it over on Sunday.' He offered his hand for her to shake. 'Is that a deal?'

She smiled, pleased to see less strain on his face. 'Yes. It's a deal.'

As she walked across the centre to the bus stop, she glanced towards the docks' office in Princes Street. The metal bridge outside it was clogged with traffic and people.

Never again would she have to consider entering that stern-looking building and ask for money.

'Hey. Mrs Dawson.'

The voice was familiar, though of late only in dreams.

Charlie Talbot came striding towards her with all the confidence of one privileged for most of his life. He wore a cap and his muffler was wrapped tightly around his throat. Like a man from the working class, he extolled to represent. All the same, she could tell he was smiling.

'Charlie.'

'Jenny. You're looking well. How are you finding your new home?'

'Oh, Charlie. Where shall I begin?'

'I take it you're on the way to the bus stop.'

His voice was warm, like butter melting on toast. She smiled at the image that appeared in her mind.

'Yes. I am.'

'Then you can tell me all as I walk with you.'

She told him how it felt living in a house with an indoor bath and toilet.

'You sound happy. I take it your children are happy too.'

'Yes,' she replied with unbridled enthusiasm. 'My girls love the new school and have made friends with a neighbour's children.'

'And you have good neighbours?'

'Yes. I do.'

They came to a halt at the bus stop. She wanted him to ask her again about going for a drink but couldn't bring herself to tell him that Roy was working away from home. To her mind, that would be encouraging him, tempting providence. Not that she would say no. She would say yes and she might regret it. The time was not ripe but one day it might be.

There was a restlessness in the queue as the bus approached.

'My bus,' she said, but wished it wasn't.

He looked pleasantly at her but more accusingly at the bus. 'That's a shame. I would have liked to hear more.'

He'll ask me now, she thought, *and this time I'll say yes.* But he didn't.

He touched his cap. 'Nice to see you again. All the best in your new home.'

His muffler fell, exposing the lower part of his face. This time, she could see he was smiling, just a brief farewell smile, and then he was gone, lost in the busyness of a late October afternoon.

* * *

It was four o'clock by the time she got home. Her girls, plus Thelma's daughters, were sitting on the pavement, their legs dangling in the road. They were eating thickly cut sandwiches.

'What have you got in those doorsteps?' Jenny asked, doorsteps being the usual term for such chunky slices of bread.

'Sugar. Alice made them.'

'You'll spoil your tea.'

'Can we stay out a bit longer?'

'In by six. It's getting dark already.'

Once inside her front door, she took off her hat and coat. The stew on the hob was thick with vegetables and scraps of meat. It was the last of both. Tomorrow she would have to go shopping at the Broadway, where the butcher would add a few scraps simply because he liked her smile.

The vegetables she'd get from the shop next door to him, sacks of parsnips, potatoes and carrots ranged along the pavement outside. Another week and she should receive the postal orders Roy had promised her. Until then she would manage and despite the privations she was happy. Her world had turned around and there was much to look forward to – if the money came through as promised.

21

NOVEMBER 1936

It was Thelma's idea to go to the pictures that Saturday and she insisted it was her treat.

'I'm paying. You got that chest of drawers for ten bob. That means I've got ten bob to spend. Your girls and my girls can come too. We can have fish and chips after.'

'I couldn't.'

'Yes you can. Now don't argue.'

'It's best I wait until I get my postal orders.'

'You don't need to. I'm paying, remember?'

'Don't you want to see what's on? It might be a picture you don't like.'

'I don't care. Bert's got to drive his mother down to her sister in Clevedon. They're expected to stay overnight. So, whilst the cat's away, the mice – that's me, you and the kids – can play.'

Jenny didn't press about paying her own way simply because she couldn't. She had only pennies left in her pocket. If only the rag and bone yard was closer. She could gather up a few old woollens and rags and see what they'd give her. Again, only pennies, but even farthings counted at present.

By six o'clock, they were approaching Filwood Broadway Picture House, known locally as the bug house.

Recalling the crummy mattress Roy had burned, Jenny shivered at any mention of bugs. Thelma had assured her it was just a local joke. 'Mind you, there's some around here who could be a bit cleaner.' She frowned at the scruffy woman in front of her as they joined the end of the long queue. 'A lot here tonight,' murmured Thelma.

Jenny eyed the poster. 'I'm not surprised. *Mutiny on the Bounty* starring Clark Gable and Charles Laughton. Everyone likes them.'

Thelma bought tickets and they filed inside. The darkness was all-encompassing, the second matinee halfway through.

'Aye, aye,' whispered Thelma. 'That one's off to the lav already.'

The film on the screen flickered and provided the only light. It was just enough for Jenny to see the woman who'd been in front of them in the queue get up and head for the toilets. She was totally alone. On her return, she had two children with her.

'Opened the lav window and let them in,' Thelma whispered again as the woman and her two offspring made themselves comfortable.

Jenny stifled her giggles. What the woman had done was dishonest but funny.

The second matinee ended and the third and final showing went back to the beginning without pause.

As a torch beam shone from the back of the picture house, the two children who had sneaked in headed for the toilets. Their mother stopped where she was, ticket in hand, ready for inspection.

By the time the ice cream seller came round, the usherette who checked the tickets was gone and the children had returned.

They stayed almost until the end of the film, Thelma

suggesting that as they'd come in halfway through, they knew what was coming so could sneak out early.

'Before the National Anthem?' Jenny whispered back.

Keeping low and silent, they made their way back up the gangway to the exit.

Outside, the smell of fish and chips from the shop next door drew them in.

Thelma bought four two penneths of scrumps for the girls and a bag of chips for herself and Jenny.

For her part, Jenny couldn't believe how much she enjoyed those chips and how much they swelled her stomach.

As they headed into Coronation Close she popped the last of the chips into her mouth then screwed up the paper. 'I was so hungry...'

'Jenny? Where the 'ell 'ave you bin?'

Jenny stopped dead in her tracks. 'Pictures,' she said without thinking as Roy loomed out of the darkness.

'Pictures! What do you think yer doin' out, wasting my money on pictures and chips?'

He swept the crumpled-up chip paper with a swipe of his hand.

Jenny's spirits sank.

'Excuse me!' Thelma waded in. 'This was my money and my treat.'

'Dad!'

Gloria flung herself at her father. Just for once, he didn't welcome the arms around him but spun her off to one side.

He raised an arm and pointed it at Thelma. 'Don't you give me any lip. What's between me and my wife is no business of yours.'

'Thelma,' Jenny said softly. 'It's all right. I can cope with this.'

Disbelief clouded Thelma's face before she jerked her chin and suggested they headed for home. She leaned towards Jenny and whispered, 'The girls can stay with us tonight if you like.'

It didn't take long for Jenny to come to a decision. She nodded. 'It might be for the best,' she whispered back.

She knew she'd made the right decision as Thelma shut the front door. At least her girls would be safe.

Alone in the darkness, Roy slammed the garden gate behind them, grabbed her arm and flung her against the front wall of the house. 'You little tart. Who said you could go to the pictures?'

He pressed her up against the wall, his hand tight against her throat, squeezing the breath out of her.

She struggled. 'Roy.' A small word and hardly escaping her lips, such was his grip.

She smelled tobacco smoke. The whole close was in darkness, yet someone was outside smoking.

'You bitch.'

Her head cracked to one side when he hit her. She fell against the privet hedge dividing her garden from next door. A frond of thorny climbing rose in the corner scratched at her face.

Her hands became claws seeking and scratching at his face, kicking at his shins, his knees, anywhere she could reach.

No matter her resistance, he remained stronger than her, his hands once more around her throat, stifling her cries for help, then suddenly they were not.

A pair of brawny hands dragged him off her. The glowing tip of a lighted cigarette flew into the small patch of lawn at the front of the house. Roy followed it, falling backwards and sprawling.

A bedroom light came on in the house next door. A head with hair contained in a hairnet protruded from the hastily opened window. 'What's going on down there? Harriet? Is that you?'

There was no answer. Whoever had dragged Roy backwards was bending over him.

As Jenny coughed and spluttered, she heard a bass voice say, 'Touch her again and I'll kill ya.'

Suddenly, it was just her standing up and Roy supine on the lawn. She felt blood from the thorny climbing rose trickling down her cheek.

The front gate slammed shut. Another one – she suspected next door – did the same.

Another oblong of light fell out from across the road. Thelma was running across. So too from the other end of the street was Maude's husband and then Cath's husband, Bill.

'What the bleedin' 'ell's going on yer,' Bill demanded.

'None of your business,' said Roy as he staggered to his feet.

Using both hands, Bill Lockhart grabbed his coat collar. 'Any bloke who knocks a woman around is a coward by my reckoning.'

Roy wasn't finished. He lashed out. Maude's husband, getting on in years, was flung aside when he tried to join in. The two men were left grappling, legs braced as each tried to wrestle the other to the ground.

When it seemed as though Bill might be getting the worst of it, there was a loud clang. Roy crumpled to his knees, then fell groggily forward to lie full length on the ground.

'That's him sorted.' Thelma stood straight and proud, a cast-iron frying pan held at shoulder height.

The minimal light from next-door's bedroom window fell on Thelma's triumphant grin.

She asked Jenny if she was all right. 'Don't worry. Your girls are fast asleep over with my two. They didn't hear a thing.'

The rest of that night passed in a blur. Bill and Maude's husband, Wilfred, took Jenny's groggy husband up to bed before wishing her goodnight. They didn't suggest she come running if there was any more trouble. This spat had been put in their way. It wasn't done to interfere between husband and wife.

Jenny wiped a flannel over her face whilst Thelma put the kettle on.

Clutching cups of tea, the two of them sat beside the diminishing heat in the fire grate where a few coals still glowed amongst the white ashes.

In response to Thelma's pressing, Jenny kept nodding and saying that, yes, she was fine. She could cope. She did not need Thelma to be there when he woke up.

'He'll pretend nothing happened,' she explained after taking a very welcome sip of sweet tea. 'If it's mentioned at all, he'll blame it on me. I had no business to be out. I should have been home with my children.'

Thelma looked appalled. 'You're a wife, not a bird in a bloody cage.' Her words were spit with venomous contempt. Her eyes blazed. She shook her head in disbelief. 'Men! I sometimes wonder how things might have been if my George's dad had lived. He was a good bloke at the time, but who knows what he might have turned out like by now? I might have killed him.'

Jenny grinned and nodded at Thelma's weapon of choice, the black and very heavy cast-iron frying pan. 'With a frying pan?'

Thelma threw back her head and laughed. 'Possibly.'

Jenny was thoughtful. 'Back at Blue Bowl Alley, I just accepted that I was his wife and that I had vowed to love, honour and obey...'

'Obey doesn't mean being a doormat.' Thelma pointed her finger, nail varnish as bright as ever.

'I know that now.' Jenny frowned. 'Back there in the Pithay it seemed that I was trapped, what with all those old buildings pressing in around me. Out here...' She looked up from her tea at Thelma. 'It does feel as if I've been let out of a cage. I would never have fought back before, but here it's different. For a start, I've got good neighbours.' She jerked her head sideways. 'Even Harriet from next door. It was her smoking outside. She dragged him off me before you and the others came along.'

'Hmm,' said Thelma thoughtfully. 'I didn't know she smoked, but there, I can't imagine smoking would be allowed indoors. I bet the house is as immaculate as the garden. If it's not all full of flowers, it will be of beeswax and lace doilies. Old family photos too, I bet. Religious ones. Sanctimonious old mare is Mother Partridge.' She added the last comment with a sniff of disapproval and drained her teacup. 'I'd better be off,' she proclaimed as she got to her feet. 'Don't hesitate to call for me if he starts any more of his nonsense.' Face set determinedly, she picked up her frying pan. 'I'll be right there if you need me.'

Jenny slept on the settee that night, at first fitfully and then more deeply, so deeply that she didn't hear him go.

'Roy!'

The house felt empty. She assumed the closing of the front door had disturbed her and presumed he'd left to go on errand and would be back later, but on checking the bedroom and seeing the postal orders left on the table, she knew for sure that he was gone.

She shook her head in disbelief. He'd gone without saying goodbye. Worst of all, he'd gone without seeing his daughters.

It was still dark outside. The streetlights were often turned off halfway through the night, the view taken that nobody respectable would be out at such a time so the lights were not needed.

She wondered if she was being too hasty thinking that Roy wouldn't be back. For a while, she stood there looking out of the window, afraid in case she saw his silhouette heading towards the house.

An hour or two passed, maybe three, before a wintry dawn finally broke. Frost lay over the grass, making it look as though someone had sprinkled it with sugar overnight.

There was no sign of him returning. There was no suitcase in the bedroom or hallway. No hat or coat hung up on the rack. He'd gone, but not only that, it seemed from the evidence that he had not intended staying for long. A fleeting visit and swiftly over thank goodness. Robin was delivering the chest of drawers to Thelma this afternoon. It was best her old friend and her husband didn't bump into each other.

After only four hours or so of deep sleep, her eyelids were beginning to feel heavy. The settee where she had spent the night eased beneath her weight as she lay back down. The bed upstairs would still smell of him.

She would change the sheets before she slept there.

As she dozed, a deep-seated instinct placed a thought in her mind. He wasn't coming back – not ever. He was as unhappy with her as she was with him. That's what his bad temper was all about. Something was seething inside, lighting his anger like a taper to a flame.

She didn't know where the thought had come from and whether it was true or not. It was just there and no matter what hardships might come, she would face them head on. She would win through.

22

Jenny had roused herself from the settee by the time Tilly and Gloria came back from over the road.

'We don't want any breakfast. Mary and Alice made boiled eggs with toast. One each. And they made buttered soldiers, that's a slice of toast cut into strips.'

'I do know what soldiers are,' Jenny responded. It was good to see her girls looking so happy. Tilly certainly wasn't missing her father and if Gloria didn't know that her father had gone without saying hello, she'd be fine. Ignorance could indeed be bliss.

'The eggs came from Mr Knight's hens next door. Alice went out and got some.'

'That's nice. I take it she paid him?'

Tilly looked unsure.

Gloria tossed her head and said, 'I suppose so. Can we get some hens and have our own boiled eggs?'

'I don't see why not – as long as you help look after them.'

'How about rabbits?'

Tilly rolled her eyes. There were times when she lost patience with her sister.

'As long as you don't make pets of them. People keep them for eating, not as pets.'

'How about goats?' Gloria added, beaming with enthusiasm.

Jenny shook her head. 'No.' She knew one of their neighbours had a pair but tending to goats was a step too far.

The subject of eggs and animals formed a nice diversion, although Tilly did ask her how she scratched her face. She blamed the climbing rose.

'It's easy to get entangled with it in winter. There's no flowers to give you warning that it's there. Now, isn't it about time you went to Sunday School?' A whole group of them were going. 'And remember to come home and take off your Sunday best before you go out to play.'

The frost was still there when Robin arrived. She'd expected to see him in his horse and cart so it took her by surprise when he rolled up in a van which rattled into the Close leaving a stream of blue smoke in its wake.

Thelma came to her front door, hands clasped together, looking overly excited for the arrival of a new chest of drawers.

Jenny dived behind the curtains when she saw Robin glance her way.

Thelma got on one end of the chest of drawers and Robin on the other. Together they manhandled it along the garden path and into the house.

Jenny moved away from the window, turning her attention to a pile of ironing that needed to be put away. Robin's appearance made her think of her childhood, of her mother taking charge after her father had come back from the war a broken man. The circumstances of that war had affected both parents, her father withdrawing into himself and screaming in the middle of the night, and her mother worn down with the effort of keeping the house going. She sometimes wondered if things would have been different if she'd had brothers or sisters, but she hadn't. Robin had been the closest thing she'd had for a brother, on account of their mothers having been in service together.

They'd been sweethearts in a childish, innocent way, a peck on the cheek the ultimate intimacy. Looking back, she perceived he was the one who'd awoken the woman within. She'd been ready for romance when Roy had come along. He'd taken advantage of her innocence and the romantic inclinations she'd got from novels. He'd taken his time, but ultimately had taken advantage of her in a physical sense. Tilly had been the result of that.

A knocking sounded from the front door just as she was placing bedding into the airing cupboard at the side of the fireplace. Perhaps Thelma had opted to use the front door rather than going around the back?

Robin was standing there, cap slightly askew on his dark curls, scarf hugging his chin. He rubbed his hands together tellingly. 'Thought I might take you up on that cuppa you offered me last time. It's brass monkeys out yer. Unless you can't...' He took a backward step. 'I'll quite understand if you say no.'

Jenny took a deep breath. She opened the door a bit wider and invited him in.

He followed her out to the kitchen, watching as she filled the kettle, lit the gas and set cups and saucers on the table.

'Did you get the chest up the stairs all right?'

He nodded. 'It went up in no time. Mrs Dawson is a strong woman. A man arrived just when we were coming back downstairs. Let himself in. Looked a bit surprised to see me until she explained why I was there.'

'Ah. That was Bert, the man in her life.'

He jerked his chin in understanding.

She asked him how come he had a van rather than a horse and cart.

'Dropped dead. Dobbin was gettin' on a bit.

Having made the tea, Jenny suggested they go into the living room.

'I bet Thelma is like a dog with two tails,' she said merrily, cup raised to lips. 'Her son won't be coming home until the New Year, but she's determined to make his bedroom perfect for when he does.'

'Seems that way.'

He set his cap on the table beside his teacup, clasped his hands together and looked at her. A fallen lock of dark hair flopped on his forehead.

She took a sip of her tea. It struck her that Robin was not his usual outgoing self. He was unusually quiet. She guessed – though didn't know for sure – the death of his mother might have had something to do with it. It had been rather sudden after all.

'How have things been?'

She noticed that his eyes had not left her face, noticed further the grim set of his jaw. 'It's up and down, not just the business, but 'er. Doreen. Gone 'ome to 'er mother and right cow she is too. Sissy Blackmore. I should 'ave taken more note of the mother first before I married Doreen. They do say, don't they, that the daughter ends up like the mother. Selfish, my mother-in-law. Bad-tempered too and...' The knuckles on his clasped hands became more prominent, almost white with strain. 'Sorry. I shouldn't be laying all this on you. It's my problem and for me to sort out.'

'I don't mind.' She shook her head and without thinking what she was doing, tucked a tress of hair behind one ear, thus exposing her scratched cheek.

She caught Robin looking at it. He frowned. 'Did Roy do that?'

She bit her lip. Her first inclination was to tell him, as she had her daughters, that she'd stumbled into the climbing rose in the dark.

'Sort of, but... you see, Roy never liked me leaving the house. Late home from grocery shopping and he'd lash out. He's been away working.' She sighed, sat back in her chair, threw her head back and closed her eyes. 'It's been heaven. Last night, I went to the pictures with Thelma and the kids. When I got home, he was waiting for me...' She stopped.

Robin waited for her to say more, but instead she looked down into her teacup, fingered the handle. Inside something was shifting. She'd noticed her behaviour changing since moving here. Coronation Close and her new friends had a lot to answer for.

'Jenny, let me take you out. As a friend.' He held up his hands. 'I promise there'll be no funny business. Scout's honour!' He saluted her in the way that a boy scout would and it made her laugh.

All the same, it was a tough decision to make – until she gripped onto the fact that Roy was away. He'd left without a word and not bothered to say farewell to his children.

'All right, but it has to be near the bus route.'

'The Bunch of Grapes in King Street fits the bill. You know where that is, don't you?'

She said that she did. Seven o'clock at the Bunch of Grapes next Wednesday.

'But first I have to run it past Thelma and see if the kids can stay over with her.'

'Shall we do that now?'

It turned out that Thelma was delighted to oblige.

'It's the least I can do. That chest of drawers fits just right in my George's room. Bert thinks so too, don't you, Bert?'

Bert came out from the living room to the front door. 'She's over the moon,' he said and laughed. 'You'd think she had royalty coming to stay. It all must be just so for my darling Thelma.'

Perhaps it was Jenny's imagination, but she thought she saw a girlish blush on Thelma's cheeks.

'I'd better be off,' said Robin, fixing his cap back on his head and pulling his scarf tighter. 'It's a bit of a drive back – but worth it,' he added.

The full force of his smile took Jenny by surprise.

23

After Robin's black van had left the close, Jenny passed the time ironing piles of laundry. Ironing gave her a chance to think and as the sweet-smelling pile grew, she began to daydream. Charlie Talbot usually figured strongly in her daydreams. Perhaps when she saw him again she would accept his offer of a drink in the pub just as eagerly as she had Robin's invitation.

The children had returned home from Sunday school, changed their clothes, grabbed some bread and dripping and had gone straight out to play. As the last of the ironing was put away, she planned the rest of her day. For a couple of hours, she would try to dig through the frosted ground where a few cabbages were defying the weather. She planned to plant more vegetables next year. So far, she'd made use of the produce left growing there, including drying and pickling the apples of autumn. Apple pie and custard for tea this evening.

Her chores done; her attention went back to the mix of feelings that just would not die down. The friends of her youth were no longer available to exchange romantic dreams, but she needed someone.

As the night beyond the living-room window drew in, she took her coat from the peg in the hallway to make her way across the road to Thelma's house.

No matter how many times she told herself that meeting Robin was innocent, she couldn't help feeling guilty. She was still married, though had a niggling doubt that she would ever see Roy again. She needed someone to talk it over with and there was only one person who could fill the void.

As she headed across the green for Thelma's house she noted on the way that the neighbourhood kids, including her own and Thelma's, were chasing each other with sticks. Around and around the trees they went, laughing and shouting, barely noticing her at all. What a change, she thought from Blue Bowl Alley. There'd been no trees to chase around back there, no grass beneath their feet. The cobbles had gleamed below the fractured light of flickering gas lights. Here, there was no flickering, the glow of the amber streetlights like small suns warming the night.

Thelma didn't hesitate to bundle her inside, offer tea and biscuits. 'Sit by that fire and get yerself warm.'

Jenny gladly did as she was ordered. 'I hope you don't mind. Only I saw Bert leave and I really need to talk to you. Woman to woman.'

'Oh,' said a beaming Thelma, teapot in hand. 'I'm intrigued. Let's fix this brew and you can tell me all about it.'

Gripping her teacup with both hands, Jenny prepared to share her innermost thoughts.

First, a little intro.

'I take it you're pleased with the chest of drawers.'

She felt the intensity of Thelma's gaze – incisive – knowing.

'It's fine. And how about that nice-looking chap who brought it.'

There was no escaping Thelma's knowing look. Jenny

reminded herself that her new friend was more experienced with men than she was and made no bones about it. It took guts to bare your soul, but who better to bare it with that someone capable of advice that wasn't hamstrung by convention.

Thelma pushed a plate of biscuits towards her. 'They're the best ones. I buy broken biscuits by the pound for the girls. They get through them quicker than I can buy them.'

Jenny knew Thelma was trying to put her at ease. Declining a biscuit but taking her courage in both hands, she came out with it. 'You know that he's asked me to meet him next Wednesday evening at the Bunch of Grapes in town and I wanted you to know that there's nothing in it. We're old friends,' she added defensively.

Thelma smiled. 'Enjoy yourself, love.' There was warmth and understanding in her eyes. 'It's your business what he is to you. Nobody else's.'

'I'm not lying,' Jenny cried, feeling an urgent need to justify herself. 'He is only a friend. An old friend.'

Thelma held her head to one side, an inquisitive look, but still incisive. 'Go on. Tell me more and I don't mean just about that particular chap. You've blossomed since your old man's been away. You're coming into your own. When you first moved in here, you were like a frightened rabbit. Now something else is breaking through, the real you in my opinion.'

Jenny drowned her surprise in a quick gulp of tea. Moving into Coronation Close had been a gigantic step from slum to something much better. It had never quite occurred to her that she had changed. It hadn't registered when she'd looked in the mirror that morning that she looked any different. On reflection, her skin glowed and her eyes sparkled. But it wasn't only that. She'd changed inside too. Moving into this house had gone some way to giving her greater confidence. Courage too. There had been only an inkling and Thelma had confirmed it.

She sighed as she set her cup and saucer down on the table. 'You're right. So much has changed. I hope that Roy stays away. I don't want him anywhere near me, yet he is my husband and the father of my girls. But…'

'But a marriage certificate is only a piece of paper. It's not a passport to happiness.'

'No. I suppose not.' Jenny looked down at her interlocked fingers, then purposefully broke them apart. Like two people, no longer needing to feel the presence of the other. 'I don't love him.'

'You mean your old man?'

Jenny nodded. 'I hate him. Moving out here has given me a clearer view of my life. I was playing the part of the loyal wife, putting up with everything because a wife is supposed to obey her husband—'

'Now look, love.' Thelma interrupted. 'You've already told me you don't want Roy to ever come home again and after what I saw last night, I don't blame you. Grab hold of life with both hands. That's what you've got to do now, and if Robin brings you a bit of happiness, then let him.'

Jenny met Thelma's forthright gaze. 'You're so wise.'

Thelma's ample bosom jiggled when she laughed. 'I don't know about that, but I have lived a bit.' Her laughter subsided. Her look became more serious. 'As you know, I have a gentleman caller. Bert is a lovely man. He's kind. He listens to what I say and doesn't put me down.'

'Roy does more than put me down,' said Jenny, harsh beatings bringing a bitterness to her tongue.

'I guessed that. But even if you're not ready for another relationship, you can still dream. You do dream, don't you?'

Charlie Talbot sprang to mind and made her smile.

'There is someone I think about a lot. Not Robin,' she said briskly. The thoughts and feelings she'd kept to herself burst out.

She told Thelma about Charlie, how she'd been smitten at the sight of him, how her heart fluttered every time she saw him. 'I bump into him every now and again. He doesn't seek me out – at least, I don't think he does. But…'

'He lifts your spirits.' Thelma leaned across the table and took one of Jenny's hands in hers. 'Look love. We're only here once. This life you have isn't a rehearsal and as far as I know you don't come back for a second bite of the cherry. So grab what you can with both hands. Yes, you're a wife and mother, but you're still a woman, a human being. Got it? Go out there and live life. It's yours and yours alone.' Then she winked. 'Do what I've always done and play the field. Go out with Robin and Charlie too, if you see him again. You don't belong to either of them. You don't belong to Roy either. You belong to yourself.'

24

To whom it may concern,

My sister and I have been council tenants for some years. Our rent is always paid on time and both house and garden are spick and span. In fact, our garden is the envy of the parks department. We grow roses that would win prizes if ever we entered them in competitions, but we are content to enjoy the sight of them in our own garden.

However, there are some around here who keep farm animals in their gardens. Chickens and rabbits kept in hutches attract rats and should not be allowed. There is even one household in our street that keep goats.

As a matter of public health, I demand that you do something about it.

Yours sincerely,

Mrs Dorothy Partridge. (widow)

'To whom it may concern? I would prefer the word sir.' Trevor Collins of the Housing Department sounded and felt decidedly grumpy. He didn't want to be here and he was certainly fed up with receiving letters from Mrs Dorothy Partridge at number one, Coronation Close.

Some of her letters had not been signed, but the writing had been the same and so had the terminology – well written – an educated woman but narrow minded.

Miss Venables was sitting across from him, pen and pad in hand. She always took notes of his comments, almost as though he was handing out his own version of the Ten Commandments. She cocked her head to one side. 'What do you intend doing about it?'

Trevor heaved a heavy sigh and sat back in his chair hands shoved into trouser pockets. He pursed his lips as he thought about it, then made a little trumpeting sound as he exhaled his breath. 'I might pop along there and see what's going on.'

'Lots of people keep chickens.'

'Yes. It keeps the wolf from the door, so to speak. As long as they don't keep pigs...'

He and Miss Venables, his able assistant, exchanged a shudder at the shared memory of a house they'd visited where pigs were kept in the garden. Worse still, they'd arrived at a time when one was being butchered. The tenant had been warned that a council house garden was not an abattoir. As far as he knew, no further slaughter took place; the tenant continued to keep the odd sow but sold off the piglets.

'Did you perceive the family who moved in recently to number two as respectable?'

Miss Venables shrugged. 'He had a lofty manner. She was quite striking; dark hair and flashing eyes.'

Trevor steepled his fingers and a sleazy smile crept across his face. 'I might call in on Mrs Partridge regarding her letter and at the same time call on Mrs Crawford, just to see if her views match those of our persistent letter writer.'

A small frown wrinkled the brow of Miss Venables. He hadn't

deferred to her for the name of the resident of number two. He'd known it already. 'Surely it would be best to speak to the husband – as head of the household.'

He nodded vigorously. 'Of course, of course. If the husband's there, I'll speak to him.'

The fact was, he knew Roy Crawford wouldn't be there. Roy was accompanying the great man himself, Sir Oswald Moseley. Trevor had had a hand in getting him the position and would himself be joining the organisation's activity when the job allowed. In the meantime, he reckoned that a woman left alone might need male company. Women hungered for sweet words and a soft caress that most men were incapable of giving. Well, Trevor Collins knew how to charm a woman and, of course, he was a man of status, thanks to his job in the Housing Department.

He opened his diary, ran his finger over the days of the week and found one that suited, one when he knew for sure that Roy would still be away. 'I'll make a note,' he said and scribbled in a specific time on a suitable date.

'What date would that be?' asked Miss Venables, who was beginning to feel slightly uneasy. 'I'll make a note of it too, just so I can remind you, should you forget.'

'No need, Miss Venables. I'm sure I'll remember.'

25

It was seven o'clock on Wednesday evening in the last week of November. The night was cold, but the slight frisson of fear and feeling slightly wicked had raised her temperature and cancelled it out.

Jenny had dressed carefully and not at all provocatively. Thelma had checked her over before she'd left.

'Hmm,' she'd said, looking her up and down. 'That's a nice coat, though a bit shapeless. I wouldn't wear it meself, though it looks good on you.'

Thelma had borrowed the coat from Bertrams, telling her superiors that she had a customer for it – in Clifton.

'What they'll say when they find out you live in Knowle West and not Clifton, I don't know. That's if they're ever going to find out. I've only borrowed it. I'll tell them the customer didn't like the cut or that they'd put on weight so it didn't fit.'

'Do I need to pay you something in case they don't believe you?'

Thelma shook her head and folded her thick arms over her

large breasts. 'They think well of me – thank goodness. They reckon I've got good taste for what looks good on a woman and for what looks best in the window display. Besides which, the customers like me. Hang on to every word I say, they do.'

'I promise I'll take care of it,' said Jenny, stroking the soft leopard-skin collar. Thelma was also loaning her a matching hat that she'd made from an old coat collar, yet another one of her jumble-sale acquisitions.

'It was the only part of the coat I could rescue. The rest was moth-eaten.'

Jenny perched it on her head and eyed herself in the mantelpiece mirror. 'All the same, Thelma, I'm forever in your debt.'

Thelma waved her away. 'Away with you. Get moving or you'll miss the bus.'

The bus made its way through Bedminster. Some shops were still open, the light from their windows gilding the night. At the city centre, the great arched lights around the central oval of frosty grass and those of trams and buses gave the old place a surreal splendour.

After alighting from the bus, Jenny made her way across to King Street. If she remembered rightly, the pub was at the end closest to the tramway centre.

King Street was much darker than the place she'd left behind. The Bunch of Grapes was on the left-hand side, an amber hue falling from the window of the saloon bar like a gold cloak onto the cobbles outside.

Waiting for Robin outside, Jenny eyed the lights, the windows and the brass door handles. Was she brave enough to go through with this? If she left now, she could get the next bus and be back home by eight o'clock.

Diminishing courage fell over her in waves. She found herself looking over her shoulder just in case Roy had once again come home unannounced and followed her.

A beery smell and a glut of conversation fell out as a laughing couple pushed open the door.

The noise and warmth were shut in and she was still outside waiting.

A brute of a man glared at her angrily and shoved her aside. 'Are you going inside or are you gonna 'ang around out yer?'

Again, the door opened to expose the light and warmth within, the sound of a piano playing and voices raised loudly in song, though slightly off key.

Grabbing her courage with both hands, she followed him in.

Heads turned. Appraising looks fell her way. Those who adhered to the old notion that women had no place in the public bar showed hostility.

Robin, leaning with his elbow on the bar didn't notice her at first. He took a sip of his drink before tipping his cap back, then straightened, as if knowing she was there even before he saw her.

She gave a little wave. He smiled in return, waved her over and it lifted her heart.

'You came,' he said when she was at last standing beside him.

'Yes.'

Even when he bought her a drink, she remained tongue-tied.

She'd ordered a sherry – at least she thought she had. This was all so surreal, her, a married woman, standing beside a man who was not her husband.

Should she tell him about Roy, where he'd gone and what he was involved in?

'Roy's not...' she began.

He placed a finger on her lips. It was warm and tasted salty.

'First, let's go somewhere quieter.' He jerked his head at the etched glass door that led to the saloon bar, the posher part of the pub where women were more welcome than in the public bar.

Plush-covered benches lined the walls. Marble-topped tables with three cast-iron legs were placed at regular intervals. The only other occupants of the saloon bar were three old women gathered around a single table. Like the three witches in *Macbeth*, Jenny thought.

She'd been worrying about how to start this conversation, but as it was, Robin made all the running, including the reasons he was there with her, spilling out the details of his own situation.

'You don't...' Despite Thelma's pep talk, Jenny had been going to say that he didn't have to, that this meeting was only a one-off and that she dare not see him again. His distraught countenance persuaded her otherwise.

'Please bear with me. I want to get this off my chest, partly to ease my guilt, but also to ease yours. I know how difficult it must have been to make the decision to come tonight. I've known Roy a while. He's a difficult type. But listen. I figure we can compare experiences – we've both had bad ones.'

So, she let him talk about his marriage, how his wife Doreen had told him that she was pregnant and being an honourable man, he'd married her.

'She didn't give birth until eighteen months later. A girl. We had a boy a year after that.'

'You're not divorced.'

He shook his head. 'You need a lot of money to get a divorce, and anyway, my wife prefers to keep me on a string. That's what I am, a puppet on a string.'

He went on to tell her about the affairs his wife had had, first with the manager of the flower shop she'd worked in, then with the landlord of a property they'd been renting.

'I'm so sorry for you, Robin. Really I am. She doesn't sound easy to live with.'

He shook his head and sipped his pint. 'Now she's back living with her mother and taken the kids with her. Every so often, I go over and get them back.' He shook his head again. 'It's them I worry about. I'm coping all right, but their lives have been turned upside down.' He fell to silence until getting up to fetch them another drink.

He'd opened the floodgates, and despite all her forebodings, she told her tale, beginning with life with Roy within four walls, then his joining the Blackshirts and beating up old Isaac, the sweet, kind man who brought her vegetables.

Robin's eyes grew large. 'I knew he was a bully but didn't know he was as bad as that.' He shook his head disconsolately. 'What did you do?'

'I couldn't do anything. Luckily, three men came along. They were down here opposing that awful organisation.' A wry smile crossed her face. 'Roy didn't know what hit him.' She hid her expression behind her half-empty glass. 'I know I shouldn't, but I was glad. Just for once he was getting a dose of his own medicine.' She shook her head. 'I know it was wrong, but...'

'Lucky those blokes came along. We need their sort to put some pride back in this country. Bullies we can do without. Hope they're still around.'

Jenny didn't agree that she hoped so too, especially regarding one of them. Charlie Talbot still figured in her dreams, how long for she didn't know. Perhaps for a lifetime, that's how big an impression he'd made on her. Was it purely infatuation? She thought perhaps it was but held onto the dream.

They talked about their children, about the past and the present, about the dreams they'd had for the future back then and how things had turned out.

His soft, gentle eyes looked into hers. She knew immediately what he planned to say next but wasn't ready to hear it. He was an old friend and her feelings were unclear as yet regarding him. All the same she felt sorry for him. He didn't deserve the treatment Doreen was dishing out.

'Yes, Robin, we both made mistakes, but we can't turn the clock back.'

Their conversation turned to their parents, Jenny's who had passed some time ago. Robin's loss of his father had been some time back too, his mother more recently.

'Even though I'm a grown man, I feel like an orphan.'

Jenny's heart went out to him. She gently shook his shoulder. 'We're both orphans now.'

They talked easily with each other, speaking of subjects and anecdotes that made them laugh. Some almost made them cry, but one thing above all others shone through: they spoke easily with one another as though they'd been doing so for years, as though the years in between had never occurred.

At nine o'clock, Jenny made her mind up to go home.

'I have to get the bus.'

'I'll come with you.'

She shook her head. 'No need. Just see me to the bus stop.'

The nip in the air had both turning up their coat collars.

Robin placed his arm around her shoulders. 'Still cold?' he asked her.

'I'm warm as toast.' She shook off his arm and kept a little distance.

'Good. Shall we take a little walk first, just to round off the evening, which I've enjoyed, I must tell you that. It was good to talk, go over old times, fill in the gaps of the years. You made me feel better than I 'ave for a while.'

'I've enjoyed it too.' So much so that she'd almost forgotten she was married. Married and out with another man, an old friend, but still another man. She'd seen the way he looked at her and didn't doubt that it was more than friendship she saw in his eyes.

They walked away from the pub and towards Castle Street but turned away from where brightly lit shops still attracted window shoppers. Not everyone was there to window-shop. Groups of girls tittered and flashed their eyes at groups of young men. Promenading up and down Castle Street and up Park Street was how those without the money for anything but walking and window shopping met up with the opposite sex.

He had a tight hold on her hand all the way to Bristol Bridge. At first, the act of allowing him to do that seemed alien, almost sinful. *Almost as though he's afraid I might run away*, she thought.

They looked down into the dank water of the river Avon. He fumbled in his pocket, brought out a fresh packet of cigarettes. Remembering she disliked cigarette smoke, he put them away again.

His focus remained on the dark water of the river.

She sensed he had something to say but feared hearing it.

Her courage came back. 'What is it, Robin?'

Without warning, he grabbed hold of her and kissed her passionately, so much so that she was breathless when his lips left hers. His hands remained on her shoulders. His look was intense. She'd been right about his intentions. In a way it sullied the evening. In another way it confused her.

He tried to kiss her again but was halted when she lay her hands hard against his chest and pushed him away.

'We can't consider marking time with each other, Robin. I'm sorry. Let's keep our distance – at least for now. Time to go,' she said to him. 'This was just a night out between old friends. We're both married, Robin, so it's all that we can be.'

The light from a streetlamp caught the disappointment in his eyes.

He seemed to shake himself back from the place he had been. 'Of course we are.'

She was relieved to leave him, to get on the bus, find a seat. She had to be sensible. Whilst Roy was her husband, she dare not do anything else.

26

Cheeks pinched pink by the crisp air, Jenny rested on the garden spade Maude's husband had given her. He had a whole shed full of gardening and other tools, the shed itself made from bits of wood he'd gathered from discarded packaging. From the same supply, he'd built a shed for his two goats.

The apple tree had lost its leaves, but the cabbages, potatoes and carrots were holding their own despite the frost. She hoped to plant her own next season and that old Mr Clark, the previous tenant, would smile down on her efforts. According to Thelma, he'd been a dedicated gardener.

'He believed in growing things you could eat – not like her next door, flowers, flowers, flowers.'

Jenny smiled to herself. Thelma had firm views about everyone who had or was now living in the street.

Her eyes strayed to the other side of the garden fence. Even at this time of year, there were still a few flowers remaining in sheltered spots next door. Pride of place went to the bulging yellow heads of chrysanthemums. Before they'd flowered, her neighbours had enclosed the budding heads with brown paper which was now removed. The perfectly rounded heads stood like a battalion of small suns, bright gold in the winter light.

The two sisters were out there, watering and deadheading, backs bent, heads hidden.

Should she say good morning? It was the neighbourly thing to do, though judging from experience, they would not respond. She decided to go for it anyway.

'Good morning.'

Mrs Partridge carried on with what she was doing. Dorothy's sister, Harriet, jerked her head up. First there was surprise. The two sisters had little to do with their neighbours.

A slight nod of the head and a strained smile. No returned greeting.

Surprised she'd got this far, Jenny persisted. 'Nice day so far. Rain later.'

She became aware of the sour gaze Dorothy directed at her sister. Harriet gave a muted nod and a mumbled yes before bending back to the task in hand.

'That was a start,' Jenny muttered to herself, picking up the garden spade and digging it into the loamy soil.

As she dug, she recalled the night she'd gone to the pictures with Thelma and Roy had returned home unexpectedly. There had been a definite smell of cigarette smoke from the person who'd first intervened. So, Jenny thought with a secret smile, Dorothy rules the roost with a rod of iron and Harriet sneaks outside to break the rules. She smokes. It was no big guess to assume that Dorothy disapproved.

Harriet, Jenny decided, could be a lot more friendly without her sister around.

She might have pursued her theory and tried again, but someone was knocking at the front door.

Pulling off her boots at the back door, she wiped her hands down her hips and headed for the front door.

She didn't recognise the man who stood there. He had a round face, small eyes and a thin black moustache – like the one her husband now sported.

He introduced himself as Trevor Collins and stated that he worked for the council.

'I hold a senior position in the Housing Department.'

He didn't need to mention that it was through him they'd jumped the queue and got this house. Trevor Collins was the man Roy had looked up to.

'Ah yes. You're also a friend of my husband?'

The minute he smiled, she knew what he was after. He had had a hand in getting Roy his new job and must know Roy was away. But he was here anyway. She was immediately on her guard.

She stood in front of the door half closing it behind her. Expression as stiff as her body, she asked, 'So what can I do for you?'

His thin lips stretched into a snakelike smile. 'We've had a complaint about people keeping farm animals. Perhaps I could come in and we could discuss your views on the matter?'

She frowned. 'I haven't complained about farm animals, and anyway, there aren't any. Only chickens. Loads of people keep chickens.'

'Do you?'

'No. I just grow vegetables.'

'Very commendable. Can I check your back garden – in an official capacity, I am entitled to.'

She was in two minds to say no but reminded herself that he was indeed a council official.

Inwardly, she sighed, but outwardly she held on to a determined demeanour. 'You'd better come around the back.'

She could see his disappointment that she hadn't let him through the front door, but he couldn't complain. After all, he had said it was the garden he would like to look at.

Swinging her arms with each step, Jenny strode purposefully along the path at the side of the red brick semi-detached.

An unobstructed view of the entire garden could be had from the end of the side path, but she took him around the back until they were standing in front of the kitchen window next to the back door.

'There,' she stated in a voice that carried. 'This is my garden. As you can see, I don't keep a cow, a pig, a sheep, goat or even chickens. Just vegetables.'

In her estimation, he wasn't looking at the garden. He was looking at her and the way he looked made her feel very uncomfortable. Despite that, she kept her nerve, arms firmly folded across her chest. If only she'd kept her boots on. Her feet were getting cold and he noticed.

'My dear Mrs Crawford, you're not wearing any shoes. You'll get chilblains. How about we go inside and you make us a cup of tea?'

'Mr Collins, you asked to see the garden. You've seen the garden. As for my neighbours keeping animals, so what if they do keep a few chickens. Almost everyone does.'

'My dear...'

He attempted to lay a hand on her shoulder. How dare he?

She shrugged it off. 'Keep your hands off me, Mr Collins, or I'll report you to your superiors at the Housing Department.'

She noticed the movement from next door before he did. A head had appeared directly next to the privet hedge dividing her back garden from that of the sisters. Behind Harriet, the sharp-featured Dorothy was also looking her way, lips pursed and eyes sharp as tacking pins.

'About that cup of sugar I wanted to borrow, do you mind if I come round for it now? Won't be a mo.'

'Harriet, we don't need...'

'Of course we do, Dorothy.'

With that, Harriet swept away from the hedge.

Trevor Collins looked put out. The steely eyes of Dorothy Partridge swept from him to her sister and back again. She looked furious.

A breathless Harriet appeared in less than a minute. 'Not interrupting anything am I, my dear?'

This, thought Jenny, *is the most conversation I've ever had with my new neighbours.*

'Nothing,' said a grateful Jenny. 'Mr Collins is just leaving.'

Looking positively churlish, jaw clenched as though crunching glass, Trevor Collins lifted his hat, said a brief 'good day, ladies' and disappeared around the side of the house.

An awkward silence descended. Jenny met the clear blue eyes of her neighbour and thanked her.

'I take it you don't really need a cup of sugar.'

Harriet shook her head. 'No. We're well stocked with everything.'

'You're welcome to a cup of tea. I'd love to talk to you.'

Harriet shook her head. 'Thank you, but no. I have to go.'

She took swift steps back the way she came. It was almost as though she'd done something terribly brave and now regretted it.

'Thank you again,' Jenny shouted after her.

Funny woman, she thought as she pulled her boots back on. As for Trevor Collins, what a creep. The very thought of him made her shiver, but he was gone now and hopefully would not come back.

* * *

Driving his little Austin car back to the centre of Bristol, Trevor Collins bristled with indignation. If that blasted woman from number one hadn't intervened with that poppycock about a cup of sugar, he would have made progress with Jenny Crawford. What a pretty little thing she was. And lonely. He was betting on her being lonely.

Another time, another place, he thought to himself. And if the occasion didn't crop up accidentally, then he'd look to orchestrate the right moment when he could get her alone and make overtures. See where it goes, he said to himself. Just see where it goes. And take your time, Trevor old son. Just take your time.

27

At number one Coronation Close, the living-room curtains were drawn back after breakfast. Daylight entered the room at nine o'clock, the exact same time the mantel clock chimed. Its dour, deep note was as tuneful as a death knell. Its casing was an abomination of dark wood and ugly carving.

Dorothy hadn't spoken to Harry for some days following him asking for a cup of sugar from the woman next door. She'd been mortified.

'How can we ever hold our heads up again. So, so embarrassing!'

Pointing out that the lovely-looking young woman from next door had been alone and in need of help had cut no ice with Dorothy. Status, not someone else's safety, was important to her.

Harry, who was quite used to being called Harriet put up with it. In time, Dorothy would have to speak.

This morning, a bright, clear, November morning, Dorothy peered out at the cul-de-sac of twelve houses surrounding the island of green grass at its heart. A cluster of mature trees made it look like a village green of old. The trees had been there long before the houses, back in the days when the estate had been fields and hedgerows. Cows had grazed where roads now radiated from Melvin Square and Filwood Broadway, twin hearts in a host of houses built after the Great War.

There was a distinct advantage in living at the first house on the left-hand side of Coronation Close. From this favoured vantage point, Dorothy could see everyone coming and going.

This morning, her gimlet eyes prowled the empty green. The milkman had finished delivering fat bottles of pasteurised milk and tall bottles of the sterilised and slightly cheaper variety. Not only had the milkman delivered but so had the milkman's horse.

'We've got manure for the roses,' she called across her shoulder.

'I'll get the shovel.'

Dorothy smiled with satisfaction. They had the best roses on the whole estate. The milkman's horse had a lot to do with that.

The downside was that number one was located immediately opposite number twelve, where Thelma Dawkins lived. Dorothy's smile vanished like morning dew at the thought of someone she regarded as a trollop. Sourness replaced satisfaction.

Thelma's children had already left for school, but she hadn't seen Thelma leave for her job in the dress shop. She presumed she had a day off. Having days off and holidays were a modern thing. Working-class people had received little time off in the past, especially those in service. One day off once a fortnight. Half a day on Sundays.

All seemed quiet in the house opposite and at least the children were not out there shouting in the front garden or on the green island in the centre of the road. If there were no children living in Coronation Close, it would be a very peaceful place indeed. Children were noisy and overly energetic. They chased around on the green, screeching at the top of their voices. They played with balls, which they were forever knocking into her garden, hitting the heads off the roses and landing in the heart of the hydrangeas.

Suddenly her attention was drawn to a movement across the road. Someone had come out of the front door and was walking towards the garden gate. A man! A man had come out of the front door. The hussy who lived there was waving to him.

Dorothy leaned as close as she dared around the curtain. Yes. She could see him and what was more she recognised him.

Her eyes narrowed and her thin, mauve lips set in a bloodless blue line. The pleasantness of the view and peaceful reverie had been well and truly sullied.

'Well I never. This is disgusting.'

Harriet started to rise from her chair. 'Oh. Sorry. I'll go outside.'

'Not you, though you should know better. Smoking should be done outside.'

The whiff of cigarette smoke lessened as the offending article was stubbed out in the only ashtray she kept in the house. The Reverend Miles was the only person favoured to smoke in the house when he visited. Dorothy always made sure to have an ashtray available when he came calling and opened all the windows once he'd gone.

'It's her over the road. That slut Thelma Dawkins. There's a man just come out of her house and it's only nine o'clock.'

The curtain provided a refuge for her torso whilst her face stayed close enough to watch the man open then close the gate.

'Is there really?'

'Yes. There is.'

'It is allowed, Dorothy.'

'She's always had men callers. Regular callers.'

'I'm not sure about that, and anyway—'

'It's that Mr Throgmorton,' she hissed. 'And him senior rent collector and a churchgoer! I know his mother. What would she say if she knew her son was calling on the likes of Thelma Dawkins at this time of day?'

'You don't know that for sure. It might be official business. He is a rent collector.'

Dorothy – who corrected anyone who dared call her Dot or Dotty – spun round, eyes thick with menace. 'A respectable man would not call on a woman like Thelma Dawkins at this time of the morning. I've a good mind to report him to the council.'

'That's not very nice.'

'Not nice!' Dorothy spluttered the same words a few more times before turning her attention back to Mr Throgmorton. In winter, he wore a gaberdine mac over his suit and a brown trilby hat jauntily pulled over one eye. His suit was dark – summer and winter; just as it should be. Dorothy liked things to be traditional, robust, and stoutly Protestant orientated.

Cigarettes and matches pushed to one side the carpet sweeper rattled over the carpet behind her. A short comment accompanied it. 'He's got a car.'

'I know he's got a car,' snapped Dorothy.

'I expect he takes her out in it.'

Dorothy took deep breaths as she often did when events and people inveigled her private world. There was always the threat of their personal domestic routine being upset by outside influences. Every day comprised of actions that never varied. She couldn't possibly allow that.

Dorothy tutted. 'I don't wish to think of him taking her out in it. I don't wish to think of what they might get up to.' She shivered. 'It disgusts me. Yes. I will write to the council.'

'Didn't you say that he had a hand in getting the close renamed? You wouldn't want him to get in any trouble.'

It was Dorothy who perched on a stepladder once a week and

dusted off the sign. Every two weeks, she washed it with carbolic soap and water. It didn't matter to her that the kids stood behind her on the green laughing at her efforts. Neither did it matter that the hand-painted sign was set atop a pole. Keeping the sign clean was her patriotic duty and nothing would stop her from doing the job.

'You don't own it,' Thelma Dawkins had said when she'd sauntered by. 'It belongs to all of us that live yer.'

Dorothy had long made a vow never to speak to Thelma, but on that occasion, she couldn't help herself.

'The sign is outside my house and is thus my responsibility. Unless you'd like to take turns cleaning it? No? I didn't think so. Good afternoon.'

With that, she'd vanished indoors, though looked out from her living-room window long enough to see Thelma Dawkins laughing with her friend Cath Lockhart, pointing at the sign, then at her living-room window, where she had been hiding behind a curtain. She'd ducked out of sight.

Her indignation had ached like an open wound. She'd been waiting for her chance to have a go at this neighbour she didn't want.

'Revenge is best served cold,' said Dorothy, her voice matching that one chilly word. 'It wouldn't be fair to report him, at least not yet. Even so, the man should have more sense than to consort with the likes of Thelma Dawkins.

In all honesty, she felt a begrudging gratefulness to Mr Throgmorton for his part in the renaming of the close. However, she had no time at all for lustful men and fallen women. His behaviour surprised her, though Thelma's did not. She was what she was.

'War widow, my foot,' she often exclaimed. 'She's too young for a start; too young and too flighty. I think our Mr Throgmorton is upright enough, but Thelma Dawkins...' Her lips curled at the thought of that painted floozy, the buttons of her silky blouses straining over prominent breasts, the clip-clopping of her heeled shoes echoing around the close. 'It's not him that's the culprit. He's been tempted by that Jezebel. She's a slut, and I'm convinced she's had more than one gentleman caller – though gentleman is hardly the right word.'

A warning look accompanied the ceaseless racket of the carpet sweeper. 'Dorothy, you don't know for sure...'

'How do we know what goes on under cover of darkness? Anyway, she can't have much of a job, certainly not enough to keep three kids.' Her eyes narrowed to slits. 'There's only one conclusion how she earns her money and I think the council should know about it.'

The rattle of the carpet sweeper ceased. 'You wouldn't!'

Dorothy glared, was brought to an abrupt halt by the sight of a dress that closely resembled a sack. The colours almost hurt her eyes. 'Whatever do you look like in that dress?'

One hand holding the carpet sweeper handle, the other pulled the gathered skirt to one side. 'What's wrong with it?'

'It's blue and green.'

A pair of narrow shoulders shrugged. 'What's wrong with that?'

'Blue and green should never be seen. It's terrible. It makes you look like a patch of purple sprouting broccoli.'

'For goodness' sake!'

A flounce of voluminous skirt was accompanied by a loud sob before Dorothy found herself alone. The horse manure forgotten about.

On this occasion, her daily routine could wait. She needed a moment to think about the words she would use in the letter she would write to the council. Would she sign her name? She wasn't sure, but she would write that letter, she would inform the council that a woman of questionable morals was renting one of their fine brick houses. They needed to know, and she was the one who would tell them.

* * *

Up in the bedroom, Dorothy's husband, who had deserted from the army a broken man was seething. It had entered his head to say that if Dorothy wanted to complain to the council about someone, how about the lecherous man who'd called on Mrs Crawford the other day. It seemed logical, but not to Dorothy. Dorothy believed she had a sacred duty to protect the interests of Coronation Close and the morals of its inhabitants. To that end, she reported to a higher authority – in this case the city council housing department.

Harry Partridge looked out of the window. The urge to punch the awful Mr Collins had been strong. Luckily, common sense had prevailed, unlike the night when Mr Crawford had come home and restraint had flown out of the window.

Thelma Dawkins didn't deserve to be hounded. It had happened before and was about to happen again. It just wasn't right. Thelma must be warned.

28

Thelma had taken today off as holiday. Bertrams was generous like that.

She hadn't expected Bert to call in on his rounds but welcomed him all the same.

Her exuberance overflowed when he handed her a present.

'Don't open it until I've left.'

Although bubbling with excitement, she promised she wouldn't.

After saying goodbye to Bert, Thelma turned her attention to the precious gift he'd brought her. She read the inscription for the umpteenth time. Accession to the Throne. King Edward the Eighth. 1936.

Using both hands, she very carefully set the precious mug in the middle of the second shelf of the dresser. After a bit of fiddling about, an inch to the left, then an inch to the right, she took two steps back.

She sighed with pleasure. Bert regularly brought her a new piece to add to her collection. Some of them were very old: from a Queen Victoria Jubilee mug, a plate commemorating the marriage of King George the Fifth to Mary of Teck, a small cup in celebration of the birth of Princess Elizabeth, daughter of the Duke of York, followed by one commemorating the birth of the younger Princess Margaret Rose. She'd whooped with pleasure at every single item. On this occasion, she could almost have fainted.

Every royal was important, but the new king more so. She'd loved him as a mere prince, though perhaps mere wasn't quite the right word. She'd read every newspaper and magazine article she could grab hold of with enthusiasm.

To her mind, the profile of the former Prince of Wales had already assumed the kingly brow and forward-thrusting jaw of a man who would mould the British Empire for the rest of his life. The mug only commemorated his inheriting the throne. Her next acquisition would be a piece of crockery depicting the date of his coronation and she wanted to be there to see it. Not in the flesh, of course, but at the picture house in Filwood Broadway. She'd seen a few films there, but Gaumont British News were bound to show the big event, the coronation at Westminster Abbey, and she couldn't wait. It would be there that the whole country, and indeed the world, would see the handsomest king ever trail down the aisle of Westminster Abbey draped in ermine.

She'd asked Betty Rawlings, an usherette who worked at the cinema, to keep her the best seat in the house on that grand day next May – a few days after the coronation – when they'd be screening it. May 1937 seemed a long time to wait, but she was determined to have the best view in the house.

Looking at the mug and thinking of Bert made her smile. 'You're a good 'un, Cuthbert Throgmorton,' she said, rolling his surname on her tongue as she might a piece of chocolate.

Next was to show off her acquisition to her friends.

At eleven o'clock, she banged on Cath's door. Cath Lockhart lived at the deep end of the cul-de-sac next door to Maude.

Maude's house was first in line and she thought she might as well invite her as well. The sound of goats bleating came from the back garden. She rapped the door knocker hard against the cast-iron plate, but there was no reply. Oh well. It would have to be just her, Cath and Jenny.

Cath answered the door with her hair in curlers and a duster in her hand.

'Fancy a cuppa? Pot's warm and waiting,' Thelma gushed.

Cath gaped at first. 'Yeah. Why not, though I'll 'ave to put a scarf over me curlers.' She looked Thelma up and down. 'Why is it you always look like a million dollars at any time of day, whereas me—'

'Stop all that nonsense. I'm asking you into my place, not the ruddy Ritz!'

'Just give me a minute and I'll be there.'

'Right. I'll call in on Jenny.'

Hips swaying in time to a happy little tune that wouldn't go from her head, Thelma glided off, head held high, like a swan floating down the river.

Cath watched her go before going back into the house to fetch a scarf to cover the metal curlers. She did like her hair to look nice when Bill came home and was prepared to suffer curlers during the day. Ideally, she'd like to be well groomed all day, just like Thelma, but it never seemed to happen.

She tied a scarf over her head and added a touch of lipstick. After eyeing herself in the mirror and noticing the red lipstick made her face look pale, she wiped it off.

'That'll have to do,' she said to her reflection and smiled. She'd been expecting Thelma to call.

This wasn't the first time she'd stood in front of the mirror. Whilst in front of it this morning winding her hair onto the curlers, the mirror had reflected movement down at the far end of the close. The figure in brown hat and trench coat had morphed into Mr Throgmorton coming out of Thelma's front door. His manner wasn't furtive so she knew he hadn't stayed there overnight. Thelma never allowed any of her boyfriends to outstay their welcome. Never had done. Never would.

She would say: 'When my kids are grown and flown, I might do, but only then if marriage is on the cards. I'm a respectable woman, no matter what people might think.'

Cath patted the curlers and plastered on a smile. No doubt she was about to find out the reason for Mr Throgmorton to call so early.

As she pushed open the garden gate of number twelve, she knew without needing to look across the road that she was being watched. Out of the corner of her eye, she detected a curtain twitch across the road at number one. Mrs Partridge or her sister were up and about. They were a strange old pair at the best of times. Their clothes were dated, their faces pale and unadorned with make-up. Dorothy's hair was strained tightly back from her pale face into a bun. Harriet's cottage-loaf style sat like a fluffy bird's nest on top her head. It always looked neat, always tidy, almost as though each hair was glued in place.

Although she could see no face at the window opposite, Cath gave a little wave. 'Nice morning,' she shouted. The movement was barely noticeable, but enough to tell her that Thelma's neighbour was in her usual spot, spying on everyone and everything that happened.

Thelma was exuberant, hands clasped together in front of her, eyes sparkling as she opened the front door. 'I've got something special to show you. It's in the living room, but we can't go in until Jenny arrives.'

The hallway was small, a tight fit for two people. An even tighter fit when Jenny arrived.

'Right. We're all here so we can go in.'

Thelma almost pushed her two friends into the living room. One hand remained pressed against the small of Jenny's back, easing her into the exact spot she required her to be. She did the same with Cath.

'Look at that.'

Thelma pointed at the new mug. Everything to either side had been moved a bit to give it pride of place.

'Very nice,' said Jenny. Quite honestly, it wasn't to her taste to have such clutter in her house. Everyone had a dresser, but Thelma's dresser looked to be straining under the weight of crockery – both her collection and that for everyday use.

'Take a closer look.' Thelma forced the mug into Jenny's hands.

'It's the king. The new one that is.'

'Correct. It's a mug to commemorate Prince Edward becoming King Edward. Bert managed to get hold of it for me. Just happened to know someone who will be supplying the council ahead of anyone else. Now you, Cath.' Snatching the mug from Jenny, she passed it to Cath. 'Read it out to me whilst I fetch the pot,' Thelma shouted from the kitchen from where came the sound of cups being placed on saucers.

Eyes round as gobstoppers, Cath froze, and her hands began to shake. The words, the letters, the numbers imprinted on the mug were a mountain she could not climb.

Recalling the scrap of letter from before, Jenny took it from her. 'You've forgotten your glasses again, haven't you.'

Cath nodded gratefully.

Jenny read it out.

Out in the kitchen, Thelma broke into a rendition of the national anthem.

Thelma came back in, a cup and saucer in each hand. She'd stopped singing.

'Give me it here.'

Jenny handed her the mug, which Thelma set carefully back in its place.

'Must 'ave cost a bit,' said Cath.

Thelma sighed with happiness. 'I don't know. Ain't it lovely, though. This is the accession mug. The proper coronation mug won't be out until next year – next May. Can't wait,' she said excitedly, hands clasped together at her breast. She looked angelic, thought Jenny, like a stone angel hanging over a grave in a churchyard. The thought was so funny that she almost burst out laughing. Thelma an angel? An avenging one perhaps. Thelma would be good at that.

She took a sip of tea. As usual, Thelma had put in too much sugar.

'It's nice. When did he give it to you?' asked Cath.

Guessing where this was leading, Thelma gave her a sidelong look.

'By the look on yer face and yer tone, you know full well that Bert Throgmorton called in early this morning. He was out this way anyway, off to see somebody in arrears. Giving them a bit of a ticking-off. I've already told you that his mother loves royalty and collects bits and pieces. He managed to get his hands on two of these, one for his mother and one for me. Mind you, they are seconds. It's got a little chip in the rim. See?'

Both Cath and Jenny examined the spot Thelma's finger was indicating. 'Oh yeah. I expect they were chucking them out. Lucky 'e rescued them.'

The three women sat there, sipping tea from chunky cups – the cheap sort obtainable from any house goods shop. Cath had long noticed that Thelma never used any of the commemorative crockery. They were for show not routine use.

Thelma rattled on about how this mug was the very latest in a long line made to commemorate accessions, coronations, marriages and births of royalty.

'Can't wait for next year. Can barely remember the last coronation.' Her shoulders heaved with yet another sigh, all her sighs contributing to the excitement of it all.

Jenny sipped at her tea and took a proffered biscuit. 'You're the ideal person to get the celebrations organised, Thelma. I take my hat off to you.'

'Not long now until Christmas and then only five months from New Year until the Coronation,' returned Thelma, bubbling with excitement.

'Just imagine how much they have to do at Buckingham Palace,' Jenny reminded them.

'Too true, Jenny. And it all takes time. For a start, there's the abbey to be prepared and all that finery to be washed and dried. Them ermines and velvets must take an age to do. Glad I ain't got to do it.'

'Don't think my mangle would cope with it,' said Cath after some thought. 'As fer me washing line...'

'The best prop wouldn't hold your washing line up,' returned Thelma. 'Everything dragging on the dirt.'

'And 'aving to do it all again,' said Cath, looking horrified as though there was a possibility of her having to do it.

Visions of regal robes being pushed through their iron-framed mangles, the rollers struggling to cope, was too ridiculous. They all burst into laughter, spluttering biscuit crumbs and nearly choking on their tea.

'What a thing!'

'We'll arrange meetings and make notes of who supplies what long before then. There's a lot to organise, but we've made a start. We can safely let things slide now until the New Year. I thought we could all dress up like dukes and duchesses.'

Cath frowned. 'I thought we was 'aving just a street party. Ain't that enough?'

Thelma looked at her aghast. 'This is Coronation Close. We've got to do more than anyone else; we're the ones honoured with a change of name so we got to show our respect.'

Talk centred then on whether they had enough material and where they could get more should they need it.

'St Barnabas. St Dunstans and the Conservatives.'

'Conservatives?'

'Not the people,' Thelma responded, spluttering with laughter. 'Jumble sales. We need to gather a load of bits and pieces from jumble sales. Churches and the Conservative association all 'ave good jumbles, nice stuff from posh people sold to suit the purse of a pauper. And we're that all right. We'll grab what we can. There's one on in a week's time. Fancy going? Yes? I thought you would.'

There was no chance of reply. Jenny had realised in her earliest days of moving to Coronation Close that if Thelma said that was your job or this was where you were going, then that was it. Thelma was the driving force, like the wheels of a tractor flattening a field of wheat.

A movement in Thelma's front garden attracted Jenny's attention. 'You've got a visitor.'

Thelma sprang to her feet. 'What the devil does she want.'

Living-room door flew open. Front door was jerked wide.

After the front door had closed, Thelma returned. Her expression was tense.

Jenny watched as she sat down at the dining table, hands clasped in front of her and jaw set like iron.

'It seems that old cow next door to you is yet again writing to the council about me.'

Concerned and curious, Jenny leaned forward. 'What about now?'

Cath's curlers rattled when she shook her head and said, 'That woman!'

'She's accusing me of running a knocking shop.'

'A what? Oh, don't get me wrong, Thelma, I do know what that is,' Jenny said when it looked as though Thelma had been about to explain.

'She's mad,' said Cath, then frowned. 'And she came here to tell you?'

Thelma shook her head. 'No. Not Dorothy Partridge. Her sister, Harriet. She came to warn me. She was going to try to stop the letter being posted, but Dorothy's gone out to post it herself.'

'I thought it was her,' said Jenny. 'Harriet, I mean. She's not a bad old bird.'

Thelma's stiff gaze went to Jenny. 'That wasn't all she said. You didn't mention that bloke from the council who called on you. Harriet heard everything; said she'd been afraid for you. What was that all about?'

Jenny felt as though she'd suddenly been covered in frost. She took a deep breath and thanked God that Harriet had been there. She related the occurrence to her two friends.

'He gave me the creeps. He's a friend of Roy's and partially responsible for getting us the house and Roy's new job. He knew I would be alone.'

Thelma gulped and sat back in her chair. 'Let's hope he doesn't make a return visit. Hopefully not, but as for Mother Partridge and her blasted letter.' She got to her feet, then sat right back down again. 'I'd like to go over there and punch her on the nose, but...' She frowned and looked thoughtful. A slow smile spread over her face. 'I'm seeing Bert tonight. Best wait for his advice. He knows what goes on. Still, at least we've been warned.'

They parted feeling apprehensive, but at least, as Thelma had said, they'd been warned.

29

The time since Jenny's arrival in Coronation Close seemed to fly by. She had a house that was slowly but surely being furnished, and a productive garden. Most of all, she had new friends, and Thelma was the best of these.

The latest dress Thelma had given to Jenny was of dark grey wool. The second-hand and dated item had been updated with the addition of white piping around the neckline and the cuffs of the long sleeves.

Jenny was so impressed with her reflection that she deftly remodelled her hair into a chignon, patted on face powder and liked her reflection even more. Even though it was broad daylight and she wasn't going anywhere, she added mascara to her eyelashes and softened a red lipstick with a smear of Vaseline.

Humming softly to herself, she began dancing around the bedroom. In her mind, she was at a dance and her partner had just told her how beautiful she looked.

'Thank you,' she whispered and curtseyed.

The daydream ended abruptly with the sound of someone knocking at the front door.

Seeing as Thelma had left for work earlier that morning, she presumed it was Cath or even Maude.

'Coming,' she called. Flushed of face, she looked forward to seeing what Cath thought of her new outfit. Thelma also made things for Cath, most of which were rarely worn. Cath liked keeping everything for Sunday best, though she didn't venture far on any day of the week.

The sight of Charlie Talbot standing at the door took her breath away.

'Charlie.'

'My word,' he said after taking his trilby hat off and looking her up and down. 'You look terrific. Are you off somewhere special?'

Lost for words, she shook her head. 'No.' She shook her head some more, desperately trying to regain her composure. 'I was just...' She gasped then laughed. 'I wasn't expecting anyone. I was just trying on this dress. One of my new neighbours gave it to me.'

He looked her up and down again before his eyes fixed on hers. 'It looks incredible.' He rolled the brim of his hat between his fingers. 'You look incredible. I wouldn't have recognised you as the same person, back there in the Pithay. Living here must be agreeing with you.'

She opened the door wider. 'You'd better come in. I'll put the kettle on. I've got tea or coffee,' she said as she busied herself filling the kettle and setting out the crockery. She took down the tea caddy and a bottle of Camp coffee.

As she waited for the kettle to boil, he stood in the doorway between kitchen and living room, staring at her, almost as though he was seeing her for the very first time.

'Shall I take your hat and coat?'

'No. I can't stay long. I came to tell you that Isaac and his wife have moved to a ground-floor flat in Lawfords Gate. It means he can get a bus to St Nicholas Market. He's determined not to give up his job.'

'I think getting up early and working there keeps him going. But I'm so pleased they've got a new flat. Does it have indoor facilities?'

Charlie grinned. 'If you mean an inside toilet and bath, yes it does. They're both over the moon. That's why I'm here. Jacob did consider writing, but forgot to ask for your new address. And Ruth being as she is... I said I would arrange to pick you up and take you to visit them. Would that be possible? Not necessarily today, but at your convenience.'

'Oh, Charlie. Of course I will. Right away if you like. I'll get my coat.'

He grabbed her arm before she could dash to the hallway. 'I think we've got time to drink our tea or coffee first.'

'Coffee or tea?'

'Coffee if you don't mind. What are you having?'

'Coffee,' she said with a smile. 'My friend Thelma converted me. It's quicker too. No more waiting for the teapot to brew.'

They pulled out a pair of dining chairs in the living room.

'Sorry I can't offer you a biscuit. The girls ate the last. I need to go shopping.'

'I've got the car outside. I can drop you off.'

'You have a car?' Her eyebrows arched with surprise. Only wealthy people had cars, though she reminded herself that Robin had bought himself an old van, but that was different. Vans carried goods. Cars only carried people.

He nodded. 'Yes. My father bought it for me.'

Jenny swallowed as she tipped a teaspoon of coffee into each cup. Anyone having a father who could buy their son a car was very wealthy indeed.

'That's nice. Milk? Sugar?'

He declined both.

Their conversation was muted. During everything that was said, he held her gaze, flattering though a little disçoncerting.

Finally she set down her cup. 'I'll get my coat.'

He followed her out to the hallway, where she retrieved coat, hat and bag.

'I meant what I said. You look wonderful,' he said as he opened the passenger door at the front of the car.

She felt herself blushing. Her gaze flicked over the houses of Coronation Close. One or two faces looked out from between the curtains. Cath and Maude were standing outside their houses at the far end of the cul-de-sac. They both waved as the car followed the road around the central green and headed off. She envisaged questions being asked later. For now, she wouldn't even think about what might be asked but centred on Charlie Talbot.

'You haven't asked me about my husband.'

'I presume he's left.'

'He's got a new job. It takes him away from home.'

She sensed a quizzical look from him, but he said nothing. It occurred to her that he might know more about Roy than she did. Although they were at opposite ends of the political spectrum, she thought it likely that they kept tabs on each other.

* * *

Lawfords Gate had four floors of two-bedroom and three-bedroom flats. Built back in the twenties, it had a homely look, its warm red brick and large sash windows a compromise between the nineteenth and twentieth centuries.

'I have a bathroom,' Ruth exclaimed, a spark of interest lifting the dullness in her eyes 'You must see it. Isaac. Show Jenny our bathroom.'

The old couple gave her a warm welcome and as directed by his wife, Isaac took her on a tour of their new home.

'We got this thanks to Charlie. He knows how to put a strong case,' said Isaac, a beaming smile splitting his face.

'And once we were moved in, he offered to call on you at your new home and let you know where we were. And now he brings you here! How wonderful is that?'

Jenny agreed that it was indeed wonderful. She smiled knowingly at Charlie. He'd said they'd specifically asked him to let her know.

'Now let me have your address and I can write to you. It gets boring here without anything to do. I like writing letters.' Ruth still had a brightness to her eyes, though her face and form were thinner, her complexion sallow.

'Of course I will.'

Charlie hooked a used envelope from out of the inner pocket of his jacket, plus a pencil. The paper was still warm. *Because his heart is beating just beneath it.* If only she could lay her hand over it, feel its beat, feel its heat.

Bent to the task of writing down the address, it was easy to hide the mixed emotions that played over her face. On the one hand, she was ecstatic at being with Charlie. On the other hand, she was devastated by Ruth's appearance. How long, she wondered, how long?

When Ruth laid her head back and closed her eyes, Jenny suggested it was time they left.

'I think we've tired her out.'

'A good tired,' said Isaac as he accompanied them to the front door. His kind face sagged with sadness.

Silently, Jenny walked with Charlie back to the car.

'Do you still need me to drop you off at the shops?' he asked her.

She thought about it. The neighbours had seen her get into his car. Cath and Maude were probably wondering who he was. At least if she came back without him and carrying a bag of shopping, the message would be clear. He was nothing to her. Just a friend. Another friend. But he wasn't. She didn't want him to be just a friend, but for now she needed to think things through.

'I'd prefer it if you dropped me off at the bus stop in Bedminster if you don't mind.'

'Whatever you want.'

She saw the disappointment in his face, the tightly clenched jaw, the way his eyes faced firmly ahead. He'd prefer to take her all the way, but she'd made up her mind.

There was only a small queue at the bus stop. He parked the car and insisted on going with her. As it began to rain, they stood back from the queue, finding shelter in a doorway. Jenny glanced at the bus queue, fearing some familiar face might be looking her way. She saw no one she recognised.

The doorway was a fitting place to shelter from the rain. Nobody would notice them here. Nobody could overhear their conversation or notice how closely they were standing.

Up until now, their meeting up had been light-hearted, yet she perceived something deeper was going on beneath the surface.

Time was ticking on. She could see the hands on the clock outside the hippodrome, like black arrows ever flying with time.

'Where do we go from here?' he said suddenly.

'With regard to Isaac and Ruth?'

'No. With regard to us. We were attracted to each other from the very first. I saw the way you looked at me and you must have noticed the way I looked at you.'

Responsibility took hold. She was not a happily married woman, but all the same, she was married. For better or worse. She took a deep breath.

She shook her head vehemently. 'I'm sorry, Charlie. I can't. I admit I was attracted to you from the first, but I've a family. I also have a husband. Do you have a wife?'

'No. I do not.'

She sighed and tried to ignore him and concentrate on the crowds, the traffic, the women pushing prams and loaded with shopping. All married. Just like her. But happily? She couldn't tell. Nobody could tell from the outside what a marriage was like.

He took out a packet of cigarettes, lit up and began to blow clouds of smoke out of his mouth and nostrils.

She said nothing whilst he did so, then he said, 'Will you allow me to make the running, not just a suggestion, but explain how I'm feeling?'

She wasn't quite sure what he meant but made out that she did. 'Yes. I suppose so.'

He took hold of her hand – just as Robin had, though on this occasion she responded differently. Was it her imagination, or could she hear her pulse in her ears?

'Right.' He pulled her close to him and held her hand between both of his. 'I've never believed in love at first sight or didn't think I did.'

'Do you believe now,' she asked him.

'Yes. I believe I do. I saw not just the person you are on the outside but also how you are inside. Your character. I saw how kind you were with the old couple. That's when I told myself that I could love someone like that for the rest of my life.'

She could hardly believe what she was hearing. If only she could hear this for the rest of the day, the rest of the week, the rest of her life. The spectre of Roy was still too strong, yet she'd believed herself in love, dared to do so in fact.

She closed her eyes and wished the moment could last forever. But it wouldn't. It couldn't. This was no fairy tale. Reality broke in.

'I'm a married woman, Charlie, and you're a few years younger than me. I have children. I have responsibilities.'

He nodded and, to her surprise, rested his chin on her head. It was comforting. Sweet. Her mind was in turmoil. 'I keep telling myself that you belong to someone else and I have no right to want you. Then I reckoned it was not about belonging. Love knows no boundaries and can happen in a split second, so why do we torture ourselves with such lies? I cannot ignore how I feel. I don't want to own you. I want to love you.'

Strands of hair were flung from her neat chignon as she shook her head vehemently. 'This is crazy. We can't. We barely know each other.'

'And yet... We want each other. We want to love each other.'

He said it so easily and with outright conviction. Loving someone wasn't about names on a wedding certificate. It was meant to be written in the hearts of the people concerned.

'That's it,' he said at last. 'That's all there is.'

No barrier prevented her from kissing him, from letting him kiss her. Hidden by the doorway, it was hard to let go, but let go they did.

'Next week,' he said. 'Same time, same place. Can you make it?'

The right words came out, the only words she could find to say. 'It's too soon. Can you give me time to think about it?'

'Two weeks' time then.'

This time she didn't hesitate. 'Yes. I can make it.'

Once on the bus heading home, she changed her mind. She was going home to her world. He was going to his. They were worlds apart with little chance of the gap ever being narrowed.

30

DECEMBER 1936

Frost coated the grass and silvered the bare bones of the privet hedges that enclosed each garden of the red-brick houses of Coronation Close. It sparkled in the light from the streetlamps where the muffled-up kids were keeping warm playing chase in the pool of light amongst the darkness.

In the back gardens, everything was total blackness except for an oblong patch of amber thrown from kitchen windows and the glazed half of the back door.

It being a Monday, Jenny had put out a line of washing that morning. Six in the evening and everything was stiff and frozen solid. Shirts, dresses, blouses and skirts looked like a row of people waiting in a queue.

Cath Lockhart had come to borrow a cup of sugar and was now helping her get in her washing.

'Blimey' said Cath, holding out a one of Jenny's nightdresses up for inspection. 'Looks like it's gonna come walking in by itself.'

Being careful not to slip on the icy path, the two of them eased their way along the washing line, unpegging each item of clothing in turn. The blue dress that Thelma had made for her was stiff as a board and refused to fold. So was everything else. Hugging the larger items in an unwieldy embrace, they gradually made their way into the house, where each item would end up leaning stiffly against the gas stove. There was a bread pudding in the oven and a saucepan of stew simmered on one of the gas rings. The smell of food cooking mixed with that of damp laundry. The smell of laundry would overtake that of cooking once the clothes defrosted.

Cath made her excuses to leave. 'Got to get me own stuff in now. I bet my Bill won't be putting on 'is long johns any time soon. Enough to freeze 'is bits off, I shouldn't wonder.'

Jenny thanked her and proceeded to get things arranged around the gas stove. The larger clothes made her giggle. Stiffly rigid, they looked almost lifelike, a gathering of chilly mortals trying to warm themselves up after coming in from the cold.

She tapped the shoulder of one of Roy's shirts that he hadn't taken with him. It felt solid even without an arm to fill it. Like a piece of cardboard.

Giggling to herself, she tapped the shoulder again. 'Can I have this dance?'

There was no reply of course.

'No need to be shy.'

She took hold of the stiff shirt, holding onto its sleeves, and did a little waltz, just a few steps around the kitchen before putting it back in place.

Underwear and other smaller items were still out on the line. There was no prospect of them drying out there. Everything needed to come indoors. In the morning, she could see what had dried and what might benefit from a turn through the mangle before being hung out again.

Out into the dark garden and up the icy path yet again to fetch the rest.

Halfway up the path, a voice cut through the cold night air. 'Is your drawers as stiff as mine?'

The speaker was Betty Brown from next door, who was close on forty years old and worked at the tobacco factory. She was also out collecting stiff laundry from a washing line that stretched the full length of the garden. A cigarette bounced at the corner of her mouth as she did so. Betty always had a cigarette in her mouth.

She was fond of saying that she couldn't live without her fags and a good cough in the morning. Besides Thelma, she was the only other married or widowed woman in Coronation Close who went out to work.

A patch of light fell out from her kitchen, giving a bit of extra illumination for her to see her way – identical to the one that fell from Jenny's kitchen.

'I'm not sure I'll get everything dry indoors by morning.'

'Yeah. Look at these long johns.' Betty held up a pair of her husband's full-length underwear. They were the old-fashioned kind that covered a man from neck to ankles.

'They must keep him very warm,' Jenny remarked with a laugh.

The glow from Betty's cigarette jiggled around like a firefly. Smoking and talking were often carried out in tandem. 'They'll need some warming before 'e puts them on, or he'll freeze 'is bits off. Don't want that, do we!'

They both laughed in the comfortable but mocking way that women do when they spoke of their spouses.

Bit by bit, every dolly peg was prised from each item of laundry, most making their way into a peg bag, some hanging from their mouths like giant incisors.

Jenny spit the line of dolly pegs from her mouth into the peg bag.

A single expletive came over the hedge from Betty.

'You all right, Betty?'

'Caught my tongue in between one of these pegs. I bought them from that gypsy woman who came 'round the door. She wanted a shilling for a dozen. I told 'er no, it's sixpence or nothing. She weren't pleased but took the sixpence anyway. She told me I 'ad a glib tongue. I reckon she put a curse on a peg to catch me tongue.'

'She was a gypsy, Betty, not a witch.'

'The same thing. All gypsies are witches.'

Jenny doubted it.

Someone came out of the door of number one, then went in again.

'Funny pair, them two. Causin' you any trouble, are they?' Betty asked.

'Not really. I speak and if they don't want to reply, that's all right by me.'

'Funny pair' Betty went on. 'Especially Mrs Partridge. Not sure whether she's superstitious or religious. Bit of both, I reckon. She never does any laundry at Easter or Christmas.'

'Then that's down to religion.'

'I've even seen 'er stepping over the cracks in the pavement.'

'That's superstition.'

'That's what I'm saying. Old witch she is.'

'What about her sister?'

'I ain't sure. An old aunt of mine used to live in the same fleapit as they did – though you wouldn't think they came from slums. But they did.'

'How did she get on with them?'

'Can't say.' The end of her cigarette glowed as she drew on it. 'I used to visit my auntie Edie before she passed away. She might 'ave been going a bit doolally towards the end. You couldn't take everything she said as true. One thing that sticks in me mind though is she reckoned Dorothy never 'ad a sister. Oh well. I can't stick out yer gassing. Got stuffed 'earts in the oven. They should be done by now.'

For a moment, Jenny stood in the gathering darkness, tingling from the frost. Why would Mrs Partridge lie about her sister?

31

Trevor Collins had a flabby jaw, a round face and small blue eyes flickering behind black-rimmed spectacles. He fully accepted that he ate too much, smoked too much and could be gruff and almost offensive at times. But he was a man with authority and considered himself respectable and very British. He also had an appetite for women, fixating on those he found attractive. He dared not pay another visit to Roy Crawford's wife yet, but he would in time. It was just a case of waiting for the right moment to come along.

He flexed his nicotine-stained fingertips, took another drag on his Woodbine and prepared himself to interview his subordinate Cuthbert Throgmorton. He was most definitely up for the task.

Bert Throgmorton arrived. Trevor exhaled a lungful of smoke before stubbing out his sixth cigarette of the morning in the tin ashtray stamped Bristol Corporation around its rim.

Bert sat opposite him looking nervous. Good, he thought. The rest should be easy.

After reading yet again the letter in front of him, he looked up. 'I've had a complaint about a woman from a neighbour in Coronation Close. She reckons that a Mrs Thelma Dawkins is using her house as a brothel. I wonder if you know anything about it?'

Colour spread like spilt paint over Bert's cheeks. 'A brothel!'

'Yes. A brothel. A house of ill repute where men pay women for certain services.'

It impressed Trevor when Bert collected himself, drew in his chin and shook his head. 'It's Mrs Partridge again in number one. She's a troublemaker.'

Trevor pursed his lips, adjusted his spectacles so that they sat at the top of his nose instead of in the middle, and lowered his eyes once more to the sheet of Basildon Bond writing paper sitting in front of him. Blue Basildon Bond. He thought it somewhat bemusing how most people preferred blue to white.

Bert tuned in to what Trevor was saying.

'This letter also says that you're one of the men who frequently calls on Mrs Dawkins. Is that so, Bert?'

The eyes of the two men met.

Bert cleared his throat. Trevor had expected him to deny the accusation. It surprised him when he did not.

'Thelma Dawkins is a widow. Yes, I do call on her, but we're both alone. There's no reason why we shouldn't. I will also confirm here and now that she is not selling...' He took a deep breath, his shoulders squaring as if for a fight. 'She is not selling her body. She has three children. The eldest, George, is away at sea. The daughters are younger and live with her.'

Trevor found himself admiring Bert Throgmorton's defiant manner. 'I'm fine with that, Bert, but you know how it is. If somebody slings mud at one of my officials, it's down to me to scrape it off. We can't have the department mired in scandal. You understand that don't you?'

Bert said that he did.

'This letter also accuses this Mrs Dawkins of having three children by three different fathers. Is that true?'

Bert's eyes flashed and anger inflamed his cheeks. 'Is it a crime to be a widow more than once?'

Trevor was taken aback by Bert's quickfire retort and the defiant look in his eyes. He shook his head. 'No. Of course not. Neither do I have any control over your private life, Bert, as long as it doesn't cast the council in a bad light.'

'It's my life and none of the council's business,' Bert responded more fiercely than he'd ever spoken to his boss before.

'Of course it isn't – as long as it's the truth, the whole truth and nothing but the truth.'

'So help me, God!'

Trevor took the letter in both hands, looking as though he was reading it for the umpteenth time. He quite often got letters from both the well-meaning and the interfering gossips who loved to make trouble for their neighbours. Being a great Sherlock Holmes fan, he liked studying the handwriting of these letters, hazarding a guess as to their background. It was a council estate, so for the most part those who proclaimed themselves 'good neighbours' had only the minimum of schooling. The spelling tended to be poor and the handwriting even poorer. However, as in this case, there were exceptions. This handwriting was well rounded, even to the point of being beautiful. The spelling was faultless.

Bert Throgmorton interrupted his thought process. 'I'm guessing it's anonymous.'

Trevor nodded. 'Most of them are.' He smiled, threw the letter into the waste basket, then leaned back in his swivel chair. 'I think we can forget about this letter, Bert. Less said, soonest mended. Seeing your woman friend tonight, are you?'

Bert didn't trust his senior not to attack again but answered honestly. 'Yes. We're good friends.'

'Ah,' said Trevor. His smug face creased into a smile. 'That's good to know.'

'May I go now?'

'Just one more thing,' said Trevor. 'Do you happen to know how the new tenant in number two is getting on? I understand her husband is away working. That she too is a woman living alone.'

Bert frowned. He couldn't understand why Mr Collins was asking the question – unless Mrs Partridge had also complained about Jenny Crawford. 'I believe so.'

He offered a cigarette which Bert declined.

'A close friend with Mrs Dawkins, is she?'

'They get on well.'

Bert disliked the sly grin and the cunning look behind those glinting spectacles. What his boss said next touched a raw nerve.

'Wouldn't it be something if the letter writer is mistaken and it's the new neighbour, Mrs Crawford, who's entertaining a fancy man, perhaps more than one.'

Bert sprang to his feet. 'If that's all, I've got a job to do.'

'Now, now, Bert. No need to take on so. I'm just trying to ensure that the tenants of Coronation Close are everything they're supposed to be.'

Bert glanced at his watch. Not being a bad-tempered man, he collected himself and said, 'If you're finished now, sir…'

'Of course, of course.'

Bert gave a little nod of acknowledgement before heading for and exiting the door.

Once alone, Trevor Collins steepled his fingers and sat there thinking of what had been said and his own personal plans for what would happen next. He didn't consider himself a judgemental man. It wouldn't matter to him whether or not dear old Bert was consorting with 'colourful' ladies.

Trevor smiled to himself. He'd always considered Bert a bit dull. Not so much now.

Still, he couldn't ignore the letter. He might as well be seen to do something – or have one of his minions do something – just a general inspection of the house to ascertain whether she was keeping it decent.

As for Mrs Crawford... Bert might have his fancy woman, but he didn't think she could possibly compare to Mrs Crawford. With some intervention from him, Mrs Crawford would be alone for a very long time. He would see to that.

Pedantic when it came to planning and being patient, he picked up his desk diary and flicked through the coming months. He found a free date. He'd make sure Roy Crawford was not around. He smiled at the thought of Roy, an obsessive who enjoyed dressing up in a uniform. He did not yet know that it was on the cards that the wearing of a military uniform – unless one was a member of the armed forces – would shortly be banned. It didn't apply to boy scouts, of course, and that he thought is what Roy Crawford is; *an adult who liked wearing a uniform.*

The tea lady knocked on his door and asked if he wanted tea or coffee. Over her shoulder, he could see her tea trolley. There were two pots on the top shelf – tea and coffee, plus a jug of milk and a bowl of sugar cubes. The next shelf down was where she kept the cups and saucers.

He opted for tea and as he supped it thought about his next moves. He enjoyed wielding power – local authority only, but who knew what might transpire in future? After all, he was beginning to cultivate those who might shortly be running the country – or even the world. Wearing a uniform didn't count for him. It was the power of ordering others around that he relished.

One step at a time though. It was a wise man who kept his finger on the pulse and knew precisely what was going on. Knowledge was power and both were aids to an ambitious man. In the meantime, he would instruct Miss Venables, his able inspector of housing, to pay Mrs Dawkins a visit.

He'd thrown the letter away but did intend writing back. He'd recognised the address of this old busybody and knew it was already on file. Best keep the nosy parkers on one's side. They might be useful in future.

He had a good memory. He remembered her complaining about Mrs Crawford's predecessor in number two. He'd been an elderly gentleman who had lived alone, grown vegetables in his back garden and kept a few chickens – as many people did.

He clearly recalled some of her complaint. '*A smell of something quite obnoxious drifts my way now and again. There is litter and, of course, litter will attract rats.*'

Following the collection of his cup and saucer, he made his way along the corridor to another office in the housing department where the housing inspectorate was located. It was their job to investigate alleged breaches of tenancies, check cleanliness, health and whether there were more people living in the house than stated on the rent book.

'Ah. Mr Collins. Good morning. Now what can I do for you?'

Very large teeth flashed between bright red lips.

Trevor was under no illusion that Miss Venables was sweet on him. Some who should know better had pulled his leg about it. He knew they were right. She did fancy him, but he'd given her no encouragement. She was as far from his fancy as a woman could be, too slim in the hips, too flat-chested and thus somewhat androgynous. She was also a bit long in the tooth – in more ways than one.

'I have a tenant of whom complaints have been made that she might be entertaining men – and perhaps even charging them for the privilege.'

'How terribly shocking.' Her face was a picture of outraged gentility.

Trevor frowned at his diary. He'd pencilled in Mrs Crawford for a visit, but would she be vulnerable enough to accept his advances by then? A woman alone could be reasonably vulnerable, but a few extra problems might make her more pliable. Only a man could truly make a woman feel safe and taken care of. Yes, Miss Venables might just do the job.

'I want you to inspect both number twelve and number two Coronation Close. As you know, Mrs Crawford in number two is a fairly new arrival and her husband is often away.' He fixed her with a look as officious as his tone of voice. 'Can you furnish me with two of your action for inspection forms, Miss Venables?'

Looking disappointed that he wasn't going to flirt – as he sometimes did – she busied herself checking some paperwork whilst he filled in the forms she'd handed to him.

'There,' he said, handing them back to her. 'Report back to me personally regarding both.'

'I shall do all you ask of me,' said Miss Venables and smiled up at him as though waiting for him to ask for even more.

He winced at her beaming face, then managed a tight smile. 'I would very much appreciate your discretion.'

'Of course.'

32

It was Wednesday afternoon when Miss Rose Venables turned up to inspect number twelve, Coronation Close having been informed that Mrs Dawson worked in a dress shop and that was the only weekday she would be in residence.

A weak sun had broken through wintry clouds and the breeze, though cold, was enough to dry a line full of washing.

It wasn't the first time Thelma's house and housekeeping had been inspected. The last one had occurred three days after she'd moved in. That inspection was normal. She hadn't heard of there being second inspections unless a complaint had been made and even some of the inspections shortly after moving in seldom happened now.

Resigning herself to the ordeal, Thelma motioned for the woman to come inside. The sooner it was over and the woman was gone, the better.

The living room was inspected. The woman ticked something in her leather-bound notebook. Next was the kitchen, last the bathroom where she glanced at the Izal toilet roll on the window ledge, then wrinkled her nose at the squares of newspaper hanging from the cistern.

'I don't have money to burn,' Thelma remarked.

Miss Venables straightened her wrinkled nose and asked to be shown the bedrooms.

First they went into each of the kids' rooms, where the poker-thin woman peered at the pillowcases and sheets.

Thelma stood as stiff as the prop that held up her clothesline, arms folded beneath her ample breasts. To say she resented this inspection was putting it mildly. But she'd made up her mind to endure.

Something more was written down in the leather-bound notebook.

Thelma seethed and couldn't help asking what she was up to.

'Up to?' came the indignant response.

'What are you writing?' Thelma demanded.

Miss Venables cleared her throat. 'I'm noting that the children's bedding is perfectly clean.'

'I told you it would be,' returned Thelma. 'It's fresh off the line. I always change the kids' bedding on a Wednesday afternoon. It's half-day closing at the shop. I'm a senior saleswoman in Bertrams Modes – an upmarket ladies outfitter.'

She said it hoping to impress. Her rigidity lessened and she almost felt proud of herself. She kept her house clean. She kept her children clean. She could have told this blasted woman that without her visiting to check. Anyone in the street could have told her she was fastidious about her clothes and just as fastidious about her house. House-proud, that's what she was.

'And now your bed.'

Pale eyes peered at Thelma from a pinched face. Today, Miss Venables' lips were a bluish purple with no trace of lipstick. From the moment, this sharp-faced harridan had entered her house,

Thelma had felt a strong urge to tell the woman to use a little make-up. A bit of colour would help alleviate the meanness of a face not used to expressing joy.

All thoughts of helping the hard woman look more amenable flew out of the window. With hindsight, she wished she'd put fresh bedding on, but for goodness' sake, they'd only been on there five days. She still felt the need to make an excuse. 'I'm about to change the bedding. Just waiting for the sheets to dry,' she said as she pushed open her bedroom door.

The room was painted pink. Bert had done it for her. The eiderdown was also pink and matched the profusion of roses on the curtain fabric. Even though it was winter, the richly coloured curtains made the bedroom seem full of an eternal summer.

The sound of garden shears could be heard from outside. Yet again, her neighbours opposite were trimming their hedges. They clipped at least once a week. Snip, snip, snip it went, sometimes all day. Thelma grated her teeth. Mrs Partridge and her sister were avid gardeners. At times, she wished they would snip off their fingers and spare her their unrelenting enthusiasm for clipping privet hedges.

It took a great deal of effort, but Thelma managed to keep her mouth shut. Even when this prim, stiff woman in tailored tweed looked sniffily at each pillow, she swallowed her outrage.

The chilly eyes turned on her as she asked, 'Why two pillows if you sleep alone?'

Thelma knew what the old cow was implying but gritted her teeth. 'When one of my kids has a nightmare, they come in with me. It's what kids do.'

'Oh really?' Miss Venables made a hissing sound between her tightly clamped lips.

'Don't have kids yerself, I suppose.'

Miss Venables response was tautly one-worded. 'No.'

For a moment, her face tightened and her lips pursed as she moved from the head of the bed to the foot.

Thelma was unforgiving. This woman had an Achilles heel and she was going for it.

'Oh sorry.' She laughed in a light, apologetic manner. 'You wouldn't, still being a spinster and left on the shelf. Well, you and a lot of others after all that slaughter in the Somme and that. Not enough men to go round was there. The prettier women collared the best of the lot.'

Perhaps in retaliation for the obvious slur, the spidery fingers picked up a corner of the bedsheet and took a sniff.

This was too much. 'What the bloody hell...'

'I have to check that no man has slept in this bed.'

Thelma muttered under her breath. 'How would you know what a man in bed smells like?'

It was plain that there was no way she was going to get any favours from this woman. With that in mind, she kept her jaw clamped shut and her hands bunched beneath her armpits. The latter was a precaution in case she lost control, grabbed the woman by the coat lapels of her aged tweed jacket and threw her out of the window. This was getting too much. She'd already inspected the downstairs rooms and found nothing amiss.

There hadn't been an inspection for years. It needed something to trigger it. Non-payment of rent was one reason along with neglect of children or licentious behaviour. The latter could mean anything but the inference from this woman was worrying.

'You have a double bed.'

'I sleep better in a double bed. It's not a crime, is it?'

The purple lips pursed. The sharp jaw tightened. 'A double bed is usually for two people.'

'Not in this house,' Thelma declared defiantly.

'Or when one of your children has a nightmare...'

There was sarcasm in Miss Venables' comment, plus a glittering satisfaction in her eyes.

Thelma glanced at the open window. It wouldn't take that much effort to throw this shrewish old maid out of it.

Pen poised in her hand; the poker-thin woman slid her fingers along the cast-iron mantelpiece – a small bedroom version of the larger one downstairs. After inspecting her fingertips, she once again wrote in her notebook.

She carried out the same procedure with the dressing table, running her fingers even between a powder compact, hairbrush and comb, mascara and tubes of lipstick.

Unable to contain herself, Thelma blurted, 'That was only dusted yesterday.'

Thin eyebrows arched as if surprised. 'Not today?'

'Do you dust your bedroom every day?'

Something was written down.

'I don't suppose you would dust every day, would you. Not having a husband and children.' Thelma couldn't help herself. She couldn't take this lying down.

Miss Venables made no comment. However, Thelma knew she'd hit a raw nerve. The bony jaw clenched and a dot of colour popped on both cheeks.

Her instinct told her in no uncertain terms that Miss Venables was out to get her by fair means or foul.

In a predatory manner, Miss Venables circled the bed, making notes all the way. Thelma regretted not changing this bed but consoled herself with the fact that the sheets were merely creased and not yet spoiled enough to put in the boiler.

The same fingers that had sought dust now picked up a pillow, felt it and, to Thelma's great surprise, raised it to the aquiline nose and sniffed. In the blink of an eye, the bedcovers were pulled back, not halfway as she'd done to the children's beds, but all the way down to the foot.

Thelma's jaw dropped. 'You going to sniff that too?'

No answer, of course, just a bending closer to the centre of the bed, eyes narrowed.

Thelma could stand no more. 'What the hell do you think you're doing?'

The council had a rule that you could be in a lot of trouble for swearing at officials, or at anyone else for that matter.

Miss Venables straightened, showed no reaction to Thelma's expletives, but wrote in her notebook. Once that was done, she held her chin high, lips clamped in a straight line. 'It's my job to check that you are not entertaining diverse men on a regular basis.'

Thelma frowned. The penny had dropped. 'Don't tell me. Someone's said that a whole regiment of blokes comes in and out of this house.'

'I couldn't possibly comment,' said Miss Venables as, straight-backed, pen and notebook now both secreted to her leather bag which was as stiff as she was, she prepared to leave.

Angry now, Thelma tramped down the stairs after her. 'That old cow from over the road 'as put her oar in. I'm right, aren't I?'

Miss Venables headed for the front door at the same stride as she had ascended and descended the stairs and made her inspection of the rooms. 'I couldn't possibly comment.'

'I've got just one gentleman friend. Just one. And that's...' She was about to say it was Bert Throgmorton but stopped herself just in case there was a chance it would get him into trouble.

In no doubt of the identity of her accuser, Thelma watched Miss Venables stride off down the garden path.

A curtain moved in Mrs Partridge's living-room window.

Thelma scowled. Mrs Partridge and sister had downed their

garden shears, gone into the house and were watching at the window.

She shouted across the road at them. 'Nosey old cows.'

The sound of the woman's determined knocking came from Jenny's front garden.

'She's out,' Thelma shouted. 'Gone up the shops.'

The angular face regarded her from over the top of her angular shoulder. 'I'll wait.'

33

Loaded with two bags of shopping, Jenny was longing to get home. Money was a bit short until more postal orders came. She'd bought more potatoes and carrots than anything else. Onions had also been a necessary purchase. A little meat would stretch a long way when vegetables were added, so she was forever making stew and suet pudding.

Walking along the shop frontages in Filwood Broadway, the smell coming out of the fish and chip shop, which was closed until this evening, tickled her taste buds. If only, she thought, as her stomach rumbled in protest. She had no idea when she would indulge again the scrumptious feast she'd tasted that night she went with Thelma to the pictures.

Breakfast had been a slice of toast cut from a stale loaf and smeared with pork dripping and salt. Lunch had been the same. This evening, she would taste some of the stew she intended to make from the vegetables and beef scraps. A few flakes of dried apple remained, perhaps enough to make an apple tart – a pastry base, of course, but no topping. She didn't have enough flour and fat for that.

No wonder I'm getting so thin, she thought to herself and sighed.

The latest postal order payment had arrived four days ago, late as usual. Her priority had been to pay the rent. Food and pennies for the gas and electricity meters came after that. She had been hoping to save up for a new wireless but worried it might never happen. Arrival of the postal orders was becoming less frequent. She'd dared write one letter to Roy telling him so; he had not replied.

Her attention was taken by a group of women who'd gathered outside a double-fronted shop that had been empty for some time. The windows had been whitewashed over, but still they were doing their best to peer through the places where a finger had rubbed it away on the inside.

She would have walked on if a familiar voice hadn't shouted out to her.

Cath pushed her way through the gathered women. As usual, her curlers were hidden beneath a headscarf. Like Jenny she'd been shopping, a big leather shopping bag bouncing against one leg, a straw one against the other.

'Finished shopping?' she asked.

Jenny said that she had.

'Might as well walk 'ome with you then.'

Jenny jerked her chin towards the huddle of women gathered around the shop window. 'There's a new shop opening?'

'There's a notice in the window. Mrs Allen from Newquay Road told me they're going to be selling furniture. Second-hand furniture.'

Cath mentioning second-hand furniture stayed Jenny's step.

Knowing Cath had not read the poster simply because she couldn't read, Jenny looked. Her surprise must have registered on her face.

'What does it say?' Cath whispered.

Taken by surprise, Jenny took a deep breath. 'It says that everything being sold is guaranteed to be free of bed bugs and woodworm. And easy payment terms are available.'

Cath expressed surprise. 'Well, that's worth knowing.'

'I dare say it is.'

Was Robin taking over the shop? She could hardly believe it.

The tooting of a car horn sounded at the same time as a black van she recognised pulled up against the kerb.

He got out of the van, swiped his cap from his head and passed the back of his hand across his sweating brow.

'Robin Hubert has arrived,' he said with a laugh and a bow fit for a queen.

The little huddle of women tittered amongst themselves. Even those with no teeth and grey hair appreciated cheekiness and a man who treated women as though each was a duchess.

Shaking her head and smiling, Jenny said, 'You are incorrigible.'

'I try to be,' he said, his smile as warm as her own.

'So you're leaving City Road?'

'I've sold it.' He nodded at the metal-framed windows above the shop. 'I'm moving in here.' He looked pointedly at her shopping bags. 'Wanna lift?'

'Can you take two of us?' Cath asked.

'Only if you don't mind getting in the back.'

Cath scrambled into the back of the van; Jenny sat in the front passenger seat.

The smell of petrol was strong, but as Robin explained, the van was getting on in years. 'Can't expect it to be perfect.'

It was a short run from Filwood Broadway back to Coronation Close. The van chugged in.

The moment they pulled up outside Jenny's house, Thelma

came tearing out of her front gate. Jenny surmised she must have been watching from her window to have raced out like that.

'You've got a visitor,' she said, nudging Jenny to look in the direction of her front garden, where Miss Venables had taken up station on the dustbin.

Robin came out from his side of the van.

The indignant figure of Miss Venables headed for Jenny.

'Mr Crawford?' She addressed Robin.

He shook his head. 'No. He's not around.'

Miss Venables sniffed as though she'd just detected an offensive smell under her nose. 'I see. When the cat's away, the mice will play. Your husband is away isn't he, Mrs Crawford?'

Jenny frowned. Who was this woman and what business was it of hers. She thought she recognised her from somewhere but couldn't quite remember where.

'Yes. I'm sorry, who are you?'

Miss Venables replied who she was and what she was there for.

Then Jenny remembered the name and this woman who had been quite officious when they had met before.

Thelma came across the road. 'She's snooping.'

'Inspecting,' said an increasingly indignant Miss Venables. 'I need to check that you're keeping the house clean and are not entertaining male visitors unless related.' Her look of condemnation was aimed directly at Robin.

Robin's expression, usually so open and pleasant, turned dark. 'Don't look at me that way, lady. I've done nothing wrong. And neither has Jenny.'

'Alone in a van together.'

A loud banging came from the back of the van. 'Will somebody let me out of yer.'

Accompanied by laughter, Robin went to the back door of the van and let Cath out.

'We were not alone in the van,' said Robin and looked quite triumphant about it. 'We had a chaperone, someone who can vouch for our behaviour all the way from Filwood Broadway.'

'She wants to check your bedding,' said Thelma, fists resting on hips. 'She's checked mine – thoroughly,' she added.

Jenny beamed at the stick-thin woman with the stern bun and a mouth that looked desperately trying to keep itself closed. 'You're quite welcome. You'll have to make it snappy. My daughters will be home from school at around four fifteen. Will that give you enough time?'

Miss Venables accepted the challenge. Whether she really wanted to get out before the children came home wasn't very clear. Whatever the reason, she did shoot around the house at incredible speed. At the end of it, she proclaimed everything to be in order.

'Thank you,' said Jenny, having laid the shopping on the table and taken off her hat and coat. Her hair swung around her shoulders. Her cheeks had been pinched pink by the cold, clear weather.

Miss Venables took in her slender form, not stick-thin as her own figure, but lithe and graceful. Her face was beautiful, her hair a glorious blur of dark, glossy tresses.

She left the house and collected her bicycle. Cycling was mostly downhill all the way. She chose to go down the hill that ran parallel to the main bus route. Eventually, the lesser road would join up with the major one.

Usually she didn't freewheel, preferring to keep control and slow the speed. On this occasion, she failed to do that. Her mind was in turmoil. Mrs Dawkins had been blowsy and statuesque, a good-looking woman by any standards. It would have been no surprise that she had several admirers. Mrs Crawford, on the other hand, was outstandingly beautiful. There had been no need for her to be investigated, so why had Mr Collins sent her there?

She had noticed a peculiar look on his face when he was giving her instructions. She also recalled that he'd visited the close recently. He must have seen her, but what...?

She spilled at too fast a speed onto the main thoroughfare that led downhill from Knowle West to the junction with St John's Lane. The brakes did not respond. Her front wheel wobbled.

The driver of the double-decker bus had no chance. The bicycle came out in front of him and there was no time to stop.

The front wheel of the bicycle spun, the spokes making a clinking noise which gradually slowed along with the breathing of the woman who had been riding it. Then both stopped. The conductor got off the bus and stood beside the driver. Then he ran across the road and threw up into the hedge.

34

It was Sunday and Jenny was undecided about meeting Charlie on the following Wednesday but was unnerved by the prospect. She needed someone to talk it over with. She needed to see Thelma. Thelma knew all about men, or so it seemed. A cup of tea and a chat always went down well at number two Coronation Close.

Just as she got to the front door meaning to go across the road and speak to Thelma, there she was about to come across the road to her.

'Thelma, I need to talk to you.'

'Anything juicy,' said Thelma with a salacious wink.

'You're incorrigible.'

'Now get that kettle on and you can tell me all about it after I give you this knitted top I got at the jumble sale. It looks and feels like silk.' She held up a dark green item that sparkled in places. 'It's got sequins on the sleeves, so is ideal for Christmas.

'I'll put the kettle on.'

'Hang on a minute.'

Before entering Jenny's front door, Thelma blew a raspberry to the gap in next-door's living-room curtains.

'That woman's like a wasp circling, just waiting to sting,' said Thelma as she set the jumper on the table and flopped onto a wooden dining chair.

Jenny fluttered around the kitchen, forcing herself to concentrate on making tea whilst she got her thoughts in some sort of order.

Teacups on table, Thelma sprang straight in. 'Out with it.'

Jenny put down her cup. 'It's like this...'

'That Robin chap is sweet on you.'

Jenny rolled her eyes. 'I've known Robin for a long time. He's just a friend.'

Thelma sniffed and took a sip of tea. 'Struck me as more than that the way he was looking at you.'

'Honestly, Thelma.'

'So what is it?'

'I'm married to a man I don't love. I'm hearing less and less from him now. I'm living on tenterhooks, worrying whether the postal orders are going to arrive.'

'Have they so far?'

She nodded. 'But the gaps in between them arriving is getting longer. I'm managing, but only just about.'

'Fancy getting a job?'

Jenny shrugged. 'Who would have me? I've got two children and if Roy does come back unannounced, there'll be hell to pay.'

Thelma rested her elbows on the table and looked at Jenny over her clenched hands. 'Why do I get the impression that isn't all you have to say?'

She bit her bottom lip hard and tried very hard to form what she wanted to say before she actually said it. 'There's a man...'

'Not Robin.'

'Not Robin.'

Thelma cocked her head. Jenny felt helpless beneath that intense gaze.

'It wouldn't be that handsome chap who took you out in his car, would it?'

'Ah! Cath saw us.'

'And she told me.'

'You didn't say you knew.'

'I thought I'd wait until you told me. I knew you would. Eventually. So who is he?'

Jenny outlined the events of that rainy day when Charlie had come to the aid of her good neighbours, Isaac and Ruth.

Thelma murmured approval. 'I like the sound of this man. Gutsy and good-looking.'

'You haven't seen him.'

'No but Cath has. She was almost tripping over her tongue.'

'Ah. The thing is he's asked me to meet him in the pub on Wednesday.' She shook her head. 'I want to, but I can't.'

'You feel guilty.'

Jenny nodded.

'Because you're married.'

Jenny nodded again. It seemed Thelma was always one step ahead of her. 'When I was living in Blue Bowl Alley, I wouldn't have dared, but now... well...'

Thelma shook her head in a warning fashion. 'Don't be a doormat all your life, my girl. Stand up and be counted. Haven't I told you that already?'

'You have.'

'Right. That's the guilt out of the way. Now how about trying on this jumper. Dark green with your dark hair – and your eyes are green too, aren't they?'

'Brown.'

'Green in a certain light,' returned Thelma.

Standing in her underwear, Jenny pulled the silk jumper over her head. 'I love it,' she said, twirling from side to side.

Thelma sat silently; her smile faded into alarm.

Jenny looked at her. 'What is it? What's the matter?'

'I'm going up the fish and chip shop tonight. Fancy coming with me?'

The lovely jumper was pulled off. Realising why Thelma's expression had changed, Jenny quickly put her other clothes back on.

'Thelma, I don't need charity.'

'What have you had to eat today?'

Jenny turned away before answering. 'I'm not hungry.'

The chair scraped the floor as Thelma got up, plastered her fists to her hips and gave Jenny a withering look. 'We're off to the chip shop tonight. My girls have made a pie, so your girls can share with them. We can walk back eating our fish and chips out of the newspaper, look up at the stars and get away from our problems. Do you agree to that?'

'Yes. All right.'

'And as for next Wednesday, go, Jenny. You might as well. There's nothing to stop you.'

'Except—'

'Don't even say it,' said Thelma, wagging a red fingernail in front of her eyes. 'You can't hide forever and in time...'

Somehow Jenny knew what she was going to say. 'The money won't come. He won't come back.'

'Correct. So you need some kind of insurance policy for when the sun goes in and it rains. You have to prepare yourself.'

Jenny gripped the back of the dining chair, summoning resolve. Thelma was good at giving advice. A bit of her courage certainly wouldn't go amiss.

'I've taken up enough of your time.'

'I'll see you later. My stomach's already rumbling at the thought of fish and chips eaten straight out of the paper.' Before Thelma had chance to leave, a sudden draught of frosty air accompanied the banging open of the back door, then the inner door separating the kitchen from the bathroom.

'Thelma. I thought you were over here.' Bert glanced at Jenny apologetically. 'Sorry to intrude Jenny, but Thelma...' back to her again. 'You've got to read this.'

He was waving a newspaper with almost patriotic fervour.

'Sorry for barging in, Jenny, but this can't wait. It's incredible. Quite incredible.'

Thelma frowned. 'What is it? Is your mother...'

He thrust the newspaper at her. 'I don't usually read the Sunday papers, but today I saw the headline and had to buy one. You'd better sit down, Thelma. Your legs are likely to go once you read it.' The headlines screamed:

The King and Mrs Simpson

Thelma gasped. 'I've got to sit down.'

She almost collapsed onto a chair.

Jenny leaned over her shoulder and read aloud the first sentence immediately beneath the headline.

A constitutional crisis has occurred...

'I don't understand. Jenny, please explain. Please say it's not what I think?'

'I'm afraid it is. It's saying is that the king wants to marry a thrice divorced American woman. If he does, there might not be a coronation. Talks on the subject are ongoing.'

Thelma looked appalled, her shocked face upturned and

looking at Jenny as though somehow, she might have read it wrong. 'He wouldn't! Surely!'

'It's all over the newspapers,' added Bert. 'They've been keeping it under wraps for a long time, then a bishop spoke out and all hell broke loose. Beg pardon.'

'No,' Thelma said at last, shaking her head in disbelief. 'No. He'll ditch her. He'll do his duty and become king. Here, let me put this filthy rag where it belongs.' The whole newspaper was consigned to the coal fire, where it curled and blackened.

35

Jenny was standing in the queue at the Co-op. Ahead of her, she spotted Harriet looking like a tent on legs.

Dorothy Partridge's sister was far from being the most becoming of women. Her clothes didn't help. She was wearing a voluminous dress of dark blue with a lace colour and cuffs that swamped any curves she might have.

Fred Stacey, the brown-coated manager, was pushing the bacon slicer backwards and forwards.

'And a pound of cheese,' she heard Harriet say from behind the net veil that hung over her face from a hat that resembled a pancake.

Fred wrapped the pound of back bacon in greaseproof paper before slipping it into a brown paper bag and writing the price on the bill pad in front of him. From there, the bill was placed into a metal cartridge. A quick pull on a wind-up mechanism, it whizzed along on the overhead wire to the cashier's desk.

Head down, Harriet made her way to pay for her purchases, handbag unclipped and purse in hand, not looking to left or right.

Once at the kiosk, she raised her head, eyeing the woman

behind the glass partition with a marked degree of impatience. There was only one woman ahead of her.

Thelma continued to be hostile towards Dorothy Partridge, which Jenny could quite understand. However, she didn't feel Harriet deserved the same dislike. On two separate occasions now, Harriet had rescued her from instances that could have had dire consequences. She decided that this was one person who deserved thanks and accordingly stepped out from her place in the queue. 'I'll be back,' she shouted over her shoulder.

Fred Stacey raised a hand in acknowledgement and continued serving.

'Harriet. I want a word with you.'

Though Jenny had spoken softly, Mrs Partridge's sister was startled. Even though her veil was extremely dense, it was possible to discern her round-eyed surprise.

Jenny clutched her shopping bag with both hands.

Harriet snatched her bill from the ink-besmirched pay desk, shoved it in her handbag and snapped it shut. She was wearing gloves made of wool and just as ugly as her dress.

A whisper came from behind the veil. 'I have to go.' Her voice seemed far softer than it had on the night when Roy had got whacked over the head with Thelma's frying pan.

As she turned to leave, Jenny stepped in front of her. 'I just wanted to thank you for wrestling my husband off me. I know it was you.'

'It was nothing.'

'And for coming around to borrow that cup of sugar you didn't need.'

Harriet shrugged. 'I did what had to be done.'

'Was your sister responsible for him calling on me? And that woman who came the other day? Was she responsible for her too?'

'No.' Harriet shook her head vehemently.

'And Thelma Dawkins? Was she responsible for the letter claiming she entertains men for money?'

Harriet sighed. 'She's got it in for Mrs Dawkins. I try to persuade her otherwise and grab the letters before they get posted but am not always successful.'

Everyone in the shop, even Fred, had stopped carrying out their transactions, and listened.

Jenny touched Harriet's arm. 'I'm really grateful for what you did.'

It occurred to her after Harriet had left and she'd re-joined the queue that Harriet's arm had felt muscular, too muscular for that of a woman.

But lucky for me, she thought, and unlucky for Roy who must have been surprised at the strength of the person who had stopped him beating up his wife. Lucky also for Harriet intervening when Mr Collins from the council had called on her.

She still questioned why Mr Collins had found it necessary to call on her. Could it be possible that Mrs Partridge had sent him a letter complaining about her? Or was the reason closer to home and driven by the fact that he knew Roy was away?

They were both members of the same organisation and of course, it was Trevor Collins who had swung the house for them and had also had a hand in this new job Roy had willingly gone to.

Deep in thought, she didn't respond when Fred asked her what she wanted. He raised his voice. 'Come on, Mrs Crawford. I ain't got all day.'

The women in the queue tittered.

One of them commented that she was miles away.

'Must be love,' said another.

Jenny coloured with embarrassment. 'Sorry, Fred. A pound of bacon please, a pound of pork sausages and a piece of scrag end – enough for three.'

'Husband not back yet?'

'No,' she said, a terse smile on her face. 'He's a bit busy.'

'As long as he's got a job. There's plenty that ain't.'

'That's right. There's plenty that haven't.'

'He'll be back soon enough.'

'Yes. I expect he will.'

She smiled as though it was something she really wanted. But she didn't. She'd never been so happy. Roy coming home would end that.

36

Jenny had immersed herself in a hot bath. She'd added scented bath salts to the water and sighed as she lowered herself into it.

'Ecstasy,' she murmured, closing her eyes.

A real bathroom. Such a luxury. She could hardly believe it. Apart from the lack of money, she was happy. And tonight...

She dipped her head beneath the water and was laughing when she came up again. Tonight, she was meeting Charlie Talbot down at the Bunch of Grapes in King Street. The prospect was exhilarating. Tonight, she would let him kiss her again. And again, and again.

Thrilled at the thought of it, she submerged herself beneath the water once again, her hair trailing out around her like shadowy fronds of seaweed.

Laughter still gurgled in her throat when she came up again, and that was when she heard something.

She tensed. The girls were over the road at number twelve. If they had come home unexpectedly, they would have come in through the back door. She'd not locked the back door, but she had locked the bathroom door.

The footsteps were not loud, but they were stealthy. At first, they seemed to come her way, and then, as though a decision had been made, there came the sound of footsteps climbing the stairs.

She thought she heard the door of her bedroom being flung open. Then the girls' bedrooms.

If it wasn't the girls, then who...?

The footsteps came thundering down the stairs, far louder, far more swiftly.

'Jenny? Are you in there?'

The door to the bathroom rattled.

'Yes, Roy.'

It was as though a fist had punched her in the head. The hot water felt suddenly cold and menace formed into faces in the rising steam.

'Just a minute.'

Not wasting time to pull out the plug, she wrapped herself in a towel and unlocked the bathroom door.

'I didn't think we had a lock on the bathroom door,' he said brusquely.

'I tend to leave the back door open for the girls but thought a bolt on the bathroom door was a good idea.'

He looked suspicious. 'Who put it on?'

'I did. I do know how to use a screwdriver. I've had to learn to do it myself when you're away.'

She was lying. Maude's husband had fitted it for her, but she wouldn't mention that. Roy wouldn't like the thought of a man – any man – entering the house when he wasn't around. He looked behind her at the hot water remaining in the bath, the windows and walls beginning to run with condensation. 'No point letting that water go to waste.' There and then he began to undress. 'Better take off the rest in here in case the girls walk in.'

'I wasn't expecting you.'

'Better get used to it. I'm home for good.'

Her heart hammered against her ribs. She forced herself to think straight. Why was he home? Why now? Why when she'd come to the decision to meet Charlie?

'I'm off to get dressed. Is there anything you need?'

'No. There's a towel in here. That'll do me.'

She raced up the stairs. Yes, she had to get dressed but not in the green sparkly top and speckled tweed skirt Thelma had given her. The skirt was hung up, closely followed by the top. She'd been so looking forward to wearing these and seeing approval in Charlie's eyes.

A dream, she thought. *Just a dream*. Reality had struck. Her husband was home. This was her life. *But why now?* she wondered again. *What had happened with his association with the British Union of Fascists? Had he become disillusioned?*

All these things went through her mind as she donned her everyday dress and tied a pinny around her waist.

She took fresh clothes down for Roy. Trousers, shirt, pullover and clean socks. By the time she got downstairs, he was out of the bath, his hair wet, a towel around his waist. Lowering her eyes, she handed him the clean clothes.

'The girls will be home soon. There's suet pudding with jam and custard for tea. I'll get something more substantial later.'

She busied herself relighting the gas and setting out plates. Keeping busy with the cotton-wrapped pudding meant she didn't have to meet the lust in his eyes. This evening loomed and not in the way she'd envisioned. Oh how different would have been the lovemaking between her and Charlie. A simple kiss, a caress, not the demands of a man who'd long forgotten how to be gentle.

He sat there silently. Whether he was watching her or not, she couldn't tell. The silence reigned heavy like the air prior to a thunderstorm.

'When you've finished with that, I've got something to tell you.'

'Bet you've brought me a load of washing,' she said somewhat whimsically, indicating the suitcase he'd left next to the zinc wash boiler.

When he didn't answer, she dared to look at him over her shoulder. He was staring down at the table, playing with the spoon and fork she'd put there with one hand. The fingers of his other hand tapped the table.

'Is something wrong?'

He caught her looking and pointed at a chair. 'Sit down.'

She knew better than to say no and, anyway, she was intrigued.

Telling her that he was going back to work on the docks was the most obvious option open to him. 'I'm going away. I'm joining the army.'

Jenny was astounded. Him becoming a soldier was a complete surprise – and something of a relief.

'I don't know what to say.'

She couldn't bring herself to say that she'd miss him because she wouldn't, but she had to say something along those lines.

'Wait until we tell the girls. I can't imagine what they'll say about their dad in the army. They'll think their father very brave.'

A slight smile lengthened his lips and the thin black moustache he still favoured. 'We're not at war. I don't need to be brave.'

'So why...?'

'I'm joining with a friend. Someone I've become very close to. We're pals.'

There was hatred in the look he gave her and a cruel cynicism to that pristine dark line tracing his upper lip.

'You don't get it do you? There's someone else in my life who I love more than you.'

In a way, she felt relief. There was also a sense of betrayal and stupidity. Surely, she should have noticed, smelt someone else's perfume on him, noticed lipstick on his collar.

I'm a fool. I should have noticed. Another woman, and here was me feeling guilty about going out with another man – even when that man was only a friend.

She frowned as she thought it through. 'What do we do next?'

'Do next? We stay married.'

Her thoughts reeled. He'd finally made up his mind about her and fallen for someone else so strongly that he was prepared to throw her aside, the house and the children.

'But if you want to be with this woman...'

'I want to be with my pal.'

She stared down at his tightly clasped hands, the way he hung his head, hiding the guilt in his eyes, the alien expression.

She shook her head in disbelief. 'He must be a very good friend indeed for you to want to go with him into the army.'

He raised his head. The look he gave her made her wince. 'You women. You don't understand how close blokes can get when they're under fire. I prefer being with men in uniform. We understand each other as women never can.'

The memory of him burning letters came to mind. He'd been close to crying over those letters. They had been from an old friend of his in the army, someone of whom he was immensely fond. Simon. She suddenly remembered his name. Simon.

'My word. My word.' Her head fell forward onto her hand. She felt dizzy, she felt sick, but thought she understood what he was saying.

'What happens next?'

'What do you mean, what happens next? Nothing will change. Not really. I'll be in the army and you'll be here with the girls. I'll get leave now and again. I'll pop back to see you and the girls.'

'You'll pop back?' She found it quite incredulous. 'You'll pop back,' she repeated and the room around her spun like a child's spinning top.

'I want to remain married. I want to remain respectable. But I don't want to be your husband. I want to be with the blokes and with Ian.'

'Ian.' She repeated the name of the man he was leaving her for. A close friend, a fellow soldier, or at least that was their intention.

She thought of his love for a uniform. There was more than one reason for him having joined the Black shirts. He'd loved that uniform. It was too far back to recall how he'd felt about his uniform during the war. She couldn't quite remember.

'Wouldn't you prefer a divorce?'

'No. That's for rich people to do and as I told you, I need to be married. It gives me respectability. Blokes – my type of bloke – get done over if they ain't married. I needs to remain married.'

Again Jenny shook her head in disbelief feeling punch drunk, a term she'd heard but never had experience of. She was his shield against what people felt about men who were attracted to each other. As of old he was being selfish, thinking of his own needs, his own position, not of hers. She glared at him, anger in her eyes and pouring from her mouth.

'You're leaving me in a kind of purgatory.'

'Well that's the way it's going to be. I'll make sure you still get the army pay on time. No fear of that.'

No fear. In effect he would be paying her to keep her mouth shut, to watch his back, to live a lie because that suited him.

Adultery was the only excuse for divorcing. She vaguely remembered that at one time a husband could divorce a wife for adultery but not the other way round. That had changed of late. The world was changing. One day it might change yet again. Divorce for other reasons might happen.

Digesting all this whilst controlling her anger took some time. All the while, she sat there as stiff as a stone statue. Once the anger had subsided something else took over. Logic coupled with her own needs. The germ of a truth grew into something more strident, a truth she thought she could live with. Roy wanted to live his own life on his own terms and be happy with the person he was with. The same applied to her. She would have the freedom to live her own life, perhaps not getting married but at least being able to do what she wanted.

The thought solidified and became more amenable. Before long she spoke softly, asking the question, 'When do you leave?'

'In two days.'

She asked him about money.

'You'll get paid when the army pays me.'

'I mean now.'

He gave her two crisp five-pound notes. She didn't ask where they had come from or exclaim that it looked as though he'd been earning a great deal of money.

'The Black shirts are generous.'

He shook his head. 'That's the last from them. The membership is far less than it used to be thanks to that bloke Hitler over in Germany. People are going off the idea. You do right by me and we stay married and I'll take care of the money. They're my daughters after all.'

She nodded, eyes downcast and her feelings in turmoil.

'Yes. They're your daughters.'

'Just tell them I've joined the army. Nothing else. Do you promise that?'

'Yes.' More nodding, more agreeing because there was nothing else she could do. Their marriage had been unhappy for both of them. Somehow, some way they would carry on living, maintaining a façade to cover the truth. Society laid down rules that didn't always suit or make sense. They would both do what had to be done.

And so it was, on a December morning when the morning mist shrouded one side of Coronation Close from the other, Roy took his leave for what appeared to be the very last time. He had said he would come back and check on his daughters, but Jenny didn't believe him.

Gloria clung onto him to the last, blubbering that she didn't want him to go. Tilly merely said goodbye and wrapped her arm around her mother.

A few of her neighbours came out to cheer him on his way. To Jenny's surprise, Dorothy Partridge was one of them, hanging onto the garden gate waving a union jack. Her sister hung back on the front doorstep, looking on but giving no sign of approval, a deep frown creasing her brow.

The white mist drifted around the frosted hedges and bare trees like the ripped shards of a bridal veil.

On the outside, Jenny gave the impression of being the loving wife left behind. Only she wasn't. Neither was he the loving husband. He was something she'd not realised before, a secret to be kept for his sake, for her sake and that of her children.

37

FRIDAY 11 DECEMBER, 1936

Thelma sat herself down and put her feet up. Bert was sitting opposite her, though making ready to go home. His mother would be expecting him.

Thelma hummed along to the music playing on the wireless, drained her last cup of tea of the evening and settled back in the chair.

After fetching his coat and hat from the hallway, Bert came back in.

'Well, I'll be off then,' he said as he pushed one arm and then the other into his coat sleeves and set his hat on his head.

'Shame you couldn't stay longer,' Thelma said tellingly.

Bert shook a finger. 'Now, now, Thelma my darling. Don't try to tempt me. You know my mother will be waiting.'

'Is she really not feeling too well?'

'No, she's not. She has not been the same since that nonsense in the paper about the king and his problems. I told her it would all blow over, but it doesn't stop her worrying.'

Thelma frowned. She'd pushed the offending article to the

back of her mind, confident that the king would do his duty to Great Britain and the empire.

The mantel clock, which was reputed a little fast, chimed ten. Thelma got to her feet. 'I'll see you to the door.'

He opened the living-room door through which he would pass into the hallway. He always gave her a goodnight kiss first before leaving and would have done so now – except the BBC intervened. The music stopped. An announcer proclaimed in a plummy voice that he was broadcasting from Windsor Castle. He went on to introduce His Royal Highness Prince Edward.

Thelma exchanged a look of surprise with Bert. 'Prince? King surely.' She turned the Bakelite knob on the walnut cased wireless.

'I wonder...' began Bert, his face visibly paling as he thought about whether his mother was listening to this broadcast. To his mind, it didn't bode well.

'Shh,' said Thelma, sinking into a chair, her attention focused on the wireless set almost as though it was showing her pictures.

'*At long last, I am able to say a few words...*'

The king! Thelma sat silently, her mouth hanging open, each word like a dart piercing her heart, especially his remark about fulfilling his duties, which she'd been sure he would not shirk. He was categorically stating that he could not carry out those duties '*without the support of the woman I love*'.

Finally, he referred to his brother taking the burden of responsibility from him as King George the sixth. All was confirmed with four simple words: '*God save the King.*'

The announcer came back to say that BBC programmes would cease for the evening.

For what seemed half an hour but could only have been minutes, Thelma sat there whilst Bert hovered by the door twirling the brim of his hat between his fingers. He shook his head. 'I don't know what mother will say.' He looked at her. 'I'd better go. She'll be worrying. Will you be all right?'

Eyes glazed and staring into the fire grate, she nodded. 'I didn't think it would happen. I know it said so a few days ago in the newspapers, but I thought it would all work out. I thought he would do his duty.'

'Seems you were wrong. In my opinion it must have been going on a while. He must have thought about this over a period of some time – years in fact.'

Thelma sat numb, eyes staring and didn't respond when Bert finally said goodnight.

* * *

Jenny had been listening to music. Her head, too, jerked upright when she heard the king giving his speech of abdication. She at once wondered how Thelma was taking it. Tomorrow was Saturday and Thelma would be working, at least in the morning. She imagined Thelma crying buckets of tears in front of the wireless, unable to believe that her idol had feet of clay. He was giving up the throne for the love of a woman.

Thelma would need her and tomorrow afternoon wouldn't be soon enough. She'd need her support right now.

First she checked on the girls, made sure they were asleep, then put her coat on.

Huddled into her coat, she passed Bert Throgmorton coming down the garden path.

'Surprising news. How is she?' she asked breathlessly.

'Stunned,' he replied, tipped his hat and sprinted for the front gate. 'Have to go. Mother will be having hysterics. Such a shock. I need to be with her.'

Normally she would have gone around the back and walked

straight in, but the side path was dark at this time of night so she rapped on the front door loud enough to wake the whole street.

When the door opened there was just enough light for her to see the stunned pallor of Thelma's face.

'I thought I would see how you were. Shocking news, isn't it?'

Thelma said nothing but stood back so she could enter. Her face was white as a sheet, her features stiff and eyes round and unblinking.

Oh dear, thought Jenny. She's taking it even worse than I thought.

Once in the living room, they both stood like statues looking at each other.

The silence and stillness was unbearable. Jenny suggested they both sit down.

'I'll make tea,' she said.

'No. There's a bottle of sherry on the dresser. And two glasses.'

Jenny took the bottle of Cyprus sherry and tipped a little into two small tumblers. She handed one to Thelma, then sat down with her own.

Thelma downed hers in one, sighed and proclaimed, 'I can't believe it. I just can't believe it.'

Jenny sipped at her drink and poured Thelma another.

Thelma took that drink more slowly. She had a glazed look in her eyes. Jenny was sure it had nothing to do with the drink. Thelma was in shock.

'I hope for his sake that he's made a wise choice. He must have done a lot of soul searching before giving up,' said Jenny.

Thelma remained as a block of white marble, her red lips a tight line of indignation. She could possibly have cracked walnut shells with her jaw.

Jenny wondered what to say that might crack Thelma's frozen expression and loosen the tightly clenched hands. Just for once, she was unsure whether the crimson fingernails were varnish or blood. What would rouse Thelma? What would reignite her worship of the royal family?

After a bit of mind searching she latched onto the more positive side of the news. 'Thanks to Mrs Simpson, we won't have a King Edward. Looking on the bright side we will have a King George. King George the Sixth and Queen Elizabeth.'

There was no response. She carried on. 'And two princesses. Elizabeth and Margaret Rose. In time Elizabeth would become queen – if they don't have any sons that is. That would make her Queen Elizabeth the Second and if she reigns as long and wisely as Queen Elizabeth the First it would be quite wonderful.'

Still nothing.

Thelma continued to sit stock-still which made Jenny wonder if she'd been listening. She couldn't be sure, but consequently felt a great urge to give her a prod, just to ensure she hadn't really turned to stone.

'Thelma...'

It was sudden, it was alarming, like a Jack in the box on the end of a spring. Thelma sprang from her chair. 'How dare he,' she shouted, racing around the room, tearing the pictures of her handsome prince from the walls, smashing every single piece of commemorative china with his picture on the side.

Jenny ducked as everything portraying the man who had shirked his royal duties was smashed, broken; wooden picture frames and newspaper cuttings flung onto the fire.

Jenny jumped to attention when a piece of burning paper fluttered from the fire grate where glowing coals glowed amongst white ash and landed on the rug. She stamped on it with both feet until the flame was gone, leaving only blackened paper.

Whilst Jenny did everything to prevent the house from

catching on fire, Thelma had slumped into a chair, her face in her hands, her shoulders convulsed in heart rending sobs.

Jenny had only known Thelma for a brief time but had never known her to burst into tears. She was pragmatic, independent, sensible and stronger than most.

Jenny touched her shoulder. 'Would you like a cup of tea now, Thelma? Or perhaps another sherry?'

Glossy locks escaped the swept-up hairstyle and fell forward around the creamy white hands with their crimson nail varnish.

Jenny did a quick check around the room, inspecting if there was anything else Thelma might throw. Happily there was not much left depicting the former Prince of Wales who had thrown off the mantle of King Edward.

Jenny touched Thelma's shoulder. 'Thelma?'

At first, there was just a shake of her head before her face appeared. Her mascara, her lipstick was smeared across her face, but she looked forthright and resolved.

'That's it then,' she pronounced in a firm voice. 'A proper royal family. A king, a queen and two princesses. What say we get Christmas over with and then plan our street party for the coronation of the new king?'

'And queen,' added Jenny, keen to take advantage of Thelma's quick recovery.

'Should be quite an event,' Thelma added, her anger replaced with hope. 'Nineteen thirty-seven should be quite a year.'

'Yes,' Jenny said softly, tears of happiness spilling from her eyes. 'Quite a year.'

For Jenny, it wasn't just about the royal family. The New Year that would herald in the reign of a new monarch promised more for her personally. She had her house and her children. She had happiness and told herself she could manage without romance for a while. Perhaps she would see Charlie Talbot again, or perhaps not. Old friends such as Robin and Isaac and Ruth were still around. The new friends and neighbours she'd made in Coronation Close gave her great hope for the future and the garden she'd always wanted would soon bear fruit. 'Roll on 1937,' she said and clapped her hands.

Thelma, the colour returned to her face, repeated the hopeful comment but also added, 'God bless the new king and his lovely family. No doubt he'll last longer than his brother, and then his daughter will become queen. Isn't that amazing?'

Jenny agreed that it was. 'Everything is quite amazing. The future is looking wonderful for all of us.'

HISTORICAL NOTES

The following is the genuine notice given to new council house tenants back in the thirties.

> The Housing Committee realise that you have been living under very undesirable conditions, and that in worn-out houses it is very difficult to get rid of vermin. But there will be no excuse in your new house. Do not buy second-hand furniture, bedding or pictures unless you are quite sure that the articles are free from vermin. Insects do not like soap and hot water, and they also dislike dusters and polish. So if in the new house you keep your windows open, and keep your bodies and clothing, hallways and stairs, furniture and bedding clean; use the duster frequently on all skirting and ledges, you are not likely to be troubled again with vermin. This sounds a lot, but life isn't going to be all work for the housewife. The new house will be easy to keep clean and it will be well worth looking after...

The foregoing is directed at working-class people moving into new council houses.

As mentioned earlier in the book, the royal affair was kept from the British public until the last minute and the establishment were worried.

There follows the opening excerpt from Gaumont British News, as shown at cinemas as the government were considering King Edward's insistence on marrying Wallis Simpson in the week preceding the abdication announcement. The Old English lettering helped to convey the message of heritage.

Our Throne

In this changing hour of the fortunes of Great Britain, it is the duty of every citizen to remember that Loyalty to the Empire is the first and only consideration.

Criticism and personal opinion must be set aside. The tradition of the throne of Britain established by the Rulers of our History is greater than the individual Sovereign.

Stand Fast

Loyalty to the Throne and to the Government which represents you will safeguard the Empire which is YOUR heritage.

MORE FROM LIZZIE LANE

We hope you enjoyed reading *New Neighbours for Coronation Close*. If you did, please leave a review.

If you'd like to gift a copy, this book is also available as an ebook, digital audio download and audiobook CD.

Sign up to Lizzie Lane's mailing list for news, competitions and updates on future books:

http://bit.ly/LizzieLaneNewsletter

Why not discover *The Tobacco Girls*, the first in the best selling Tobacco Girls series from Lizzie Lane.

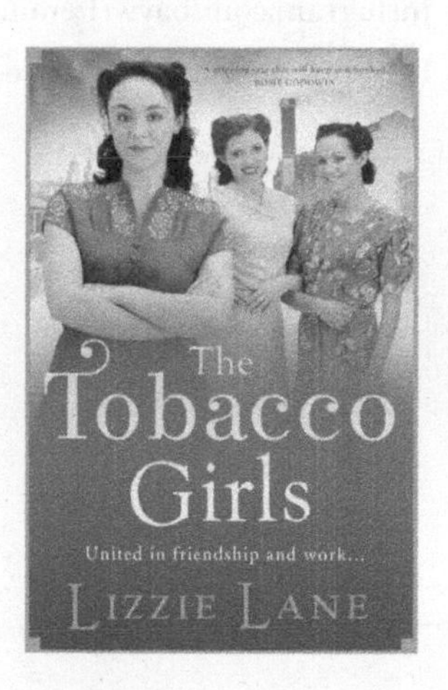

ABOUT THE AUTHOR

Lizzie Lane is the author of over 50 books, a number of which have been bestsellers. She was born and bred in Bristol where many of her family worked in the cigarette and cigar factories. This has inspired her new saga series for Boldwood *The Tobacco Girls*.

Follow Lizzie on social media:

facebook.com/jean.goodhind

twitter.com/baywriterallat1

instagram.com/baywriterallatsea

bookbub.com/authors/lizzie-lane

Milton Keynes UK
Ingram Content Group UK Ltd.
UKHW042347020923
427891UK00004B/55